SO
THIRSTY

Novels by Rachel Harrison

The Return
Cackle
Such Sharp Teeth
Black Sheep
So Thirsty

Short Story Collection by Rachel Harrison

Bad Dolls

SO THIRSTY

)

Rachel Harrison

Berkley

New York

BERKLEY
An imprint of Penguin Random House LLC
penguinrandomhouse.com

BERKLEY and the BERKLEY & B colophon are registered trademarks of
Penguin Random House LLC.

Library of Congress Cataloging-in-Publication Data
Names: Harrison, Rachel, 1989- author.
Title: So thirsty / Rachel Harrison.
Description: New York : Berkley, 2024.
Identifiers: LCCN 2023059701 (print) | LCCN 2023059702 (ebook) |
ISBN 9780593642542 (hardcover) | ISBN 9780593642559 (ebook)
Subjects: LCGFT: Vampire fiction. | Novels.
Classification: LCC PS3608.A78368 S6 2024 (print) | LCC PS3608.A78368 (ebook) |
DDC 813/.6--dc23/eng/20220304
LC record available at https://lccn.loc.gov/2023059701
LC ebook record available at https://lccn.loc.gov/2023059702

Printed in the United States of America
1st Printing

Book design by Nancy Resnick

For my friends. Forever wouldn't be long enough.

SO
THIRSTY

1

Sunlight severs me from sleep. I grasp at a fading dream, catch its last breath, quiet and wispy as a cobweb. It feels tragic, but I already forget what the dream was about. Something good. Was I at the mall again? I'm always dreaming about this mall. It's the same mall, except a little different every time. The stores change, the layout. The fountain to throw loose change into while wishing to strike it rich.

I'll have to tell Naomi. She also has a dream mall. It's a cornerstone of our friendship.

Someday we'll meet in the dream mall, she'll say.

How do you know it's the same mall? I'll ask.

It's obviously the same mall.

I take her word for it. She speaks with such certainty, it's impossible not to.

Sometimes when I bring up the dream mall, she'll go on a rant about capitalism infiltrating our subconscious. Sometimes she'll try to interpret, say the dream is about choices, about decision paralysis, or insecurity, or identity; then she'll eulogize her beloved dream dictionary, which she accidentally left on a train when she was a teenager. It was a gift from her favorite aunt, who bought it from a clairvoyant in Prague—irreplaceable.

I've never asked her why we've yet to find each other there, at the dream mall, what that could mean. I'm sure she'd have an answer. Naomi has an answer for everything.

I yawn, shut my eyes tight. I call the dream back to me, make a silent plea with sleep, but they're both gone, so I might as well get up.

My morning routine looms. As I lie under the covers, the simple task of brushing my teeth feels monumental. Then everything that comes next. Applying moisturizer, vitamin C serum, SPF, foundation, blush, mascara. All this effort just to look half-decent. To look alive.

And then making coffee, and logging in to work, and checking email. Slathering peanut butter on a slice of almost-stale bread that I'm too lazy to toast. Smiling at Joel when he offers a cheery *Good morning.*

He snores beside me now, impervious to the morning light, its brightness amplified by a fresh dusting of ultra-white snow. Joel could take a nap in an Apple Store, on the surface of the sun. Doesn't bother him. He always forgets to close the blinds at night. So do I, but it's too early for accountability. At seven thirty a.m., there's only blame.

I roll onto my back, tongue the drool crust at the corners of my mouth. A face materializes, just for a second. There was a man in my dream. His image has already escaped me. Not someone I know, I don't think. A stranger, maybe? Or a figment of my imagination.

What would have happened between us had the sun not interrupted?

Joel grunts, twitches, then resumes snoring. Sometimes I feel guilty for dream cheating, even though I know I shouldn't, considering. . . . But, turns out, seven thirty a.m. is too early to contemplate the complexities of monogamy and the enduring hurt of infidelity.

I get a leg free of the covers, put a cold bare foot on the carpet. I lost a sock in the night. Like the dream, it's now gone forever. I don't know where all my missing socks go, but wherever they are, I hope they're happy.

I thrust myself to standing and stumble into the bathroom, shivering, my knees stiff. I avoid the mirror as best I can. Lately, my reflection has been the bearer of bad news. *You're tired,* it tells me. *You're sad. You're getting older.* Last week, I spent over an hour examining a line on my forehead that I could have sworn appeared overnight. The line shouldn't bother me as much as it does.

It really bothers me.

It instigates these spells of debilitating angst that punctuate a bland, general malaise. Upon the arrival of my new forehead wrinkle, I Googled "existential crisis" directly after I Googled "Botox." I'm aware that my imminent birthday is exacerbating this angst.

But it's not like there's anything I can do about it. There's no cure for getting older, no solution for the harsh seep of time, save for maybe an attitude adjustment, a positive outlook, which I'm incapable of. Best I can do is acquiesce.

I don't know. I don't know. I'd talk to Naomi about it, but she couldn't relate. Her life is a wild, glamorous adventure.

I squirt out some toothpaste, brush my teeth with my back to the mirror, turning to the sink only to spit.

"So, I know you hate surprises," Joel says, scooping some coffee grounds into a refillable pod. He pops it into the Keurig and turns to me, rubbing his stubble like he always does when he's nervous.

"I hope that's the end of your sentence," I say, and lick a knife clean of peanut butter, then stuff it into the dishwasher, which is somehow already full. "I emptied this last night. I know I did. Do we have a ghost?"

"A ghost that uses all our dishes while we sleep?"

"Yeah," I say. "A midnight snacker. A hungry ghost."

He laughs and shakes his head. "Sloane."

"I'm haunted by chores! Also—sorry—there's no more milk."

"Really? I thought we got more. . . ." He opens the fridge, because he can never just believe me. He rummages around, validates the absence of dairy.

"Ghost must have gotten to it," I say, imagining an ethereal floating milk mustache. "You should try it black."

"I'm not cool like you."

I grind my own beans, prefer a French press. Maybe because I'm a snob, or maybe because, freshman year of college, I lost my virginity to a random guy at a party and in the morning, in his grimy off-campus apartment, he put on a Jimmy Campbell record and made me coffee with a French press, and I felt special for five seconds. Felt cool. Like an adult. Like I wasn't a girl anymore. I left that morning thinking, *This is the kind of woman I am. The kind who takes a lover. The kind who drinks strong French press coffee.* I never saw the guy again, but leave it to teen me to let a complete stranger spoil me to the ordinary, to allow myself to be ruined for what's simple and easy in favor of some romantic notion of who I imagined I would be.

I've abandoned enough of that idealized self. The French press is my last holdout.

Though it is kind of a pain to wash.

"Guess I'm going out," Joel says, sighing. "Do we need anything else?"

I shrug. "Not that I can think of."

4

"Oh," he says, tossing up his keys and catching them in the opposite hand. "Birthday surprise. You want to hear it?"

"Okay," I say, battling a sudden bout of stress-induced nausea.

"This Thursday through Sunday, I booked you a cottage at the Waterfront in Auburn. For you and Naomi."

"Naomi?"

"My coconspirator."

I screw and unscrew the lid of the peanut butter jar, fidgeting until I figure out how I feel.

"This is the exact reaction I was hoping for," Joel says. He's joking, but I can sense the frustration lurking under the surface. I can see its dorsal fin.

"I'm . . ." I start. "That place is so expensive."

"It's a big birthday," he says, and my existential angst returns, batting around my chest. Is it a big birthday? Is thirty-six big? "Plus, it's off-season."

"Naomi's coming?"

"Yep," he says. "Girls' weekend."

"But she's in Europe," I say, my voice at a mortified pitch. "I think."

"Not this Thursday through Sunday. I've been planning this for a while. You don't need to worry about anything," he says, which, of course, makes me worry. "All right. I have to go get the milk; my first meeting is in twenty."

"Okay. Thank you, Joel. Thank you."

He nods and slips out through the door to the garage.

I walk over to the front window to watch his car pull out of the driveway, tires interrupting the perfect powdering of snow. I'm still holding the peanut butter, and I'm struck by this riotous impulse to chuck it at the wall. Instead, I return it to its rightful spot in the pantry. Then I roam around the house clenching and unclenching my fists, compulsively sighing.

I'd call Naomi, but I know she wouldn't pick up. And what would I say?

I'm so excited! I can't wait to see you!

Or, *Why didn't you tell me? You know I hate surprises. I don't feel like celebrating my birthday. I'd rather just ignore it. If you ever bothered to ask me how I was doing, you'd know that.*

Or, *Do you think this is a generous gift from a guiltless husband, or do you think it's suspect?*

I park myself in front of my laptop and attempt to get some work done.

Joel comes back with the milk, which he leaves out on the counter, either absentmindedly or with the expectation that I will put it away. At around five o'clock, I log out and go down to the basement to pedal the stationary bike for half an hour while staring off into space. Then I come upstairs and put a pot of water on the stove to make pasta for dinner. I step into my knockoff UGGs and take the kitchen recycling out to the bin at the side of the house. The bin is already full, overflowing, and a cherry seltzer can falls onto the icy pavement. I reach to pick it up and notice something small and furry and still in the dark, wedged in the narrow space between the bin and the house.

It's a mouse. And it's dead.

If the mouse were alive, I'd be screaming, flailing. I'd wish it were dead. But because it is dead, I wish it were alive.

I don't want to just leave it there, let its corpse freeze to the driveway, so I get a garbage bag and a pair of plastic gloves from the garage and pick it up, wrap it in the bag, toss it in the trash.

Someday me, too, I think, carefully removing the gloves and throwing them on top. *Someday I'll be dead in a bin and none of this will matter.*

This sudden grimness provides a nebulous sense of relief, like tonguing a sore in the mouth.

I let the lid slam down and wheel the trash and recycling to the curb, go inside, wash my hands vigorously. Then I get my suitcase out of the closet.

I consider that maybe I do need this weekend away. More important, maybe I want it.

2

Your luxury experience awaits at the Waterfront Collective retreat, resort, and spa. An oasis nestled in the heart of—"

"Are we really doing this?"

"Nestled in the heart of the Finger Lakes. The—"

"Naomi."

"The picturesque American village that we call home has been at once restored *and* transformed, the perfect location for the ultimate escape."

"You done?"

I hear a big, deep inhale through the receiver, and I understand that, no, she is not done. "From our modern yet cozy cottages, to our lavish spa, to our fine-dining restaurants, discover a vacation experience like no other. Welcome . . . to the Waterfront."

"Should I applaud?"

"Well, yeah. That would be nice," Naomi says, breathless from her dramatic reading of the hotel website. Not hotel. *Collective. Vacation experience. Ultimate escape.* "This place is posh as fuck. Are they even going to let us in? We don't play tennis. I've never eaten a scallop. What even is a scallop?"

She knows what a scallop is, but she likes to pretend her par-

8

ents don't have money. I play along with the charade. "Maybe we'll find out."

"Never taken a picture with an American flag draped over my shoulders at the beach at sunset. I don't wear white. I've been arrested, you know."

"I know. I was there."

"The first time. Not the second."

"A shame to have missed it."

She shrugs. I know her so well, I can sense it. We're on different continents, but we might as well be in the same room. I can picture her in front of me. How she's sitting. Her legs tucked to one side, her feet pointed. Wearing a pair of men's boxer shorts and a crazy lace bra. Some combination of Hanes and La Perla she can somehow make work. If I didn't love her so much, she'd be insufferable.

"Ooh, you can get married here. This venue is insane. A sprawling estate with exceptional lake views, originally built as the summer residence for some crusty old chin beard . . ." She trails off.

"Do you want to get married?"

"Fuck no," she says. "Damn. I'll need to pack extra sweaters to tie around my neck. WASP cape."

"Do you not want to come?"

"Of course I want to come. I'm coming. Flight is booked out of Munich."

"You're talking like the Finger Lakes are fancy, Miss Flight-out-of-Munich. You've been traveling around Europe for the last, what? Three, four months?"

"And I'm coming back to the States with a vague accent to prove it."

"Great. Can't wait."

"It's not as bougie as it sounds. It's work. Most days I'm wrangling at least one hungover man-child, or getting groupies to sign

NDAs, or chasing *Rolling Stone*, or spending a tragic amount of time on the band's Instagram. Some days I'm a glorified roadie. Plus, the showers over here have no water pressure. And the toilets are weird."

She's not being dishonest, but she is downplaying her journeys for my benefit, so I won't be so jealous. I'm both grateful and a little insulted. "Still . . ."

"Sure. Still . . ." she says. "But fuck it. I get to see you!"

"I hope this goes without saying, but you don't need to fly back from Europe for a weekend."

"Your *birthday* weekend," she says, and I flinch so hard, I almost fumble my phone. "And the timing worked out. European leg is done. Lee and the band fly home right after me. You and I will get up to some trouble, some birthday debauchery—you know, classic high jinks . . ."

"Right, right."

"Then I get to go back to being a PR bot slash rock star's girlfriend." She lets out a dramatic sigh. "You know, their last show is Friday, they fly back Saturday, and he's got everyone back in the studio next week. And not where we live, in New York fucking City, no. In Pittsburgh. His new hometown dream studio that he had to open, in Pittsburgh. So now I have to haul my ass there to document the creative process. I think he's afraid of losing momentum. He's relentless."

"You fell in love with the ambition of an ambitious man."

"And you failed to talk me out of it. This is on you," she says. "Anyway, I should probably go. Start to pack. Lee's out with the guys, and it's easier to get shit done with him out of my hair. Mr. Ambition is salty about having to survive a few days without me."

"He just can't bear to be parted from you," I say, swoony like an animated princess.

She snorts. "All right. Later, angel. Meet you in paradise."

"I'll see you there."

I set my phone screen down on my desk. It's eleven seventeen a.m., and I'm supposed to be in a meeting. I saw Naomi calling and wondered if she was canceling. I don't know why I always assume the worst.

It's typical Naomi to call at inconvenient times. When I'm supposed to be in a meeting. When I'm doing my weekly Saturday cleaning, rubber gloves on, bleach in hand. When I'm asleep at three a.m. She doesn't understand time zones, or home maintenance, or nine-to-fives, but she's so authentically freewheeling and oblivious that it's impossible to be mad at her for it. It's her finest magic trick, transforming her most frustrating qualities into part of her charm.

I take a deep breath and a sip of my now-tepid coffee, dial into this meeting late, prepared to apologize for my tardiness, but no one seems to notice my arrival, or that I hadn't been there in the first place.

It's one of those miserable January days so frigid it's difficult to breathe. The wind is ruthless, stinging any exposed skin. I feel the baby hairs on my neck and at my temples go frosty. I reach to pull my hat down, and my fingers suffer. All feeling in my extremities fades. The cold infiltrates my brain, and I imagine my thoughts cased in ice like the branches of the peach tree in the front yard, which has been scrawny and barren since September.

I stand in the driveway, waiting for Joel to come say goodbye. He went inside to get something and has been gone for too long, leaving me here to freeze.

The door opens and he comes shuffling out holding a small

gift-wrapped box. The paper is gold, edges clean, tape invisible. There's a neat pink ribbon tied around it, an impeccable bow teetering on top.

"Another present?" I ask.

"Not for now," he says. "For your actual birthday. Day of."

"Open it in the car as soon as I pull away?"

"You would. Present shaker."

"I'm not a present shaker. I'm patient and normal."

He raises an eyebrow and I pout.

"All right," he says. "Got everything you need?"

"Yep. Do you?"

"I'll survive."

"Okay. Love you," I say, and give him a quick, dry kiss—our lips winter chapped. "And thank you. I'll see you in a few days."

"Sloane?"

"Yeah?"

"Have fun."

"Don't I always?" I say, opening the car door and climbing inside. I set the present down on the passenger seat, put the heat on full blast, and give Joel a wave before driving off.

I steal a look in the rearview. At the house. At my beloved peach tree. At the shimmery snow-covered yard. At Joel. He remains in the driveway watching me, seeing me off in his puffy coat and aviator hat, and I think about how he leaves his dishes in the sink and his socks bunched up in the laundry basket, so I have to individually unbunch them or else they'll never dry. I think about how he can be so condescending over such stupid, insignificant things, like my not knowing how to put more peppercorns in the grinder. I think about how he chastises me for not carrying cash and for avoiding the dentist. I think about how he lied about the first girl but didn't deny the second. I think about whether staying with someone is really a choice, or if it's a complete lack thereof.

I turn the corner and Joel disappears.

At the first red light I hit, I reach over to the passenger seat and shake the gift-wrapped box. Something shifts inside.

"Hmm."

The light turns green, and I drive on, waiting for some excitement to set in. But all I feel is this kneading of dread. This impulse to turn around, go home. I don't really desire my life, but I'm reluctant to leave it. There's comfort in the mundane, safety in the routine. In waking up and knowing exactly what my day will look like.

I fear breaking my routine will break everything.

And I fear wanting too much out of this trip. I fear want in general. I made a promise to myself years ago to always temper my expectations, protect myself from disappointment. So this trip will just be miles on the car, a few nights in a picturesque cottage, some time with Naomi that will be good. That will be fine.

And then I'll be a year older, and the peaches will fall from the tree, and I'll avoid my reflection, put cream on my neck.

The tang of blood awakens me to my teeth's nefarious inclination to gnaw on the delicate flesh inside my cheek. A violent nervous habit my body executes without permission. I never realize I'm doing it until it's too late.

I swallow, and the blood drags down my throat. It seems thicker than it should be, and it leaves me uneasy. I swallow again. Again. I can't undo the damage, can't erase the flavor.

All I can do is shudder at the aftertaste.

3

I choose a back route, no highways, hoping for a scenic drive. The sun melted the ice, the snow, leaving the roads slushy. Everything drips; everything is wet, the snow-covered hills gone muddy and soft. I pass by antique malls and dilapidated barns and rusty tractors and the occasional cow. I pass through small towns with general stores and unsavory political signage. A lot of Christmas decorations are still up, strands of lights drooping, wreaths browning, nativity scenes missing wise men, Santas covered in muck. I pass by beautiful lake houses and wonder what the owners do for a living. Who can afford such houses? What decisions did they make? What mistakes did I make?

I sing along to "American Pie" because no one is around to judge me. I think about Buddy Holly dead in a field. The Big Bopper, Ritchie Valens—who was only seventeen. I think about Patsy Cline, also killed in a plane crash. Before her death, she supposedly said, "Don't worry about me, hoss. When it's my time to go, it's my time." I wonder if she was able to maintain that attitude as the plane went down.

I hope so. It seems the cruelest fate, to die scared. But maybe that's the only way.

I put on "Walkin' After Midnight." I wonder if I should start calling people "hoss." If I could pull it off.

When I arrive in Auburn, I crack my window and inhale. Pure, crisp winter air. There's music playing, big-band jazz. There's a quaint Main Street with a movie theater that has a classic marquee, and an ice-cream shop, a bar called the Pharmacy, a pharmacy called the Drug Store, some retail shops that I know must be overpriced, gouging tourists like me. There's a Chase bank, which shatters the illusion of the old-fashioned, the 1950s "aw, gee, shucks," "take a nickel to the soda fountain for a cherry-lime rickey," "call your sweetheart on a rotary phone," "listen to a transistor radio," meat-loaf-and-mashed-potatoes Americana.

At a traffic light, I make a right onto a tree-lined street. Grand Victorian houses are spaced evenly, set back on clean lawns—all with hibernating gardens and ornate birdbaths or fountains, each with its long driveway neatly plowed. Any remnants of snow are white, unsullied. Again I wonder, *Who lives in these houses? How do they have this kind of money, living out here? What do they do?*

This place is a postcard, a fantasy. A profound trepidation materializes in my chest, spreading quickly to my limbs, giving me pins and needles. I shudder and close my window. The GPS advises that I make a left in four hundred feet. All I can think about is going home.

But it's too late for that, and there's a car coming up behind me, so I go ahead and take the left.

The road winds down a wooded hill, and through the skeletal trees I get glimpses of the lake glittering beneath the rapidly setting sun. The main building reveals itself at the bottom of the slope—a titanic stone mansion with an elaborate porch, countless arched windows, tall chimneys. The whole structure is swathed in thick vines, which contribute significantly to its air of Gothic romance. Aptly named the Waterfront, it seems to rest precariously on the edge of the lake, at least from this vantage point. I pull around the circular drive and park in front of what I assume to be the entrance. There's an awning—an extension of the porch.

By the time I open my car door, there's a porter, a boy who might be fresh out of high school or college—I can't tell. He wears a ridiculous old-timey uniform. He must hate it.

"Hello, ma'am," he says. Ugh. *Ma'am*. "Checking in?"

"Hey. Yes," I say. "Okay to park here?"

"Yes, ma'am." Again with the "ma'am."

I follow him inside to the lobby, a two-story foyer with a grand staircase, dark walls, gilded molding. There's a marble counter to the side, and another adolescent appears behind it, a bony girl in a similarly old-fashioned getup. She bounces upon seeing me, smiles widely, revealing gapped teeth encased in plastic aligners.

"Hello. Welcome to the Waterfront Collective retreat, resort, and spa. My name is Mary Beth. Do you have a reservation with us?"

"Yes. Should be under Parker."

She stoops behind a gold MacBook. "Ah! Yes, Ms. Parker."

Ms. Thank God.

"I see we have you with us for three nights in our Whispering Woods Cottage."

Heaven help me if Naomi finds out that's what it's called.

"If you'll please give me a moment, I'll get you your key cards," Mary Beth says, opening a drawer. "And here we are! Will you be taking advantage of our valet service? We have a heated garage, convenient for winter months. We can escort you to your cottage, and then for your stay we have a shuttle service available as well."

"Uh, sure." I drop my Mazda fob on the counter and pick up the small black velvet envelope with two matte crimson key cards. Fancy, fancy.

"Have you stayed with us before or is this your first time?" she asks. She's using a sort of fitness-instructor voice. Overenthusiastic, with an ever so slight undercurrent of condescension. She's young, and I can tell that she's performing her idea of adulthood, using this affectation in an attempt to appear professional. I used to do it, too. You never feel old enough, until the day you don't feel young enough.

"First time," I say.

"We're so glad to have you! I'm delighted to tell you about our amenities. . . ." She chatters on about the spa, the wellness center; about snowshoe rentals, snow tubing, ice-skating, cross-country skiing. She takes out a pamphlet, then proceeds to read me the entire pamphlet. She talks about how the Finger Lakes region rivals Napa when it comes to wine. She lists every restaurant and store on Main Street.

"Matthew will take you to your cottage," she says, gesturing to the porter, who hovers at my back. "Please let us know if you need anything. Thank you for choosing the Waterfront Collective. We do hope you enjoy your stay!"

"Ready?" Matthew asks me. Something about how he says it gives me the impression that he's annoyed with me. Completely uninterested in my existence. Or maybe he's perfectly pleasant, but Mary Beth was so bubbly and saccharine that he seems stoic in comparison. I don't know. He's not looking at me.

It pinches a little, that no one really looks at me anymore. Not like they used to.

"Ma'am?"

"Sorry. I'm ready." I give a thumbs-up for some reason. He grabs my fob off the counter and then opens the lobby door for me. I realize this isn't an act of chivalry, that I'm probably expected to tip him. I hope I have cash.

I follow him out to my car, where he opens the passenger-side door and gestures to me.

"Oh. Um, okay," I mutter to myself, climbing in.

He gets in on the driver's side, adjusts the seat.

He pulls onto a gravel drive behind the main mansion.

"I have a friend meeting me here. She's taking a car service from Syracuse. Is there . . ." As he waits for me to finish my question, I begin to feel like it's a stupid one. ". . . transportation for her? Should I direct her to the cottage or . . . ?"

"She can check in at the desk. The shuttle will take her to you," he says, making a left onto a dirt road. Tucked back in the trees, there's a contemporary cottage, white, with a red arched door. It's tall, two stories, and oddly narrow. All windows at the front. A stone chimney rises up off the steeply pitched roof.

Matthew puts the car in park and makes quick work of getting my suitcase out of the trunk. I grab my bag, Joel's mystery gift, the key cards.

The ground here is hard and crunchy, winter frozen. The trees sway, and it really does sound like the woods are whispering.

Matthew drags my suitcase up to the cottage door.

"Thanks," I say when we reach it. "I can take it from here."

I fumble around in my bag for my wallet, then gracelessly search for an appropriate bill. I give him a five.

"Thank you, ma'am. Enjoy your weekend," he says. Doesn't sound like he means it. He bows slightly before getting back into my car and driving it away. Hopefully to that heated garage. It's a seven-year-old Mazda, though, nothing worth taking for a joyride.

I burrow inside my coat and take a moment to look around, wonder how close the nearest cottage is. Who's inside it, what they're doing, and if they're doing it in matching plaid onesies. It's too cold to continue to stand here speculating.

Blowing into my hands, I admire the view of the lake—the water dark and eerily still. The sun has gone pale as it sinks behind the trees, steeping the horizon in a tawny haze.

Shivering, I turn around, slip one of the key cards out of the velvet envelope, and tap it on the scanner. There's a faint click, and I twist the knob, open the door. I'm greeted by an aggressive woody scent and a soft wave of light. I grab my suitcase and step inside, letting the door shut itself behind me with a heavy thunk.

It's tricky to figure out how I feel about the space because I'm too busy anticipating what Naomi will think of it. What she'll make fun of or comment on.

It's small but open. To the right there's a floating staircase that leads up to a loft. To the left is the fireplace, rustic white stone. There's a leather couch in front of it, covered partially by a chunky knit throw blanket. There's a modern kitchenette in the corner, a basket of apples on the counter. A café table and chairs. Under the staircase are two doors. One to a surprisingly spacious bathroom, all white marble and glass, with a double vanity, a waterfall shower, and a freestanding tub. It smells of fresh linen. There are fuzzy towels, and two luxe robes that I know Naomi and I will end up in.

The other door leads to a bedroom. There's a four-poster bed and a midcentury dresser, some funky wallpaper to make it a little less West Elm. The lone window is covered with heavy curtains. I pull them back to check out the view. The lake is there, obscured only partially by the trees. This will be Naomi's room.

I lug my suitcase up the stairs to the loft. There's a daybed; a nightstand with a twin-bell alarm clock; one of those flat TVs that can look like pieces of art, only it's on a stand, not mounted, so the jig is up. The ceiling is vaulted, which helps it not to feel too top bunk, too cramped. Especially with the windows. At the back and the front, just walls of glass. Through them the trees, the lake. It's a stunning view. But I don't get any curtains, so I guess I'll be up with the sun.

My phone vibrates in my pocket, startling me. I take a breath, shimmy it free from my jeans. A message from Naomi. Be there soon!!! Don't have any fun without me. Seriously. Not even a little.

Wouldn't dream of it, I reply.

"Soon" is a vague term in Naomi-speak. Could mean ten minutes, could mean an hour.

I hate not knowing how much time I have to kill.

I use the bathroom, wash my hands, sample the complimentary lotion. It smells too strong, too floral. I attempt to wash it off, rigorously soaping my hands, running the water hot, despite knowing I'm stripping my skin of its natural oils, which I've read in numerous articles is very bad and will age me faster. Women's hands are the tell. There are no fillers, no lifts for withered, veiny witch hands. At least not that I know of. Not yet.

I take a quick glance in the mirror. There are bags under my eyes that I need an ice cube and concealer to correct. I take my hair down and put it back up, smoothing some flyaways that pop right back out. It's exhausting to care this much.

I slog back upstairs to my suitcase, get out my cosmetics bag, which is the size and weight of a concrete block. I take it into the bathroom and get to work. I put on a podcast about Chernobyl while I primp, because there's nothing like hearing the grisly details of acute radiation syndrome while staring at your own face to really put things in perspective.

I know Naomi doesn't care what I look like, that she'll just be happy to see me. She's also high on something half the time, so everything and everyone is beautiful to her. But still, it feels necessary that I do this, that I attempt to put myself together. Otherwise I'll be too preoccupied for any chance of a good time.

It's moisturizer, foundation, concealer, blush, highlighter, mascara. Lipstick.

But lipstick is never just lipstick. It's a sort of soul-preserving lie, like putting on armor before battle. You can die wearing armor, but you'll feel better about your chances. Confident on the front lines before the arrows fly.

I go for my most expensive tube, a splurge purchase from a designer more famous for couture than for makeup. I read online that it's the best there is, that it has a cult following, which made me sad but also made me buy it. It is pretty. A satin-finish crimson red. The shade is Killer.

"Sure," I say to myself, and blot with a tissue. "Sure."

Then I rewind the podcast thirty seconds in case I missed something crucial about the rupture of the reactor core.

I wonder if anyone living near the plant had any inkling of doubt. If, as they passed under the shadows of the smokestacks, they'd ever considered the worst-case scenario. I think I would have, but who knows?

Besides, anticipating the worst-case scenario doesn't prepare you for the worst-case scenario. Just gives you the opportunity to be smug in the face of disaster.

4

She doesn't need to knock. I can sense her. I can smell her, somehow. Her signature smoky vanilla perfume. She says it makes her feel like a sexy campfire.

I'm at the door as the shuttle pulls up. I open the door and there she is.

She wears a faux-fur bucket hat, a 1970s denim halter jumpsuit with wide bell-bottoms, cowboy boots, and her Penny Lane jacket—orange suedette with fuzzy pink trim. Her long black hair is in a thick braid that falls down to her ass. The only makeup she has on is some metallic green eyeliner, artfully smudged. No lipstick. No mascara. No foundation—she doesn't need it.

We stare at each other for a moment, and then she tackles me to the floor in an aggressive hug.

"I'm going to fucking eat you!" she yells into my hair as her arms wrap around my neck.

"I'm dying," I say. "Help! Help!"

"Sorry. Do I smell like I've been traveling for twenty hours?" she asks, letting me go.

"You smell like you."

She gasps. "Do I *always* smell like I've been traveling for twenty hours?"

"Stop. You smell famous and you look like a Spice Girl."

"Aw, I'm blushing."

We sit up, catch our breath. Her hat was knocked off in the wild embrace. She picks it up and puts it on the couch, goes back outside for her massive suitcase and an obnoxious carry-on that I doubt fit in the overhead bin.

"Do you need help?" I ask her.

"Yes, generally speaking," she says. "But not with this. It's my cardio. My strength training. Joseph Pilates can suck my— Ooh, I like the length."

She reaches for my hair, then grazes my collarbone with a manicured nail. "Shorter. Edgier. It looks good. The color, too. Going more strawberry than blond. Closer to your natural."

"Is it edgy? I worried it was too suburban."

She cradles my face in her warm palm. "You never post pictures of yourself. Last time I saw you, you were platinum."

The last time we saw each other was at Levi's birthday party. Joel and I drove six and a half hours to Brooklyn for what turned out to be a sort of grunge rave in a Bushwick warehouse. The music was so loud it hurt my bones. I saw Naomi for about ten minutes, as she dragged me to the bar to take a shot of something, told me she loved me more than salt and missed me like candy, and that she'd be right back. I didn't see her again until the next day, when we had an awkward brunch at one p.m. Lee didn't show, Joel was anxious to get on the road home, and Naomi had to excuse herself to go throw up in the bathroom. I followed her in to hold back her hair.

She apologized profusely. "I never get hungover. You know this."

"I know."

"It's him," she'd said. "I swear it's not me. It's *him*."

I didn't have to ask her to elaborate. I knew she meant Lee.

Naomi's trouble on her own, but with him? Fire, gasoline; gasoline, fire. They have that sort of wild passion that makes you roll your eyes, scrunch your nose. That makes you so jealous you don't know what to do with yourself. They're good for each other in that sense, because they understand each other, can keep up. But sometimes Naomi needs someone to reel her in, like I can. Levi can't do that. I appreciate that she's with someone who never tries to turn down her volume, dim her light. But now and then, I worry he'll turn her up so high that she'll explode.

They've been together on and off for a decade, and sometimes I wonder if they'll ever get married, elope. Other times I wonder if they'll kill each other.

His party was almost a year ago. A scary thought. The older you get, the faster time goes, as if the sand becomes finer the longer it sits in the top of the hourglass.

"You look the same," I tell her.

"Is that a compliment?"

"Yeah. Of course it is."

"Well, shucks. Are my nips out?" she asks, reaching into her jumpsuit to adjust. She looks around the room. "This place is very . . ."

She pauses, tilts her head.

"Not into it?" I ask. "I won't be offended. Joel picked it, not me."

"Pinterest chic. Luxe basic. Like, coming down the hill and seeing that mansion, I was thinking, okay, we're going to drink fucking hot toddies and layer scarves and flirt with the ghost of a railroad tycoon. Like, asking reception, who was that man at the bar last night? And they'd be, like, what man? Pan up to the portrait of him on the wall; he's been dead for a century. That whole thing."

"Right."

"But now, here, this is a different vibe. This is, like, drink hot chocolate, hashtag *so blessed*. Like, someone who would ask to speak to a manager wouldn't need to here, because this place was designed specifically for them. Like—"

I interrupt her because otherwise she'll just keep going. "There's funky wallpaper in the bedroom."

"I mean, go figure," she says. "But is there a ghost we can tag-team?"

"I don't know, Nay. Did you bring your Ouija board?"

"Fuck! Knew I forgot something," she says, grinning. "Is that real fruit?"

She walks over to the basket of apples and picks one out. She tosses it up in the air and catches it with the other hand, then takes a confident bite.

"Is it plastic?"

She shrugs. "Might as well be."

"How was your trip?" I ask her.

"The tour, or coming here?"

"Both."

She takes another bite, then sets the apple down on the counter. "Good. Bad. Fun. Exhausting."

"Band must be doing well, though."

"Yeah. Don't get me wrong—I'm grateful. 'Kitchen Floor' pays the bills. But if I hear that song one more fucking time . . ."

She turns to me, puts a finger gun to her temple, and pulls the trigger.

"It's still weird to hear Lee on the radio," I say.

"Yeah," she says, sighing. "The song is so thoroughly mediocre. I can't wrap my head around it. That's their big hit? Depresses the shit out of me."

Thoroughly mediocre is generous. "Have you had the talk yet? About them getting someone else?"

"Not yet. Mm. I gotta get that authentic fruit taste out of my mouth," she says, pulling a handful of Dum-Dums from her coat pocket. She started with the lollipops to help her quit smoking. They were effective in that she doesn't smoke anymore, but she's been on a lollipop a day for about three years now. "Want one? Think I've got a cream soda."

"My favorite!"

She hands me the cream soda–flavored one and selects a blue raspberry for herself.

I appreciate the treat but suspect it's a means of deflection from talking about work. Naomi studied photography in college and had some success working in fashion after graduating. She started managing PR for Levi's band as a side gig, to be supportive. But then Data Ave took off and took over both of their lives.

For the past year or so, she's expressed to me some dissatisfaction in working with Data Ave. With Lee. She's talked about wanting to get back to being an artist. When I asked her why she couldn't do both, she lost it.

"Because it's not fucking possible! It's not a part-time thing, Sloane. It's consuming. Twenty-four seven, for years now. How did I end up on my boyfriend's payroll? How did I end up in this position? Where *my* life revolves around him?"

I didn't know what to say, how to respond. I could sense in that moment that I was failing her, but I couldn't figure out what to do about it. What the right advice was.

"I'm sorry," I'd said, finally.

"It's fine. It's fine. Never mind," she'd said, changing the subject. Like she does now.

"So, what do you want to get up to?" she asks me. "You look hot. We should go out. You want to go out?"

"Whatever you want," I say, unwrapping my lollipop.

"Let's go into town," she says. "It's so cute and quaint. We can walk around, get some dinner. How's that sound?"

"Sounds pretty PG."

"Well, we're doing a mountain of cocaine first," she says. Joking, maybe. "Where's the bathroom? I have to pee. Takes me, like, fifteen minutes to get in and out of this jumpsuit."

"Just there." I point, and she twirls away.

"Thanks, birthday girl!" she says. "Ah, damn. I forgot your crown."

"No Ouija board, no crown. What's even in that giant suitcase, then?"

"My victims," she says, cackling.

5

An hour later, we're shivering in front of the cottage, waiting for the shuttle to take us into town.

"Let's just go back inside," I say. "It's taking forever."

"I never used to get cold," Naomi says, ignoring me. "I used to be out in the middle of winter in fishnets and a leather jacket and I was *fine*."

"You weren't fine. You were drunk."

"Offensive," she says.

"Where *is* this shuttle? They said five minutes, and it's been twelve minutes. No. Thirteen minutes."

"Impatient," she says. "It'll get here. And it's such a beautiful night. Look at the lake! The moon!"

"I can't feel my toes."

"When they thaw, you'll appreciate them like you never have before."

"I appreciate my toes all the time."

She's skeptical. Eyebrows raised, lips pursed.

"What? I do," I say, though I can't remember the last time I thought about my toes. "I should've kept my car."

"If you drove, you couldn't drink. This is better. Ah! That's it," she says, pointing to a white van bumbling toward us.

"Or we're about to get kidnapped."

"Relax. There's resort branding on it."

"Maybe that's part of the ruse."

"It'd be a good ruse," she says as the van pulls up. The door slides open, and the driver greets us. I'm relieved that he appears to be in his sixties and that the entire resort isn't staffed by college kids.

"Hello! Good evening! Heading into town?"

"Yes, thank you, Todd," Naomi says, climbing into the van. Either he was her driver earlier or she's spotted a name tag that I can't see. Or she's intuited his name through psychic clues, mind reading. Or his name isn't Todd, and she's testing to see if he'll correct her. Hard to say.

"Any destination in particular, or . . . ?" He's got a thick Midwestern accent and it endears him to me.

"Anywhere on Main Street," I say, getting in and scooching onto the seat beside Naomi. I press my hands to the heating vent. The door closes automatically, making a horrible whirring sound.

"How's your night so far?" Naomi asks him.

"It's good, thank you. Would you like some music?" he asks.

"Yeah, okay," I say. "Sure."

He presses a button, and a second later, it's "Everyday" by Buddy Holly.

"I was just thinking about Buddy Holly," I say.

"No, you weren't," Naomi says. "You were thinking about death."

My mouth falls open as I eject a strange noise.

"What?" Naomi asks. "Am I wrong?"

I always forget how well she knows me—better than I know myself. It's saved me in the past, her intimate knowledge of my heart, my mind. I've used it for clarity, for comfort. But sometimes this knowledge feels invasive, unwelcome. Sometimes it terrifies me.

She makes eye contact with Todd in the rearview mirror. "We're very pretty but very grim."

"Hmm?" he says, as if he hasn't been listening.

The drive to Main Street is short, only a few minutes. We pull up to the curb in front of one of the shops.

"This okay, girls?" Todd asks.

"Perfect," Naomi says sunnily.

The door opens, and I'm about to step out when Todd says, "Now, you give me a call when you're ready to go back, and I'll pick you up. As long as it's before one a.m. You have the number?"

"Think so," I say.

"Good. Be smart, girls. Be safe."

"We will. Thank you, Todd," Naomi says, following me out of the van. The door shuts and he's off down Main Street. She turns to me. "Why the face?"

"I don't like 'ma'am' or 'lady,' but somehow 'girl' is worse."

"What would you prefer, Goldilocks?" she asks, patting me on the head. "What would be *juuusssst* right?"

"I don't know," I say, shaking her off. "I don't know."

"God," she says, looking around. "What a sweet little American town. Smells like apple pie and willful ignorance."

She threads her arm through mine. "You hungry? You want to eat now, or you want to shop?"

"If by 'shop' you mean *go into every store and not buy anything*, then shop."

"Done!" she says, pivoting on her heel and dragging me into a small store that sells artisan soaps shaped like mythical creatures— mermaids and unicorns and fairies. The prettiest of fictions.

———

After exploring every shop on Main Street, we get a tiny booth at the Pharmacy—the only bar in town. It's eccentric but sophisticated. Exposed brick; built-in bookcases brimming with tchotchkes, like rusty funnels, apothecary bottles, antique syringes, crystal skulls, plaster molds of teeth, and fraying books. There's a fireplace, inside it a neon sign made to look like a fire, glowing red and orange and yellow.

The ceiling is distressed tin. The lighting fixtures are all art deco with bulbs emitting a dim purple hue. The drinks are expensive, and the food is outrageous.

Naomi and I split some truffle fries as we sip our first cocktails of the evening. I ordered a Negroni; she got something called Soylent Green.

"What's in that, again?" I ask, pointing to her glass.

"Very funny."

"No, really. I'm asking."

"Gin with cucumber, mint, and lime." She slides the glass across the table. It's a beaker, actually. They serve their drinks in beakers, shots in test tubes.

I take a little sip. "Mm, mm. People-y."

She laughs, taking her drink back. She looks at me for a moment, and I can almost hear her wheels turning over the music in the bar, some mellow indie rock playlist. She's analyzing me, and under her keen gaze I'm at once both desperate to know what she's thinking and filled with such dread that I might prefer to stay ignorant.

She parts her glossy lips but, whatever she's about to say, she's interrupted by "Kitchen Floor," Data Ave's big hit.

Naomi downs her drink. "I can't escape."

She signals the waiter and orders two shots of vodka and a tonic with lime.

"I don't do shots anymore," I tell her.

"Good, 'cause they're both for me. Don't give me that look—you know I'm a lush."

"I can ask them to change the song."

"Fuck the song."

"Do you want to talk about it?"

"Talk about what?" she asks, looking over her shoulder for the waiter. For her shots.

"Why don't you tell me about Europe? Let me live vicariously through you. Please."

"You should have come with me."

"I have a job."

"It's remote."

"I have a house. I have . . . It's . . ." It's too difficult to explain logistics to a free spirit. "Come on. Don't make me beg."

"That's what he said." She winks at me, and I roll my eyes.

Her shots arrive, she takes them in quick succession, and then she tells me her stories, slurring through tall tales of tour adventures. Outsmarting a pickpocket in Berlin. Befriending an Italian heiress in Rome, getting invited to her villa somewhere on the Amalfi Coast. Drinking the best wine she's ever tasted with a view of the Tyrrhenian Sea, passing around rare artifacts from the ruins of Pompeii stolen from an archaeological dig and kept in a private collection. Drinking gin and tonic out of cans in the shadow of the Tower of London, communing with the spirit of Anne Boleyn.

At some point, she goes up to the bar for another drink, leaving me alone at the table to pick at soggy calamari and the undesirable remains of charcuterie. Tiny sour pickles and colorful stinky cheese and mounds of congealed mustard. She was the one who ordered it, but she hasn't eaten much; frankly, I don't know how she's still standing. Her tolerance to alcohol has always been much higher than mine; she's a born party girl.

She's made a friend. Some tall, strikingly handsome stranger with curly dark hair and tattoos, dressed like a hipster pirate. He appears somehow completely out of place but also like he's part of the decor, like the bar is his home and he can never leave. There's a weird aura about him.

Naomi's into it.

I anticipate her returning to the table, but minutes pass. Half an hour. She hasn't looked back once, hasn't taken her eyes off the stranger. She's had another shot and another drink, maybe a tonic. I'm keeping tally on a napkin. What else do I have to do?

Focusing on Naomi, I've lost count of my own drinks, which is unlike me. *Is this my second or third? Maybe third?*

It must be because I think I'm imagining things. Because I think someone's staring at me. In the corner, a man whose face is half concealed in shadow, half washed out by a red neon sign. He leans back against the wall, but his shoulders hunch forward, his head angled down. His hair, almost as long as mine, hangs over his eyes. Something about him is familiar but I can't place him. Maybe if he were closer . . .

There's a prickly heat rising from somewhere inside me. Exhilarating. Uncomfortable. What if he comes over here?

Someone breaks a glass, the sound shattering the delusion I have about the man in the corner. He's not looking at me. No one's hit on me in a bar in years, and that's not going to change tonight. I take another sip of my drink, finish it off. I pull out my phone and text Joel, wait for him to respond. Wait for Naomi to come back.

This whole thing isn't a new experience. Naomi's been abandoning me to flirt since we were fourteen. The night she and I solidified our relationship, went from classmates to actual friends, we were attending Meghan Fitzpatrick's birthday party. We'd gone to the movies to see some forgettable rom-com and then migrated to the mall. Everyone split off into groups, and somehow Naomi and I ended up in the food court, just the two of us, licking cinnamon sugar from a shared Auntie Anne's pretzel off our fingers.

"What kind of music do you listen to?" she asked me. I'm sure we'd spoken before then, at school or in dance class, or at some other mutual friend's birthday party, but this is the first time I remember.

"Why?" I was being defensive—a strategic choice. She was the coolest girl in school; I was desperate to be her friend, but I didn't want her to know that.

"Sorry, what?"

"Why do you want to know? So you can judge me?"

She started to laugh. She has the most delicious laugh; I had to bite my lip not to smile, to maintain my stone-cold façade. "I mean, obviously."

"What do you think I listen to?"

"I think you listen to Fiona Apple."

She was right. I did. Still do. "Okay. What else?"

"The Yeah Yeah Yeahs."

Right again. "Okay, and . . . ?"

"The Strokes," she said, and sipped her soda. "And then, like, Billie Holiday. On vinyl."

"Okay, fine, you have me all figured out. Congratulations."

She laughed again, snorting root beer through her nose. She wiped her face with a napkin, then started pressing those little buttons on the plastic lid of her cup, fidgeting with the straw. "So. Who's judging who here?"

I looked at her, lowering my eyebrows, inquiring.

"You thought I was going to judge you, but you judge me."

"No, I don't."

"Yes, you do! You've been judging me this whole time. You assumed I asked you about music so I could, like, figure out if you were cool. Like I'm some total uppity hipster bitch. But I was only asking because I already think you're cool and was genuinely curious."

I was taken aback. She was right again. And—*and*—she thought I was cool. Naomi Rowe thought *I* was cool. She wore Doc Martens to gym class and didn't even get in trouble, because she was a track star and won a bunch of medals and could do whatever she wanted. She'd hang out with Coach Laura on the bleachers while the rest of us did jumping jacks. Everyone had a crush on her. She got straight As. Never had an awkward phase. Perfect teeth without orthodontic interference, flawless skin without ever agonizing over benzoyl peroxide or salicylic acid. She always showed up to school in some inspired mix of thrift-store finds and designer labels under her varsity jacket, inspiring trends throughout the halls.

"To be fair," she said, filling the silence, "I can be a total uppity hipster bitch."

"I guess me, too."

"Want to go try on ugly dresses?"

"Yeah, okay."

She took my hand and dragged me to JCPenney, where we picked out horrible mother-of-the-bride-type gowns for each other. We paraded in and out of the dressing rooms giggling like lunatics.

Afterward, we went back to the food court to meet up with the rest of the girls and wait for Meghan's mom to pick us up. But the girls weren't back yet, so it was still just us. That was when we discovered that we both have dream malls. We were describing our respective malls and splitting a milkshake when this boy approached us. Approached Naomi. Some cute skater kid who was old enough to drive. They flirted for a while; then he offered Naomi a ride, and I watched her toy with the idea of taking it. I think she would have had the other girls not shown up a few minutes later, Meghan in her garish pink birthday dress, her braces gleaming under ruthless fluorescent lights.

"Sorry," Naomi told the boy. "Not tonight."

She gave him her number, then took my hand again as all of us headed out to the parking lot to pile into Meghan's mom's minivan.

"It was a fake number," she whispered in my ear as we sat smooshed in the back seat.

"Really? I thought it was true love."

She laughed, squeezed my hand, and said, "I think this is. I think I love *you*."

I dropped all my defenses, the façade. "I think I love you, too."

6

She squeezes my hand now as we wait outside the bar after calling for the shuttle. It's past midnight but shy of one, dark and bitter cold. My toes are numb again, my fingers, my face. My wrist aches like it does sometimes, just to remind me it was once broken. Little flurries whirl around, not really sticking to anything.

"We should just walk," Naomi says, hiccuping. "Can't be that far."

"We're not walking," I say, craning my neck to look for the van.

"Why not? It'd be an adventure. The night is young!"

"First off, you can barely stand."

"I could run a fucking marathon right now," she says, and she means it. Her endurance while she's drunk is pretty remarkable, her resolve transcending intoxication.

"Okay, sure. But it's pitch-black and it's snowing."

She attempts to catch a snowflake on her tongue. "Not enough to eat."

I look down at my phone. Still no reply from Joel, which has me sick to my stomach. I tap a frozen finger on the screen to open the weather app. "Great. Now the forecast is all snow. We could get hit with up to four feet. What if we get stuck here? I have a meeting Monday and I didn't bring my laptop."

"It's New York in January," she says, her tone shifting, going sharp. "It snows. There are plows. You always assume bad shit is gonna happen."

"You always assume it won't."

She doesn't say anything, just blinks at me. There are flurries caught in her eyelashes.

"This is what you do, Nay. You put me in this position. You make me feel like I'm crazy for being practical."

She throws her hands up, shakes her head. "It's some snow, Sloane. Not an apocalyptic blizzard. But you can't see that because you're always reading about the fucking Carolean Death March."

I'm surprised she remembers. I told her about it a few years ago, after I fell down a Wikipedia rabbit hole.

"You're obsessed with disaster. Right now it's Chernobyl. Before that, Aberfan. Before that, the *Hindenburg*," she says. I can't tell if she's teasing or being mean. "Remember when we went to the cape for June's wedding? You brought a book about Columbine to the beach. You love a tragedy."

"Maybe that's why I'm friends with you."

"Hey," she says, eyes wide and glassy. Hurt.

"Well . . ." I mumble, looking down at the sidewalk. She called me out, and I got defensive. But I'm not walking it back.

The shuttle pulls over to the curb. We stare at each other as Todd opens the side door.

"Good evening, girls! Bringing you back to Whispering Woods?"

"Yes," I say, stepping into the van. Naomi lingers on the sidewalk with her arms crossed, defiant. I give her a minute before I lean my head out the door and hiss, *"Get. In."* Like she's a stubborn toddler and I'm her exasperated mother.

"Maybe I'll walk," she says, digging a lollipop out of her pocket. "It is a *beautiful* night."

"Naomi. You're embarrassing yourself."

She unwraps the Dum-Dum, gives it a lick. "No, I'm not. I'm embarrassing you."

"Just get in the van."

She laughs coolly and finally relents, climbing in.

Todd clears his throat and shuts the door. I'm sure to him, or any other outsider, it sounds like we hate each other, like we're in some vicious fight. But this is a form of unconditional love. Of release. We gift each other the freedom to gnash our teeth, to growl and gnaw. Behave badly. Be terrible. Because we'll love each other through it and no one else will. Because this ugliness is not permitted anywhere else. At least, not without consequence.

"Don't be mad at me," she says, resting her head on my shoulder. "Don't be mean to me."

"I'm sorry," I say, staring out the window. "I thought you were being mean. And you left me alone all night to go flirt with that guy."

"I struck up a conversation with a nice, handsome gentleman," she says, doing her best Blanche DuBois. "I am terribly sorry."

"Okay," I say.

"That's not why you're upset, though," she says, dropping the Southern belle shtick. "There's something else."

She's right, and it's *so* annoying. My skin feels like a straitjacket. "Don't make me say it."

"Talk to me. I'm right here."

It's Joel. Why isn't he responding? What is he doing? Why did he send me on this trip? And why am I asking myself these questions when I know the answers?

"Sloane?"

"I don't know, Naomi. Take a wild guess."

We're already back at our cottage. Todd opens the door. "Good night, girls."

"Good night, Sir Todd," Naomi says as we stumble out of the van. "I miss you already."

The air feels like tiny ice daggers stabbing my face, leaving my lips raw. I hurry up to the cottage door, slam the key card against the lock.

"Look at the lake!" Naomi says. "It's so pretty. Fuck. Should we live here? I want to live here."

I open the door and step inside. "Come on. You'll freeze."

"All right, all right," Naomi says, her boot heels click-clacking as she steps over the threshold. "Ooh, should we start a fire?"

"Let's just regroup in the morning," I say, massaging my temples as I start up the stairs.

"No," she says. "Let's stay up and brush each other's hair and gossip about people we don't know."

I look back at her.

"I'm sorry I got caught up at the bar," she says, kicking off her boots. "I had too much Soylent Green."

I sigh. "I know you did."

"I can't help it. I just love people."

"I know you do."

"You most of all."

"So you say."

She frowns at me. I've hurt her feelings again, and now I feel like a villain.

"Okay. I'll try to stay up," I say, plopping down on the couch. It's dark in here. I don't know where any of the light switches are and I'm too tired to hunt for them. "But I don't think either of us should attempt to start a fire."

"Don't trust me?" she asks, cozying up, pulling a blanket over our heads. "Did you do this at sleepovers when you were a kid? Make blanket forts?"

"Probably. I don't really remember," I say. "I barely remember yesterday."

"That's not true. You remember everything."

"I remember some things in very specific detail. The rest is hazy."

"Mm. We would have had fun as kids," she says. "My only regret in life is that I didn't know you sooner."

She can be so sweet sometimes. I wish it made me feel something other than unworthy.

"That and the Playboy Bunny tattoo," she says.

I laugh.

"Hey! You're supposed to say, *No, it's cute.*"

"Are we being honest here?" I ask.

"I don't know. Are we?"

I yank the blanket down, freeing my head. "I can't breathe under there."

"Come back," Naomi says. "Trade secrets with me in the safety of the blanket fort."

She's doing her best to get me to confess. She knows something's wrong, and she's working me. She'll get it out of me eventually, so I might as well tell her now. I give a quick eulogy for my pride—*You had a rough go of it. Goodbye*—and then tell her the truth.

"I think he's doing it again," I say. "And I don't know what bothers me more, the fact that he could be cheating or how little I actually care."

After a beat, she says, "You know, I've tried to be there for you in the way that you need, I've tried to give you space, and I—"

"Naomi, it's fine. Can we just—"

"No, let me finish," she says. "I don't know what it's been like

41

for you. And I don't pass judgment. I trust you, and I've trusted that you're dealing with it in the way that's best for you. But maybe I fucked up. Maybe I should have stepped in sooner."

"I don't need your help. I'm a grown-up."

"You've been a grown-up since we were teenagers. Have you ever thought about, like, trying to be happy?"

"Don't be cute," I say, standing.

"I'm serious!" she says, grabbing my hand before I can walk away.

"What does happiness even look like, Nay? Is it even real? Is anyone happy? Are you? I'm sorry. I'm . . . I'm not trying to chase some unicorn just to find out it's a horse with a cone glued to its head. I just want to be in my house with my things and watch a movie on a Friday night and garden on the weekends and . . . I don't know. Buy groceries. And it's not lost on me how that must sound to you, but what am I supposed to do? Get a divorce? End up alone, stressed about bills? Let me just . . ." I take a breath. "Everyone has their problems. This is mine. I'm not going to upend my life over it only to wind up miserable in a different way. It's not worth the risk."

Silence squirms around the cottage. The walls seem to inch in. That woody smell grows rapidly in strength, becomes cloying. The air is too warm and too dry; it scrapes against my skin, claws at my throat and eyes. Through the windows, the walls of glass, I can see flurries scurry across the dark.

The quiet becomes unendurable. Naomi squeezes my hand.

"What?" I ask.

"You've always settled for less because—" She stops, shakes her head. "I wish you saw yourself the way I see you."

I give a hollow laugh. "Yeah. I guess me, too. I think I'm going to turn in. I'll see you in the morning."

"Okay. Good night, Sloane. Love you."

"Love you, too."

Up in the loft, I sit on the bed and stare at my phone.

I should have some water. I should take off my makeup. I should apply my nightly retinol, my moisturizer. I should change into my pajamas. I should forget what just happened, everything I said, everything she said.

I shouldn't have had so much to drink. I shouldn't have eaten so much goddamn cheese. I shouldn't have come here. I really shouldn't have come here.

I should go to bed. I should just go to sleep.

I shouldn't do what I'm about to do.

Maybe Naomi's right. Maybe I love a disaster.

Because I open up the doorbell-camera app I installed on my phone that I pretended to be too tech inept to use so Joel wouldn't worry about it—if he even would have thought to worry about it. And it takes me a minute, because I actually am tech inept, but I do figure it out. I do find her. Three and a half hours ago, right around the time I texted him, I see a car that I don't recognize pull up in front of the house. I see a woman walk up to the front door, think better of it, and promptly change direction. Probably heading in through the garage.

It's hard to tell, because the camera isn't particularly good and she doesn't get close enough to it, and it's nighttime, so the footage is blurry, that unnerving black-and-white, but she looks pretty. She looks young. Younger than me.

My shoes feel too heavy, too difficult to remove. I leave them on, fall sideways down to the mattress. I let my phone slip from my hand, disappear somewhere. I pull up the blankets, hoping I disappear somewhere. Underneath them, into sleep. The wind whirs outside, rattling the windows.

"Go away," I tell it. "You can't come in. You can't come in."

I close my eyes as the room starts to spin.

———

When my eyes open, the haze of sleep is slow to fade. There's music. The trees dance to it.

Tap-tap-tap-tap.

It's almost like jazz. Like the faint, nostalgic jazz of Main Street. Only it isn't.

Tap-tap-tap-tap.

No, it isn't like that at all. Because it isn't pleasant, this music, this sound. It's insistent.

Tap-tap.

There are windows on either side of me. Pure glass. The woods. Nature. There are no curtains to pull. There's nowhere to hide.

Why would I think that?

I need to go back to sleep; the longer I stay awake, the harder it will be. But it's loud. I turn over, stare at the ceiling. It's so tall, pitched so high above me.

Tap-tap.

Is it getting louder?

It's the wind. That's all. All it is.

Tap-tap-tap-tap.

Wind at my window, shrieking with urgency.

But it's not only the wind. There's a whisper hiding underneath. A voice. And a . . .

A clinking. A chattering.

My teeth.

I reach for my trembling jaw, hold it still. My hands are freezing. *I'm* freezing. There's no blanket. Where are the covers? Why am I still wearing my shoes?

A sourness bubbles up my throat. I swallow it down, run my tongue over unbrushed teeth. I shudder.

Sitting up to remove my shoes, I catch a glimpse of the moon, a slim crescent shining like the blade of a sharp knife. The sky is black and starless. There are no more flurries, and without them, the scene is ominous. The threat of a storm looms; I feel it in my gut.

I pull off one of my shoes. The other. I let them fall to the floor with a *clunk-clunk*.

What follows is stark silence, and I understand immediately that it's a listening silence. That the wind and the whispering have ceased to press their ears to the windows. That they want to know if I'm awake. That they don't want me to hear what they're saying.

I hold perfectly still. Hold my breath. Make no noise.

Why this paranoia? Why am I so afraid, so fearful of the wind? Of these big, big windows. Of a view of the sky.

The whispering resumes, and my eyes slide right, toward the front of the cottage, and somehow slowly but all at once, a dark silhouette appears at the glass. A figure.

There's someone at my window. There's someone out there.

Only there can't be. I'm on the second floor.

It's a tree. A shadow. It's not what it looks like. Or it is, but I'm dreaming, and this isn't real; it's a nightmare.

It must be a nightmare, because that isn't a shadow. It isn't a tree. The shape of it, there, at the glass, at the corner of my eye— it's—

When was the last time I had a nightmare?

Tap-tap-tap-tap-tap-tap-tap.

It's coming from behind me now, and my head swivels on my neck so fast, I get dizzy. There's a branch. I see it. Up to the left.

Tap-tap-tap-tap.

"Shh," I tell it. "I'm trying to sleep."

I yawn, for a moment forgetting about the figure, or for a moment certain that when I turn back it won't be there. Or that the source will reveal itself to me. An explanation. Logic.

But I turn back and it's still there. Hovering.

I shut my eyes tight, and when I open them again, the silhouette is gone. No figure haunts my view. I let go of the breath I've been holding captive.

The heat wheezes on, blows in from some hidden vent, and the tapping resumes, the wind. My stomach churns.

This should be when I shrug and go back to sleep. Except there's this sudden sense of doom that I can't shake. The sense that something is off, that something is wrong. There's a fluttering of nerves. Panic.

Then I remember why.

Here I am, alone, awake, and scared in this strange bed, while there's another woman busy in mine. In my bed, my home, my safe place tarnished.

Tap-tap-tap-tap.

The doom squeeze intensifies. I pull the covers over my head, grip them like a parachute on the way down.

Here I am, alone in the dark, with my sour breath and my chattering teeth and my life on the precipice of catastrophe. The night keeps the snow under its tongue, but the cold wind persists in its tapping at my window, loud and gloomy as a prophet.

Just the wind. Only the wind.

7

"Wake up! Wake up! Wake *uuuuuup!*" Naomi climbs into my bed. She pushes me over to make room. "It's birthday eve!"

I groan. "What time is it? Why are you doing this to me?"

"It's almost eleven, sleepyhead."

"No, it isn't," I say, opening a single heavy eyelid to check the nightstand clock. It's ten forty-seven. "Shoot."

"Golly gee, you slept in!"

We look at each other and take a quick, silent vote on whether we should acknowledge last night's conversation, continue the discussion, or sweep it under the rug for as long as possible, linger in sweet denial. The latter wins.

There's no point in telling her what I saw on the doorbell camera. I shouldn't have even looked.

Why did I look?

"You're still in dreamland," she says, taming a flyaway, gently pressing it to my skull.

"Mm," I say, rubbing my eyes and wracking my brain for a more pleasant thought. "Oh, I've been meaning to ask you, do you think I could get away with calling people hoss?"

"Hoss?"

"Yeah," I say, and yawn into the pillow to spare her my breath.

"Let me think about it."

"You need to think?"

"Yeah, I need time to think. I'm not just going to say yes and then have you out here trying to pull off something you can't pull off. But I don't want to say no and deprive you of an opportunity."

"But your initial reaction is no?"

"I'll have my answer to you by end of day," she says. "Which is in, like, an hour. Come on. Up, up, up! I want to take you to brunch. I need coffee. And a cheeseburger. Not necessarily in that order."

She hops up, taking the covers with her.

I whine.

"Birthday eve!" she says, grooving toward the stairs, my blanket draped over her head like a veil. She turns back toward me, curtsies, leaves the blankets, descends the stairs. "Another beautiful morning to caffeinate! Ah, caffeine. My favorite socially acceptable drug."

She goes on chattering, but I stop listening. I roll out of bed and hobble over to my suitcase, contemplate what to wear, if it even matters. The days it's most critical for me to feel good about myself are the days it seems most impossible.

It's jeans and an unsexy sweater.

As I'm buttoning my fly, my gaze lifts to the window at the front of the cottage. No snow, yet. But there's something else. A smear on the other side of the glass.

It's . . . a handprint. It looks like a handprint.

My nightmare comes slithering back—the figure at my window—and with it an ambiguous whispering. Faraway voices I can but can't hear. I step closer, closer to the glass. It's exactly where the silhouette appeared. Residue from a bad dream.

An obliterating headache erupts between my eyes. I pinch the bridge of my nose. I'm hungover.

I dismiss the window smudge. It's not a handprint, because it can't be a handprint. It's just muck.

I look down at my own hand. At the two slim bands on my ring finger.

"Sloane!" Naomi calls out. "I need sustenance!"

I fight the urge to climb back in bed and sleep all day. To sleep forever.

"Coming," I say.

We're too impatient to wait for the shuttle to take us into town, so we walk to the main mansion from our cottage. We arrive shivering and starving, our hair wind crazed, like a pair of wolves. We're out of place in the dining room, which is formal, all decorative molding and heavy drapes. There's a limited menu—a choice of yogurt with whipped honey and berries or eggs Benedict. Naomi throws a small fit at the lack of cheeseburgers on offer but is appeased once she gets her coffee, a butterscotch latte with a perfect heart in the foam.

"Aw," she says, snapping a picture.

We each order the eggs Benedict, which come with a side of thin, crispy fries. Naomi asks for ketchup and the waiter seems offended, but he brings it. He's another kid—maybe early twenties? I never noticed or cared how old people were until suddenly everyone was younger than me.

Naomi turns the bottle of ketchup upside down and spanks it with a flat palm, over and over, until a red mass finally bursts free of the bottle's neck. It oozes onto her plate, saturating everything. Messy. She smiles, satisfied.

I shake my head.

"*Gour-met,*" she says, licking some ketchup off of her thumb, licking her lips.

I take a sip of my coffee. It isn't strong enough.

Though we made an unspoken agreement not to revisit last night's conversation topic, and though I resolved to keep the doorbell camera discovery to myself and try to put Joel and his cheating out of my mind, it's still there, and it's taking up space between us. I'm reluctant to admit it, but it's been taking up space between us for years.

"I made us plans tonight," she says, piercing a ketchup-coated French fry with her fork.

"Plans?"

"For your birthday. Something special."

"You're not going to tell me what?"

"If I told you, you'd have time to talk yourself out of it."

I've suddenly lost my appetite. I look down at my plate, and the poached eggs are like alien eyes staring back at me. "You're really selling this, whatever it is."

"This is part of the present. Caution to the wind," she says, setting down her fork and reaching across the table for my hand. She gives me a sweet, pleading puppy-dog look. "Have you no faith in me?"

"Okay, you win," I say, sufficiently guilted. "Whatever you want to do tonight, I'll go along for the ride."

"I don't want you along for the ride, though. I want you in the driver's seat. Revving the engine like a motherfucker."

"Not the engine-revving type, Nay. Never have been."

"You could be, though. It's not too late."

I snort.

"Come on. I promise. It's gonna be good."

I pick at my fries. "Well, if you promise."

She laughs. "No faith. Zero faith."

"Can you blame me? Within a week of us being friends I got my first detention," I say, diving into nostalgia to escape the present. "Trouble."

"You're so full of it!" she says, threatening me with her fork. "That was not my fault. I wasn't even there that day!"

We argue about an incident with our honors English teacher, Dr. Hopkins, who rarely assigned books by women and, when he did, spoke about them in such an overtly misogynistic way that I finally blew a fuse and called him out on it, earning myself a detention.

And yes, it's true that my frustrations with him had been long-standing, existed even before Naomi and I had started to hang out. But she was the one who confirmed my frustrations were valid, who, when I brought him up, said, "That guy hates women." She corroborated everything I'd been silently seething about for months. And whether she'd meant to or not, she gave me the confidence to confront him about it.

Because when you're fourteen and the coolest person you've ever met is in your corner, you feel invincible. You feel immortal.

Naomi is trouble, but more often than not, she's the kind of trouble I need, that I'm not brave enough to stir up on my own. My nerves settle about tonight's surprise plans. At the very least, I could use the distraction.

The waiter comes by to clear our plates.

"How was everything, ladies?" he asks, expressionless, his voice void of enthusiasm.

"Amazing," Naomi says, looking up at him, batting her lashes, petting her long neck. She flirts with everyone. She'd come on to a scarecrow in a corn maze. It's not about whoever she's flirting with. It's not about desire, or at least most of the time it isn't. It's about power.

The waiter smiles at her, showing signs of life. "Can I get you anything else? More coffee? Another latte?"

"Just the check. Thanks, hoss."

She turns to me, grinning.

8

Naomi lifts up one of my dresses. "Where did you get this? From the *Sister Wives* collection?"

We're back in the cottage after spending the afternoon at a wine tasting. We behaved badly, ignoring the sommelier and making stuff up. *I'm getting notes of citrus fruit and man tears. This one is full-bodied, peppery, intense, and satisfying, would pair nicely with left-over pizza and an episode of* Cold Case Files. *This one is jammy, very jamlike, very Bonne Maman.*

Now we're wine buzzed—blundering and impish—as we get ready for tonight's mystery activity.

"Very funny," I say, snatching the dress out of her hands. "And I don't remember where I got it."

I do. I just don't want to admit that it's from Target. I doubt she would care, but part of me is still the girl in the food court wanting her to think I'm cool.

"I'm sure it's cute on you," she says. "Perfect for church."

"All right, I get it. I need to dress conservatively for work, not show up on calls with full cleavage. And I could never pull off . . ." I gesture to the getup she's in. A denim minidress, fishnets, her cowboy boots, a cropped cardigan with fringe.

"False," she says, taking my hand. "Let's go play dress-up."

There's no point in resisting. I let her drag me to her room and choose outfits for me.

"If I knew what we were doing I could dress myself," I say as she rifles through her giant, overstuffed suitcase. "I don't know what's appropriate."

"Are you wearing cute underwear?"

"Are you kidding?"

She laughs maniacally. Which could mean she's kidding, or it could mean she's dead serious. I'm too afraid to learn the answer.

We come to terms on the third outfit, a vintage T-shirt long enough to pass as a dress over a pair of black faux-leather leggings and under a long camel-colored cardigan. I'll wear my own boots. My own frumpy winter coat.

"Let's get some music on," she says as we move into the bathroom to do our hair and makeup. She slides her phone over to me. I let my own die, avoiding contact. Avoiding reality. "You can DJ."

"You'd so readily relinquish your power?"

"For you and you alone," she says. "Don't play anything depressing."

"And you accused me of having no faith. Let me do my thing," I say. I put on "Another Night" by Real McCoy.

"Oh, okay, okay. I see what we're doing here," she says, dancing around, swinging her hips.

"You forget that I can be fun, too."

"Never. I never forget that," she says, heating an eyelash curler with the Waterfront-provided blow-dryer. She starts to sing. "'Another night, another dream, but always you . . .'"

"'In the night, I dream of a love so true.'" The words "love" and "true" leave a vinegary taste in my mouth. The bathroom shrinks around me, becomes claustrophobic. In the last few hours, I'd been successful at not thinking about Joel, about his ulterior motive for sending me on this trip. His choice to brand it as a present for me.

I remember his other present. The gift box that's currently up in the loft, that's wrapped in gold paper with a pretty pink ribbon.

I'm tempted to go open it, but then I hear his voice in my head. *Present shaker.*

His voice was what first attracted me to him. We met standing outside of a bar in Morristown, New Jersey. It was December, and the trees in the park across the street—the Green—were all wrapped in bows and string lights. I heard Joel's voice—he was saying something about how public executions used to be held on the Green, right where Santa's house was now set up for the season—and I turned to look over at him, and he looked back at me. I remember thinking that everything about him was ordinary except his voice. He has this 1930s radio voice.

He walked over and introduced himself. He was confident but not cocky, well put together but not showy. I liked him immediately. I liked that he knew nothing about me, my past. He seemed like the perfect person to start over with, start fresh. I remember thinking that he seemed right. I remember that word, "right." Not charming or sexy or handsome or polite. *Right.* Like trying on something that fits, that distinct feeling of relief in the dressing room.

I could tell straightaway that he was nothing like my father; or any of the men my mother dated postdivorce; or any of my high school boyfriends; or Smith, my first love, who tossed my heart in a meat grinder before setting it on fire, who made it impossible for me to trust anyone, especially myself.

Joel took me inside and bought us ginger beers; I was sober at the time, and I appreciated that he didn't seem to mind. We sat talking for so long that we closed down the bar. He was witty and he was smart, studying law at Seton Hall. He wasn't religious, if you didn't count Sunday worship of the Buffalo Bills. He liked hiking and cooking and watching documentaries. He was stable, financially and emotionally—came from a happy family. He told me that after he graduated he planned on moving back to western New York, and I knew then that I wanted to go with him. I pictured this nice life with us together; I could see it so clearly. It seemed very low-risk, very easy, very practical, which was exactly what I'd been searching for. A partner. Someone to split the bills with, share the burden. And the joys, too, I guess.

We've been together ever since that night, the night we met. Almost fourteen years. In those fourteen years, I've caught him cheating three times. The first time was just after we got married. The girl messaged me on Facebook. She said it'd been going on for a while, that she wasn't the only one, and she felt bad, and fuck him. When I asked him about it, he denied it, and I didn't believe him, but I pretended I did. I deleted my Facebook.

The second time was four years ago. A different woman. One of his coworkers. I found texts on his phone. This time, when I confronted him, he copped to it. He apologized and told me he loved me, that it was a one-time thing, and it would never happen again. I stopped looking at his phone.

The third time was last night.

"Another night, another dream, but always you." The song plays again. The air is thick with hair spray, and for some reason it makes everything seem surreal. Like I'm lost in the mist, crossing into the Twilight Zone.

I'm not quick to dismiss his indiscretions because I'm so in love with him. I do love him, but it's never been about that. Nothing about my compliance is for his benefit. It's for my own. It's because I made a choice. I committed to the life I built with him, a life I like just fine. That's familiar. That's comfortable. I fear losing it if I lose him.

I fear the unknown.

It's true that I can't control whether he's faithful, but as long as I turn the other cheek, I know he won't leave. That gives me some semblance of control over the situation. Over my fine little life.

"Earth to Sloane," Naomi says.

"Yeah?"

"You're out in space."

"I'm not," I say. "I hate space. It's so smug."

"For real. It's always like, *I'm so dark and deep and unknowable.* Who cares?"

"Nerds," I say, rubbing my forehead. My hangover headache is back with a vengeance. The wine was a bad idea.

"You know what, though? I fuck with Carl Sagan. He could get it. If he were still alive." She picks up her phone. "Sorry, but you were sleeping on the job. Lost your DJ privileges."

And now it's Lesley Gore, singing, *"It's my party and I'll cry if I want to, cry if I want to . . ."*

"Too on the nose," I say.

"Uppity hipster bitch," she says, knocking my hip with hers.

"Takes one to know one," I say, grabbing my red lipstick. The shade Killer.

Once again, we stand shivering outside the cottage, waiting for the shuttle. At least I assume we're waiting for the shuttle. Naomi will neither confirm nor deny.

I'm not particularly jazzed to venture off campus for this surprise, and normally I would put my practical, no-fun, buzzkill foot down, but right now I really don't have it in me to fight.

The wind whips off the lake, through the trees.

"Why are we doing this, again?" I ask.

"Hmm?" Naomi says. She's hunched over, checking her phone.

"Waiting outside. We did this last night. The shuttle is never on time. Let's go in."

Naomi doesn't respond. She puts her phone in her pocket and stares down the dirt driveway. She's uncharacteristically anxious.

"Nay?"

"I don't like it in there at night," she says.

"What?" I ask. A gust of wind lands like a kick in the teeth.

"In there. In the cottage. Too many windows. It's creepy, don't you think?"

The memory of my nightmare returns, heavy and searing, like someone has dropped a hot stove on my chest. Above me, behind me, is the window with a smear that looks like a handprint.

"Did you see something?" I say, my voice too high.

"Yeah. Too many horror movies. Obviously."

"Right," I say, sinking my head between my shoulders.

"Oh!" Naomi says. "There he is."

I force my gaze against the tantrummy air. There's a car approaching, but it's not the hotel shuttle. It looks like the goddamn Batmobile.

"Um, what is that?" I ask. "*Who* is that?"

"It's Ilie," she says. "The guy from last night."

"What guy?"

"The guy I met at the bar," she says. "He has a house on the lake. He's staying there with some friends. He gave me his number and told me to call him if we were looking for a good time. So I called him."

If my face weren't frozen, I'd be giving her a death glare.

"We'll hang out," she says. "Meet some new people. It'll be fun!"

"The thing is, I know you're familiar with the concept of stranger danger, but until we're tied up in this guy's murder lair, you're not going to believe it's a real thing."

"Well, if that happens, you can tell me *I told you so*," she says. "Your favorite."

"Naomi. I'm not getting in a car with someone I don't know. That *you* don't know."

"I do know him. I know his type. He's a rich European. Old-world old money. We're gonna go over there and drink top-shelf liquor and do the best fucking drugs and stay up and talk and—I don't know—get naked."

"What?" I shout, so loudly, the wind withers.

This argument is happening too late. The driver slams on the brakes right in front of us, and the passenger-side door opens.

"Good evening, my loves," says the impossibly handsome stranger apparently named Ilie. He has a strong accent I can't quite place. Russian? "Come, come. Let me take you to the party."

Naomi turns to face me. She puts her hands firmly on my shoulders, looks me in the eye, and says, "You have to live your life, Sloane. You have to *live*."

Then she lets me go. She turns back around and climbs into the car.

Snow starts to fall, flakes as thick and wide as doilies. I forgot to check the weather forecast.

Naomi beckons me from the passenger seat. She lifts up a lollipop, waves it around. She singsongs, "I have candy."

"That's not funny," I mutter, staring down at the ground, which is powdered with snow. It's sticking.

"Sloane," Naomi says. Something about her tone snaps my head up. She's pleading with me.

"Come, love," Ilie says, grinning. "I don't bite."

This isn't my decision. It's Naomi's, and she's already made it, so I get into the car. Because I won't let her go alone. I can't.

She's all I have.

9

The Batmobile is a two-seater, so I end up sitting on Naomi's lap. She giggles at Ilie as I reach back, searching in vain for a seat belt.

"Don't worry. I am safe driver," Ilie says in his thick accent. He's speeding, sliding all over the snow-slick road. "Very safe."

"Yeah, I can tell," I say. This car probably cost more than my house, but does it have airbags?

"Sloane, yes? It is very nice to meet you. I tell Naomi, I am very glad she is calling. My name is Ilie," he says. He lets go of the wheel to shake my hand. I give it a quick squeeze, but instead of taking the wheel again, he gets out a pack of cigarettes, puts one between his lips, and lights it.

"I don't usually smoke in car, but," he says, shrugging as he finally takes the wheel again, "it is special occasion, yes?"

"It's Sloane's birthday," Naomi says.

"Tomorrow," I say.

"Happy, happy birthday," Ilie says. "You must make wish. It will come true."

I can't get over this guy. He's so good-looking and so ridiculous. He wears tight satin pants and a sheer black button-up that's not sufficiently buttoned. The top buttons have been given the night off. Silver necklaces disappear into a forest of dark chest hair. He's like a caricature, only he's too hot to be a caricature. Like if a young Colin Farrell were to play Rasputin in a sexy, not-at-all historically accurate biopic.

"Don't worry. It is not far," he says, zooming past Main Street. "Tonight you will meet all of my best friends. We like to meet new people. Interesting people. Like you."

He winks at us, then takes a sudden, hard right, barely missing a tree. Then he slams on the brakes as a gate opens to a private drive.

I don't even flinch. I've temporarily transcended fear. It could be in a cool, enlightened, "Whatever will be, will be" way. But more likely I'm experiencing existential despondence.

Ilie rolls through the open gate, and I watch in the side-view mirror as it slowly shuts behind us.

And just like that, my fear is back, waving red flags in both hands.

"Why are you closing the gate?" I ask. "I thought this was a party."

"Everyone is here," he says, unfazed. "We close gate so no un-invited guests. Very exclusive."

"Right," I say. Naomi pinches my side. I reach down and pinch her back. She yips.

"See? I tell you it is not far. This house I get not so long ago. This region they say has good wine. Lots of tourists. Good invest-ment. Good place. Very beautiful. Quiet. But I think too quiet. I need some fun, you know? Some excitement."

"And that's where we come in?" Naomi says.

"Yes, yes. You are right," Ilie says, once again slamming on the brakes. I almost go flying through the windshield. "Ready? You tell me what you think of the house. My house."

Ilie comes around and opens the passenger-side door for us. I tumble out onto the driveway, which is slippery with snow. It's accumulating fast, and I realize we might not be able to make it back to the cottage tonight—a realization that I might have had sooner if my life weren't coming apart like wet paper.

It's difficult to see the house through the snow and wind, the wintry hemorrhage. It's an extensive ranch. Maybe midcentury? It sits atop a slight hill, surrounded by trees.

Ilie wedges himself between me and Naomi, offering us each an arm.

"And they say chivalry is dead," Naomi says, bowing her head to him as she threads her arm through his.

I'm too nervous to touch him. One, because I don't trust him. And two, because he's so attractive it makes me uncomfortable, makes me want to turn and run away as fast as I can. Makes me want to evaporate.

He slides his hand up my arm, brings his face to my face. "You are shy, love? I promise, this night you will remember forever."

His eyes are wide and hazel, his lips pink, his teeth brilliantly white but chipped. His breath is sour.

"Sloane?" Naomi says. I feel her looking at me. Turns out, you never get too old for peer pressure.

I give a resigned sigh and take Ilie's arm. He leads us up a pathway to the front door. It opens before we get there.

"Look at these stunning creatures!" says a tall, bone-thin woman with the most glorious golden blond curls. "Welcome. Come in. Please."

We step over the threshold into a dimly lit hall. There are candles *everywhere*. Flickering flames cast shadows that crawl up the walls, which are covered with artwork—extravagantly framed oil paintings of flowers and landscapes and seascapes and castles. The colors shimmer in the candlelight as if the paint were still wet.

"You may take off your shoes, your coats. Make yourselves comfortable. Our home is your home," the blonde says.

Naomi takes her shoes off but leaves her coat on. She won't be parted from it.

I slip off my boots and hand the blond woman my coat. I have no such attachment to mine.

"Thank you," I say to the woman. She's dressed in a velvety purple gown. She looks like a high-fashion model. She's all angles. Her features are intense, her skin like glass. She wears no makeup, at least as far as I can tell.

"Of course," she says. She speaks with an accent similar to Ilie's. Maybe it's not Russian. I don't know. I'm not well traveled.

She hangs my coat on a freestanding rack that I'd mistaken for an abstract sculpture. It looks like a giant, mangled paper clip. Mine is the only coat it carries on its silvery arms.

"This is Elisabeta. Our Elisa," Ilie says. "She has mean face, but she is very sweet. Come. I introduce you to everyone."

Elisa drinks in Naomi. She approaches her, slips two fingers under her chin, and then kisses her right on the mouth.

My jaw drops. I swear it hits the floor.

The kiss lasts for a solid minute.

Eventually, Elisa pulls away. She strokes Naomi's face with the back of her hand, then says, "Yes, let's go to everyone."

I lag behind, let Ilie and Elisa walk ahead. I grab Naomi by the sleeve of her jacket.

"Um, what was that?" I whisper.

"A friendly greeting?" she says, laughing a little. "Don't over-think it, okay? It's cultural."

"Oh? What culture, exactly?"

"Hey. Just be present. Open-minded. Have you considered the possibility that this could be the best night of your life?"

"No," I say.

She blows a raspberry.

"Most I can hope for is that it's not the worst. Or the last," I say.

Bringing my voice down to a whisper of a whisper, I add, "He closed the gate."

"Overthinking," she says. She takes my hand and spins me around. "Come on. Would it kill you to loosen up?"

"It might."

She gives me this look that makes me want to swallow my tongue. She's serious. She's rarely serious. "You want to pretend you're some dull suburban normie. We both know that's not who you really are. Be honest with yourself for a second. Don't you want to let your hair down?"

"Not here. Not now. This whole thing is weird. These people, this place. Let's call a car while we still can. The snow—"

She lets go of my hand. "You assume the worst, and it's this self-fulfilling prophecy. You think you're in control, that you're playing it safe by never taking any chances or leaving your comfort zone, but—"

"That's not fair. Don't bully me for using common sense."

"Someday you're gonna look back on your life and there'll be nothing but regret."

She starts after Ilie and Elisa.

After my wrist surgery I randomly started reading up on the *Hindenburg*. One rainy Thursday afternoon during summer break, Naomi drove me out to the memorial in Lakehurst and we walked around the field where the zeppelin went down in flames.

That was when I told her I'd decided to drop out of NYU and move back to Jersey.

"Without the scholarship, I'll never be able to get out from under the debt. Even with the scholarship it was a lot," I'd said, trying to get at an itch inside my cast. "It just isn't worth it. Risk a lifetime of debt for what? A degree is a degree."

"I probably shouldn't smoke a cigarette here, right?" she asked, not acknowledging anything I'd said.

"Probably not." I waited for her to call me out, bring up the Smith ordeal and my subsequent spiral, which resulted in my GPA's nosedive, costing me my scholarship, and culminating in my drunkenly falling off a curb and breaking my wrist in front of a Saturday-night crowd on St. Marks Place, almost getting run over by a cab, the front tire missing my skull by an inch. The other, less practical, more shameful factors in my decision to drop out.

Instead, she said, "Not to be insensitive, but I feel like it's pretty obviously a shit idea to ride in a giant gas-filled sky balloon."

"Yeah," I'd said.

"Worth it for the view, though. Don't you think? Worth the risk?"

"View is fine from here."

I knew the point she was trying to make, but it was the wrong place to make it. I knew the charred spirits roaming the field with us would be on my side, would agree with me. If they had it all to do over again, they would have stayed safely on the ground. Never taken the risk.

But now here I am, having spent the last sixteen years with both feet firmly planted, making every decision with careful consideration, leading the most risk-averse life I could conceive of. And it still blew up in my face.

Maybe Naomi's right. I don't have any control. I never have.

So I might as well join the party.

I follow Naomi down the hall, which opens up to a sunken living room.

There's a giant stone fireplace with a hearty red fire crackling inside. There's an elaborate candelabra on the mantel, the candles lit, wax dripping. There are no windows, at least none that are uncovered. The walls are all draped in heavy fabric, and there's an array of rugs and blankets and fat pillows covering the floor. There are several backless couches with bodies strewn across them. The room smells of smoke and incense and sweat. It looks like an opium den.

Ilie says something in a foreign language, and the bodies begin to twist awake, sit up, become people. I count four. Two men, two women. One of the men is in the corner, cast in shadow. The other, illuminated by firelight, is shirtless, with a lit cigarette dangling precariously from his lips. He's sinewy, covered in tattoos and gnarly scars. Both of his nipples are pierced. His white-blond hair is buzzed. He looks about the same age as Ilie, late twenties or early thirties. He's got a square jaw and a pronounced brow ridge, though the brows themselves are so faint, they're practically invisible. His eyes are reptilian green.

I'd put him among the most intimidating creatures on the planet.

Just as I think this, he smiles, gold teeth glinting.

"Hello!" he says, his voice unexpectedly high and pleasant. "I am Costel. Nice to meet you."

One of the women pops her head over his shoulder. She's petite with a blunt, dark bob, a heart-shaped face, a pointy chin. She wears a white silk slip dress, the straps loose and sliding down her arms.

"I am Miri," she says. "Ilie, you were right. They are so pretty! So, so pretty."

"You doubt me?" Ilie asks, stepping down into the living room and crossing to Miri. He ruffles her hair, then grabs a fistful, a brief flash of violence that turns my blood cold.

Miri gasps, then giggles. They stare at each other for a moment, and I hold my breath until Ilie releases his grip on her hair. He pats it back into place, then kisses her on the forehead.

Anxiety skitters around my ribs. There's clearly something off here, but Naomi has me doubting my own intuition. Am I hesitant because I've spent the last decade and a half living as a dull suburban normie, or because I'm a person with keen judgment and basic survival instincts? I don't know. I can't tell.

"Tatiana? What do you think?" Ilie asks, turning to the other couch, where a woman lounges, wearing a long, lace-trimmed sleeping robe. She has cherry red hair styled in perfect Old Hollywood waves. She looks like she's ready for a boudoir photo shoot.

She gives us a once-over through a cage of false lashes. Then she points lazily in our direction. "Keep an eye on that one. She will steal something."

I assume she's talking about Naomi. I'd be offended on her behalf if only it weren't true.

"And that one has bad posture."

I know she's talking about me. Also true, but I'm still offended. I roll my shoulders back.

"To answer your question, Ilie," Tatiana says, sliding a thick, beautiful thigh out of her robe. I can easily identify her accent as French. "Yes. They are fine for the night. Did you offer our guests something to drink?"

"Ah!" Elisa says, clapping a hand over her mouth. "I forgot. What a terrible, rude, very bad host. Sloane, Naomi, something to drink?"

"Yes, please," Naomi says. "Whatever you have. We like everything."

Miri, the small brunette, has now climbed onto the lap of shirtless Costel, and they're making out. Absolutely going at it.

Ilie stands over them, watching. Grinning.

Tatiana leans back and her robe falls all the way open, revealing a maze of lingerie.

I'm getting the sense that this a very particular kind of party.

"Perhaps some wine?" Elisa asks us.

"Um, actually, do you have anything stronger?" I ask, star-ing daggers at Naomi. "Gin, whiskey, tequila, vodka, a horse tranquilizer . . . Sorry—is there a bathroom?"

"Yes. Back through there, first door on your right."

"Thanks. If you'll excuse us . . ."

I catch Naomi by the wrist and pull.

10

We squeeze into a small, dated powder room. Dirty mirror, peeling wallpaper, disintegrating tile, clumps of dust gathered in the corners. The toilet and sink are a sickly green. The bronze fixtures long ago lost their sheen.

Naomi pulls down her stockings and sits on the toilet. "I'm sorry about what I said before. I just think—"

"Um, I can't believe I have to ask this question, but is this an orgy?"

"God no." I experience a brief, sweet relief. Then she says, "Well, I mean, it might be."

"What do you mean, *might*? I don't think there's any middle ground when it comes to orgies. It either is or it isn't."

"I'm not sure," she says. "There was an implication tonight would be wild, but Ilie never said anything explicit."

"Yeah, we need to go."

She grabs some toilet paper, wipes, flushes, pulls up her stockings, and pulls down the skirt of her dress. She crosses to the sink and washes her hands.

"Nay—we didn't sign up for this."

"We don't have to do anything we don't want to do."

I slap my hands to my forehead in disbelief. "You mean *I* don't have to do anything *I* don't want to do, because you're clearly into it!"

"So, what if I am? Lee and I went to a party like this in Amsterdam and it was honestly the hottest, most insane experience of my life."

"But Levi isn't here, is he?"

"Neither is Joel."

I'm surprised she'd go there. Now I'm fuming.

"Just because he cheats doesn't mean I—" I can't stand to hear myself say it out loud, say that I wouldn't cheat. Because maybe it's the truth and maybe it isn't, but neither makes me feel good. "What about you? Lee would be okay with this?"

She takes my lipstick out of her bag. Reapplies Killer. "We have an agreement."

"What kind of agreement? Why have you never—" I stop myself because I realize I already know the answer to this question. Naomi's never told me that she and Levi have an open relationship because of the infidelity in mine, which is so insulting and embarrassing I wish I could crawl into a deep, dark hole and never come out. Turn into Gollum, only a more depressing version, with nothing to love.

"It just never came up," she says. A lie to spare my feelings that has the exact opposite effect.

"All right," I say. I take a turn on the toilet as Naomi fixes her lipstick in the mirror, dragging her pinkie nail along the edges of her lips, her finger coming away red.

"The idea of a party like this is a lot, I know, but in practice, if you just go with it, it's so freeing. So *fun*. Remember fun, Sloane?"

"Were we not having fun?"

"That's not what I meant," she says.

"Sure," I mutter. I'm distracted by a clanking noise, followed

by a low, distant groan. It doesn't sound like a pleasurable groan.
It sounds pained. "Do you hear that?"

She doesn't answer.

"Nay?"

"You know what?" she says, whipping around as I make myself
decent and elbow her out of the way to wash my hands. "No. I'm
not going to let you do this. Make me feel bad for embracing the
night. For taking you here. For getting you out of your fucking
house with your snooze-fest husband who can't keep his dick in
his pants, who doesn't make you happy, who you won't leave because you got your heart broken once in college and have been
fucked up about men and sex and yourself ever since."

"Let up, Nay. I'm here at your orgy. You go do whatever you
want. I'm not stopping you."

"No, we're talking about this."

"Is there no hand towel?"

She shakes her head, looks up at the ceiling. "You're not ever
going to confront it, are you? You're just going to bury it."

"I bury everything," I say, giving up and wiping my hands on
my T-shirt.

"You deserve more than—"

"It's not about deserving, Naomi. That's what you don't understand. Life isn't some, like—I don't know—fairy tale. Not everyone gets to frolic around the world, partying with bands and
movie stars and heiresses and counts. Not everyone gets what
they want."

"That's bullshit! You're trying to make this about me and whatever you think my life is like. But this has nothing to do with me.
This is about you giving up." In her voice there's a quaver that
destroys me.

"It's too late," I say. "I made my choices."

"It's not too late! It's not."

71

She takes my left hand and slides off my engagement and wedding rings, the two simple white gold bands I asked for because I felt weird about Joel spending thousands on flashy jewelry when that money could be put toward a house, or my debt.

I let Naomi do it. I let her slip the rings into her jacket pocket.

"You should fuck someone tonight," she says. "Maybe you'll come so hard you'll remember who you really are. Happy birthday."

She pushes past me and opens the door. She pauses to make sure I'm following.

"You could have been a great poet," I say.

"Maybe in my next life."

I go with her, back to the party. Not because I want to. Because I can't hide in the bathroom all night. It has a weird smell.

"Elisa is worried," Ilie says, stabbing at the fire with a long cast-iron poker. "She thinks she makes bad drinks."

"Gin and tonic," Elisa says, looking genuinely distressed as she holds up two giant cobalt wineglasses. "I can try again if it is too strong."

Naomi accepts the drinks for us, then passes one of the glasses to me.

"Cheers," she says, and takes a fearless sip. "It's perfect."

I bring my glass to my lips, slowly tilt it back. Pure gin. Normally it'd be too much for me, but under these circumstances . . .

"Yeah, agreed. Perfect," I say.

Elisa claps. "Wonderful!"

She embraces Naomi, kissing her on the cheek. I take another gulp of gin.

I hear that distant clanking sound again, just for a moment. It's there and it's happening and then it's gone. Then it's quiet, save for the pop and hiss of flames, and the soft slurping of Costel and Miri making out.

Ilie leans the poker beside the fireplace and turns his attention to a record player set on a retro stand. "We need music, yes?"

He slides an album out from a stack on the floor, a seemingly random selection. It's *Who's Next* by the Who. I don't know if "Baba O'Riley" is the right song to set the mood for group sex, but I'm not going to offer up my opinion on the matter, since I won't be partaking.

Ilie looks at the album in his left hand, then down at the record player, then back at the album. With his right hand, he fiddles with the tonearm. I can tell he doesn't know what he's doing. He doesn't know how it works.

"Technics SL-1200. Original model," I say, stepping in. I slip the record out of the sleeve and put it on the platter. "Pretty nice record player for someone who doesn't know how to use it."

He chuckles. "It come with the house."

"And the extensive collection?" I say, gesturing to the stack on the floor and the albums stuffed into the stand.

"Yes, yes," he says.

"That's lucky." The song starts to play, filling the room with that famous, mesmerizing ostinato.

"Oh, yes!" Ilie says, his eyes igniting with recognition. "I know this one. Good music."

"How long have you had the house?" I ask him.

He ignores me and starts to dance around the room. He sweeps Naomi away from Elisa, and they spin and laugh and touch each other, and I stand perfectly rigid, right where I am, my hands pulled into fists, gnawing on the inside of my cheek until my mouth fills with blood and I swallow it down, hoping my suspicion goes with it, but it doesn't. It's stuck between my teeth like a stubborn piece of meat. Now that it's here, I can't get it out. Can't be rid of it.

The thought. The suspicion.

This isn't his house.

"*'Let's get together before we get much older!'*" Naomi sings, orbiting Ilie as if she is the earth and he is her sun. Elisa stays close, a tenacious moon.

As I watch them it's like they're playing a game, only no one's explained the rules.

I'm not alone in their audience. Costel and Miri have come up for air. Tatiana models her pink manicure as she covers her mouth to hide a sly smile.

Urgent nausea alerts me to the fact that it's starting, that whatever is going to happen here tonight is about to be happening. I look over my shoulder. There's the candlelit front hall, and then two other hallways off the living room, but they're dark and I don't know where they lead, and I'm afraid to wander around this house that may or may not belong to these people.

I believed that the crazy Batmobile belonged to Ilie; it seemed like the kind of car someone like him would drive. But this house? It doesn't seem like the kind of house a young überwealthy person would buy. It's dated, and not in a kitschy, fun way. There are water stains on the ceiling. Or maybe they're just shadows. Maybe I'm searching for things that aren't there. Searching for excuses, for justification to keep myself on the sidelines.

Ilie stands behind Naomi; Elisa stands in front. Ilie holds her waist; Elisa holds her face.

I stare down at the floor, at the patchwork of ugly rugs and blankets and pillows.

Someone moans.

Christ. I really don't want to be here for this.

I beeline to the far corner of the room, beyond the reach of firelight, and settle on the floor. I'm tempted to turn toward the wall, like a kid in time-out. I regret not bringing my phone, regret leaving it to die. But what would I do if I had it? Message back and forth with Joel, playing dumb? Check the doorbell camera again?

Everything Naomi said to me in the bathroom, in the hall, has me in my head, has me questioning. What if I can't keep doing this? What if I can't go on as this version of me that continues to let this happen? That accepts less because it's easier than longing for more.

My eyes flick up. Miri is naked, bent over a couch. She looks at me and smiles, bites her lip, then waves me forward with a single come-hither finger.

What if I want to? What if I've buried my desire so deep that I don't even remember what it looks like? Sounds like. Tastes like. Feels like. What if I want to get fucked by someone just for the sake of getting fucked? What if I let go of my reservations? What if I didn't anticipate the worst possible outcome? What if I didn't give a shit if it was Ilie's house or not? What if I let myself be guided by something other than fear?

What if Naomi is right? What if it's not too late?

All of a sudden an ember appears, fizzling near my shoulder, and I nearly jump out of my skin.

There's someone next to me. A man. He smokes a cigarette.

"You scared me," I tell him, bringing my hand to my heart, as if that'll prevent it from beating out of my chest. I take a sip of the gin.

"You're scared?" he says, passing me his cigarette. "Good. You should be."

11

My breath hitches in my throat. I watch in horror as my hand reaches out for the cigarette, accepts it, brings it to my lips. My body has gone rogue.

I take a puff without inhaling and pass it back to the man, whom I can't really see, his face obscured in shadow.

"How scared?" I ask. For some reason, I'm now more intrigued than afraid.

"Depends," he says, then pauses to take a long drag.

Spellbound, I wait for the rest, until I can't any longer, until I have to ask, "On what?"

"How brave you are."

"Oh," I say. "Not at all."

"No?"

"No."

"You admit to being a coward?" He's British, his accent haughty.

"Not being brave and being a coward are two different things," I say.

"How so?"

I think for a moment. He passes me the cigarette again, and

this time I inhale, welcome the poison into my lungs. I wash it down with gin. I haven't smoked a cigarette since I was twenty.

"Cowardice is selfish," I say. "It's an active choice to do the wrong thing. Not being brave . . . it's passivity. And no one suffers but you."

"You suffer?"

"No," I say. "Well . . . we're off topic. You were warning me."

There's a very loud grunt. Costel is taking Miri from behind. I avert my eyes, my cheeks scorching red.

"You were brave enough to come here," the man says.

"I didn't know I was coming here until I was here," I say, and finish off my gin. "And I didn't know the, um . . . I didn't know what kind of party it was until about five minutes ago."

"If you did, you wouldn't have come?"

"No."

"Why don't you leave?"

"Do you want me to leave?" I say, surprising myself.

"I'm asking."

"I don't have a car. And I can't call one because I don't have my phone. And the weather is bad. And I'd have to convince Naomi to come with me, and it's pretty much impossible to talk her out of doing something she wants to do."

I gesture to the room, to the giant knot of bodies.

"You wouldn't leave without her?"

"No," I say. "I wouldn't."

"You're a good friend," he says.

"Thanks. Thank you. For your, um, approval. Sorry—it's a little hard to carry on a conversation when . . ."

Someone's getting spanked. There's the distinct sound of a hand smacking against skin, at a very specific cadence. There's a chorus of incredibly enthusiastic, sensual moaning. I haven't watched enough porn to confidently say this sounds like live porn, but it sounds like live porn.

"Not brave enough to join in?" the man asks me.

"I'm not interested in joining."

He leans forward, leans in close to me, close enough that I can finally see him. Through a tangle of totally overgrown dirty-blond hair, his eyes find mine. His face is almost too pretty, too perfect. But there's some asymmetry about it, some elusive chaos in its terrain. It's what I find most attractive about him. The mystery of what makes him more strange than beautiful.

He lifts his chin, flaunting a jaw sharp enough to cut glass. "Because you don't want to, or because you are a coward?"

"You're sitting in the corner, same as me."

He laughs. "This is true. But I am a coward."

"Why did you tell me I should be scared?"

"Never mind."

"Never mind?"

He sighs and leans back, vanishing into the dark. "You wouldn't believe me if I told you."

"I don't believe anything you say."

He rocks forward and stands up. He's tall, must be over six feet, with long limbs, a narrow neck. "Would you come with me if I asked?"

He extends a hand. His palm wide, his fingers reaching.

"Where?" I ask.

He grins, revealing dimples and big white, crooked, magnificent teeth. "Does it matter?"

Behind him, there are things happening that I've only ever heard frat boys joke about. Things I had no idea people actually did. I can't decide if I find it amusing or upsetting. I see Naomi's naked back pop up from behind a couch. She appears to be actively involved.

I never envied her adventurousness. I was bold in my own way, until I decided not to be. But there's an ugliness percolating in my chest, a venomous resentment rising from the depths.

The truth is, I doubt she brought me here because she thought it'd be good for me, that it'd break me out of my shell or help me get my mind off the Joel situation. Whether she realizes it or not, this isn't some benevolent excursion to bring me back to myself. We're here because she wants to be here. Because this is her kind of reckless endeavor.

It inspires this need in me to spite her. The question is, do I spite her by sitting in this corner with my arms crossed or by taking this man's hand and letting him lead me somewhere?

Or do I take his hand not because of Naomi, or because of Joel, or because of all the decisions I've ever made in my life that haunt me, that make me doubt myself and my ability to choose anything, to do anything right? Do I forget all that and take his hand for the simple reason that I want to? That I really, really, *really* want to?

I look up at him, at his enormous round, brown eyes, at his excruciating beauty, and I slide my hand into his. There's a slight shock, an electric current that passes through me, that I might be imagining. The touch of him makes my insides fizz, like I'm a shaken can of cola, like I could erupt. His skin is cold, his palm calloused.

He gently pulls me up, and my knees creak as I stand. My legs give, angry at me for sitting on the floor, and I stumble into him.

I mutter an apology, staring straight into his chest. He wears a ratty old sweater that has holes, that's far too big. It looks grimy but smells clean. He smells like bergamot.

I want to put my ear to him and listen as if he were a seashell.

Who even am I? What is this complete and utter anarchy that's occurring under my skin? My blood rages through my veins; my heart's thrashing in full riot mode.

I take a step back. Embarrassed by own my thoughts, I attempt to compensate by playing it cool. "Lead the way."

But he doesn't move. He stands right where he is.

It's all sensory overkill. The smell of the fire and the incense and the sweat, which is now the most dominant note. "My Wife" plays, one of my favorites on that album, and it's almost but not really louder than the fire and the moaning and the sound of bodies on bodies on bodies. My vision is gin blurred, and my eyes struggle to adjust to the shifting firelight and the shadows fighting to claim the space.

There's the taste of juniper and tobacco, and there's my hand in his. This new touch.

When was the last time I was touched by somebody new?

After a minute or maybe an eternity, he turns his back to me but doesn't let go of my hand. He leads me out of the living room, and we turn down the hall on the right, pass the powder room, continuing on. We move by a series of doors. They're all shut.

On the left there's a door that suddenly, terribly, catches my attention. Another step and it's at my side. And it's moving. The door rattles, rebelling against its frame, and the knob twists, as if there's someone on the other side trying to get out. As if they're locked in.

And I hear it again. The clanking. And a short, guttural groan.

"Hey," I say, yanking the man's hand.

He stops but doesn't turn around to look at me. He tucks his hair behind his ear, a signal that he's listening, and that he's an asshole.

The regret comes swiftly. Why did I follow this strange man down this dark hallway? At best there's disappointment; at worst there's danger. Why did I allow my want to decimate my logic? Why is it always a battle between the two?

"What's behind this door?" I ask. Maybe I'm braver than I give myself credit for, though I'm not sure what it matters, what it's worth.

"The cellar," he says. "There's a draft. It knocks. Huffing and puffing. We lock it out."

He takes another step, pulling me along with him.

"I've lived before in many drafty castles," he says. There's a change in his accent, so subtle and so fluid, I barely catch it.

The way he just pronounced "many." There was a heaviness to it. It betrayed him.

"Castles where?" I ask.

"I would tell you, but you said before, you don't believe anything I say," he says, his accent consistent.

"Should I?"

He stops again, this time turning to face me, wearing a grin like a fox with feathers still in its teeth. It's so unapologetically devious that I want to smack it off him.

He stoops his shoulders and lowers his long, serpentine neck so we're eye to eye. "I can't honestly tell you that I'm good. But I am honest."

"I'm not charmed by a bad-boy persona," I say, the lie sticky on my lips. "I think it's boring."

He laughs, and it's this loud, clumsy laugh. An authentic laugh. It wraps itself around my dread and squeezes until it bursts into excitement, into this eagerness to touch him, to stick a straw in him and drink, drink, drink.

"You should know it's not a persona," he says, again giving me his back as he continues to lead me down the hall.

"And you should know I'm not impressed." I hear myself say it, and it sounds like something I would have said at seventeen. Am I reconnecting with my true self or being an idiot?

"Here," he says as we arrive at the foot of a winding staircase. He bows slightly, gestures for me to go ahead.

"You first," I say. "It's too late to pretend you're a gentleman."

He raises an eyebrow, and then his face falls to a frown, as if I've hurt his feelings. Then he starts up the stairs. I follow him, taking a final glance over my shoulder back down the dark hall.

That one door, the cellar door, is still rattling on its hinges, and I wonder if it's possible for a draft to be so persistent. To have such strong arms.

"Let's see if I earn your trust with this view," he says, just as the hall vanishes behind me, as the stairs twist and I arrive somewhere new.

We're in a conservatory. Glass walls, glass ceiling. All around us there's the night, the falling snow, the intricate patterns of shadow and frost.

"What do you think?" he asks.

"Not bad," I say, and he laughs again.

That laugh.

12

I shiver watching the snow come down. It's cold in here. There are plants wilting against the glass. There's some dusty patio furniture. A stack of magazines on the coffee table. *Architectural Digest* and *Life in the Finger Lakes*. There's a worn copy of *The Power Broker*.

I don't believe for a second that any of these people have a keen interest in Robert Moses.

Whose book is this?

Whose house is this?

The man circles the room and lands in a chair, draping himself across it, limbs swinging. He wears a long, thick silver chain tucked into his sweater. It glints in a patch of moonlight.

I take a good look at him. As I stare, my heart takes off, beating faster and faster until my head catches up and I realize he reminds me of someone, only I can't remember who.

Right now I'd give anything to be younger, for no other reason than to escape this feeling. Rewind to a time before this was possible, before I'd lived enough to discover a ghost in a stranger's face.

"What is it?" he asks me.

Have I met him before? In life? In a dream?

I shake my head. "Nothing."

"Mm. Do you lie for my sake or for your own?"

I don't know how to answer, so I don't. I move back toward the stairs. Above me a mound of snow slumps from the roof, lands with a dense thud.

"Tell me something true," he says.

"What is this? Truth or dare?" I ask without turning around. I press against the wall. Beyond the glass, the snow is piling up. How much more will fall tonight? I imagine this view completely obscured. I hear Naomi's voice: *It's some snow, not an apocalyptic blizzard.* But how would she know?

"Have you ever played truth or dare?" he asks.

"I never played any of those games." If I had, maybe I'd be less scandalized by the X-rated spin-the-bottle debauchery happening in the other room.

"I've never played either. Would you play with me now?"

I look over at him. He wears the biggest, goofiest smile, delighted by his own idea, and it's infuriatingly endearing. I snort.

"I'm serious. What else are we to do?"

There's an insinuation, and it sends a spark rocketing up from the arches of my feet through my core and out of the top of my head. Sweat breaks over me like a wave.

"Okay," I say, sitting down in the chair opposite him, crossing my arms and legs, creating a barrier with my extremities because I'm nothing if not committed to deluding myself.

"Your turn," he says.

"Truth or—" I can't even finish. It's so absurd.

"Or . . . ?"

"Truth or dare?"

"Dare."

"Dare?"

"Yes. Dare."

"I thought you'd pick truth, since you're Mr. Honest."

"I am. That's why truth isn't exciting. For me. Maybe not for you since you lie."

"I don't lie."

"A lie!"

I could strangle him. Put my hands around his neck and . . .

"What's my dare?"

"I'm thinking."

"Don't think too hard. It's a game."

"I dare you to speak with your real accent."

He sits up in his chair. "This is my real accent."

I sit up straighter in mine. "No, it isn't."

He laughs, lets his head back, runs his fingers through his hair. "You're cheating."

"How am I cheating?"

"That wasn't a dare. It was truth."

"Okay. I dare you to tell me why you're using a fake accent."

He leans forward, hands on his thighs, eyes narrowed. "It's my turn."

"You're not going to do my dare?"

"I am doing your dare. This is how I speak. Truth or dare?"

"Truth."

"Who hurt you?"

The question hits me like a fast pitch. I fall back against the musty cushion, my jaw slack.

"That's not—"

"Not what?" he asks. "Did you change your mind? Would you prefer a dare? Because I have something in mind . . ."

He grins his devious fox grin.

"Your question is presumptuous."

"So was your dare."

I wish I weren't wearing these leggings. I know better than to borrow Naomi's clothes. They don't fit right, and they're always impossibly uncomfortable. There's a tag scratching my lower back. And they're not real leather, but they might as well be—they're sauna hot.

"Are you going to answer?"

"I don't know how to answer."

"It's a simple question."

"It's not. It's vague and . . . and . . ."

He raises his eyebrows. "And . . . ?"

I'd rather be back courtside at the orgy. "And nothing. I'm not playing this game."

"You're quitting on me?" he asks, pouting.

"Nobody has hurt me."

"Then why are you hurt?" he asks, slipping a metal case out of his back pocket and getting another cigarette. He lights it with a Zippo. "I can tell."

"How?"

He exhales. "I've been around."

"That so?"

"I don't look it. But I'm old. And wise."

I scoff. "Wise."

He pouts again, ashes his cigarette on the floor. "Don't be cruel."

"How old are you?"

"It's not your turn," he says. "It's still my turn."

"I answered your question. Nobody hurt me."

"You will think I'm lying. About my age."

"Tell me anyway."

He nods, takes a drag. "I am five hundred and ninety-two."

The audacity. "You are *such* a liar!"

That grin slinks out again. "See?"

I stand to get away from him, walk over to the far wall, the musty scent from the cushion clinging to me like a parasite.

"I'm sorry," he says. "I suppose I'm no fun to play with."

Outside, the snow falls with purpose, as if fleeing the dark of the sky. There's nothing peaceful about it. It's frantic. The glass walls must be thick, because I can't hear the storm. It's eerily quiet.

I assume Naomi will finish eventually. Come find me.

I hate not knowing how much time I have to kill.

"Fine. Dare," I say. "And if I do it, I win."

"With the dare I have in mind, I think we'd both win," he says. The way he says it, and the way he looks at me when he does, I can't. I lose my nerve.

"All right, old man," I say, returning to my chair. "What if we drop the game and have an honest conversation? Just talk."

"Whatever you want," he says.

I realize I still don't know his name. "You could start by telling me your name."

"Henry," he says, tossing his cigarette to the floor and stomping it out. He doesn't look like a Henry, and maybe my face reacts without permission, because he adds, "But in the spirit of truth and honesty, that isn't the name I was born with. That name was ugly, with an ugly history. I changed it."

"I'm Sloane," I say. "Sloane is my mother's maiden name. Sometimes I feel like it suits me. And sometimes someone says it and I can't believe they're referring to me. There's a complete disconnect. I'm no more attached to it than my Social Security number."

I'm rambling. Whatever. Killing time. Just killing time. Just talking. Nothing else is happening here. Or going to happen. He's strange and arrogant and I'm married. I look over at him, and he looks back at me.

I really like the way he looks at me.

"Is there a name you think would better suit you?" he asks with such genuine interest, I regret not having kissed him already.

When was the last time anyone made a genuine attempt to know me? Beyond the checklist of basics. When was the last time anyone made any effort to gain insight into my interiors?

This is wrong. This is bad.

This is platonic. It has to be.

"That's a good question," I tell him. "Maybe something simple and old-fashioned."

"Like . . . ?"

"Hmm. Like . . . Eleanor. Or Esther."

He laughs his giant-nerd laugh, snorting at the end. "You are not an Esther."

"Not now. But I could be. If I chose to be. Like you chose to be Henry."

"I suppose names are only part of our identities. Not all of them."

"They're foundational."

His lips pull to the side, brows sink as he thinks. "Did finding out my name change your opinion of me?"

My turn to think. "Yes. But every new thing you learn about someone influences your opinion of them."

"Do you form strong opinions of people?"

"Generally, yes. Do you?"

He nods. "Most people are predictable. I observe them, come to my conclusions, and give them the opportunity to prove me wrong, and they never do."

"Never?" I shift in my chair. I wish it were closer to his. We're separated by the coffee table, a valley between us.

"Very rarely."

"Have I proven you wrong?"

"No," he says, wearing a smile I haven't seen before. "You bewilder me."

My cheeks sizzle; I'm blushing so hard, I can likely be seen from space.

"That's why I brought you up here. Tried to engage you in playground games. You're an enigma. I can't quite figure you out."

I open my mouth to dispute him. Tell him I'm not an enigma. I'm ordinary. My life is tedious at best, sad at worst. I take an Epsomsalt bath every Tuesday night while listening to true-crime podcasts. I vacuum and do laundry on Saturday mornings, then go to Wegmans around noon, where I buy the same things every week, maybe switch up the flavor of seltzer. I batch cook Bolognese sauce once a month. I stare at the soup recipe that's been saved to my desktop for two years and I know I'll never make but for some reason won't delete. I waste hours researching eye creams. I call Naomi. I call my parents, FaceTime my brother maybe once every couple of months. I keep in touch with friends who live far away via text, and sometimes I get coffee with acquaintances who live nearby, but it's always surface level. When anyone asks me what's new, the answer is always *Nothing*.

I work remotely as a project manager for a food distributor, and once a quarter I fly to Chicago to go into the office and see my coworkers face-to-face, and we'll go out to dinner and I'll walk back to the hotel afterward, mellowed from exactly two glasses of wine, and I'll stop in a 7-Eleven for an electrolyte drink so that I'm not at all hungover in the morning.

Joel and I go for hikes in the summer, to the movies when it's cold. We go to the local diner, where we talk about finances or retirement or things we need to do around the house. He goes to the gym, goes out with friends, goes out. Travels for work. I stay home, and I read, and I cook, and I bake, and I garden, and I clean, and I watch TV, and I breathe. That's all I do. Breathe.

But Henry doesn't need to know any of that. We agreed to be honest, but I can be honest without telling the whole truth. Why not give him his mystery?

I say nothing.

He stands up and slowly comes toward me. The way he moves, the way he walks . . . he has this supernatural grace.

There's no question now. No doubt. Only clarity. Only want.

I want him to touch me. I want his hands on my thighs, my waist. In my hair.

But he passes me. Circles around the back of my chair, and I'm reacquainted with the brutal sting of disappointment.

He wanders to the window. He's quiet.

"If I hadn't gone and sat in the corner, what would you have done tonight?" I ask him. "Would you have stayed and watched? Would you have joined in, eventually?"

"No. Years ago, maybe. Yes. To feel something. To feel different. Good. But it's fleeting. And empty. Meaningless. I find no satisfaction in it. Though I understand how there's satisfaction to be found."

"What would you have done, then? If you weren't here with me?"

He reaches over and plucks a shriveled brown leaf off a drooping plant. "I would have gone and wallowed. Sat alone in the dark, longing."

"Are you being smart with me?"

He turns around, leans against the glass with his hands behind his back. He's keeping them from me. "We agreed to tell each other the truth. That's the truth."

"If you say so."

"You don't trust anyone. Not even yourself. That's why I asked who hurt you. Trust is something that's broken. That's lost. That's taken from us. Who took it from you?"

I'm drowning in all the sweat from these leggings, and from this back-and-forth, from the physical distance between us that's now too great for the intimacy of this conversation. I stand up and I go to him, and the closer I get, the closer I want to be. I leave maybe an inch between us. And I tell him.

"No one took it."

His brow furrows.

"You want my sad story? It isn't particularly interesting. It's not some heartrending saga or Greek tragedy. I'm easily defeated."

"Tell me."

"Okay . . . Well, when I was young, I was ambitious. I wanted to go to a good school. Somewhere I could make connections. I thought I'd be a lawyer or a CEO. Someone powerful. I grew up poor, worrying about whether Mom remembered to pay the electric bill, if Dad remembered to buy us food on our weekends at his house. I didn't want that for my future. I wanted something better. Shinier. And so I worked hard and got a scholarship to NYU. But when I got there, it wasn't some perfect dream. I made friends, but I felt . . . I felt different from everyone else. Lonely. Until I met Smith."

Henry's hands come out from behind his back. He hovers them at my waist, leaving enough space that he's not quite touching me, his open palms just skimming my oversized T-shirt. What lucky fabric.

"I'd never been in love before, and I fell hard and fast for someone who had a short attention span. He was into me for about six months, and then he wasn't. Broke it off out of the blue first semester sophomore year. I didn't take it well. Especially because . . . See, this is the part—this is the part I don't tell anyone, never tell anyone, because they'll either feel sorry for me or blame me, and whichever one it is, it always makes me wish it was the other. So"—I stop to laugh and to swat away a rebel tear—"he'd asked me for pictures over the summer, right? And I was nineteen and stupid, so I sent him these pictures. Naked pictures of myself. And he sent them to someone, who sent them to someone, and yeah. They got around. And I was already, just, completely heartbroken. It sent me over the edge. Now I had this reputation. I thought, why not earn it? Why not live up to it? So I became the slut they all said I was. But I couldn't handle it sober, so I started drinking. Partying. Slacking off in my classes. It's scary how quick I got so out of control. Even Naomi was like, *Relax*. But I couldn't. Because, and this is important, important to note, to understand . . . because I loved *feeling* it all."

I pause. "No. That's not right. I loved feeling it *all*. I loved waking up with a pounding headache after drinking too much the night before. I loved throwing up until my throat was raw. I loved sobbing on the subway, so loud, the whole car would stare at me. I loved getting high with a stranger in the bathroom of a random bar in the afternoon. I loved hooking up with—well, I wasn't discerning at the time. I loved the walk of shame. I loved missing class, getting emails from my adviser that I wouldn't respond to, just to steep in the stress, punish myself. I loved the wind in my hair as I was free-falling, which is crazy, because I was such a rule follower growing up. So conscientious. But . . . I don't know. I don't know where I was going with this. A few weeks before the end of second semester, I was drunk and fell off a curb. Almost got run over by a taxi. It *juuust* missed me. I could've died. Instead I just smashed my head. Scraped my face, my whole arm. Broke my wrist. Shattered it, actually."

I lift my left arm, twist my wrist so it clicks, so it makes that heinous noise. So it aches.

"But I knocked some sense into myself. Came back to reality. I remember lying in the hospital, wondering how I got there. I went through all of it, step by step. Every mistake I'd made that led me to that moment, that horrible, disgraceful moment. It wasn't Smith's fault. Or my parents'. Or anyone else's. It was *my* fault. I'd made bad decisions. A lot of them. I promised myself that from that day on, I'd be more careful. I'd use my head, not let myself get carried away by emotions. I'd temper my expectations. Protect myself from disappointment. And I thought it was a good plan, but I'm starting to wonder if it was yet another bad choice."

Henry grips my waist. Tightly.

"There it is. Is your mystery solved? No one hurt me. I hurt myself," I say. "I . . . I don't know why I just told you all that."

"Because I asked," he says. "I'm glad you did. We may come to understand each other, Sloane. If we do not already."

He slides one hand to the sweat-damp small of my back, the other up to my neck. He could choke me with this one hand if he wanted to. It's big enough. Strong enough. But his grasp is unthreatening. His fingers stroke my jaw, lift my chin.

We stare at each other, and his eyes are so big, this color I've never seen before. A color that seems to change as I stare, from brown to green to yellow . . .

He whispers a question. "May I?"

I let my lashes go heavy, let the world around me disappear. And then it's his lips on mine.

Then it's me getting exactly what I want.

13

His mouth is cold, and he tastes like tobacco. Right now, that's all I know. All I'm aware of. The universe is this. A cold mouth. Tobacco.

He kisses me harder, reverses us, puts my back to the wall.

Is this happening?

Are my hands in his hair? It's a greasy nest and I want to live in it.

Are my legs wrapped around him? Is he holding me up? Pressing me into the glass wall?

This unfamiliar sensation arrives, racing through my whole body. It's powerful and overwhelming and revelatory, so vital I fear that if it stops, if it goes away, I might die. I really might die. This electric feeling, this blissful burning, is as essential to my survival as oxygen.

I pull him closer to me.

He carries me to a love seat, which is even mustier than the chair but I couldn't care less. He's on top of me. His shoulder blades are like the edge of a cliff I'm hanging off of. What'll happen if I let go?

I don't want to find out. I can't.

I can't.

I can't.

I—

"Wait," I say, coming up for air. "Sorry."

I take a gasping breath and apologize again. I'm not sure what I'm apologizing for, or to whom. To him, to Joel, to myself.

Henry sits back on the love seat, giving me space. He tucks his hands under his thighs, either to show that he's respecting my boundaries, or to restrain himself.

I pull myself upright, attempt to pull myself together. Once I wrestle my breathing back under control, I look over at him, and he's staring straight ahead, wearing his wiliest grin yet. I can't think of anything clever to say, so I say nothing, and we sit in silence for I don't know how long. So long, it stops snowing.

Finally, he speaks. "I like you, Sloane."

"You don't know me," I say. And in the impulsive, temporary fog of post–making out optimism, I add, "Yet."

"*Yet,*" he repeats. "Might I hope to know you better?"

I'm flattered, but I can't help wondering why he's bothering with me. He could go find someone else to sleep with. Easily. He looks like a grungy nineties rock star, like a Renaissance portrait of Kurt Cobain or Gavin Rossdale. Like the rogue prince in a dark, lesser-known fairy tale.

Why me? Because I'm here in front of him? Because Naomi is preoccupied?

I was maybe pretty when I was younger, but I can't remember the last time I looked at my reflection and saw anything but flaws. Time has etched itself into my face and made my own body a foe, fickle and unforgiving, more a cage than a vessel.

What is there about me to desire, other than my proximity, my availability? That I'm close and have a pulse.

"What do you like about me?" I ask, even though I'm nervous about the answer.

His grin inverts and his expression goes grave, and my worry spoils to terror.

"You don't need to lie to get me to . . . Nothing's going to happen between us tonight. Nothing more."

"That's not what I'm after," he says.

"Tell the truth."

"You won't believe the truth. Any of it," he says, looking forlorn. "And I want you to stay."

Ominous but intriguing. "I don't think I can leave. The roads . . ."

"I don't mean stay the night. Just tonight. I mean stay with me."

"Oh," I say. Of all the turns this night has taken, this might be the most unexpected. He's a romantic. Or he's messing with me. Probably that.

He stands, goes over to the wall, and presses a hand to the glass. "What you said, about feeling different. Lonely. Imagine that sustained over years. Lifetimes."

He paces now, swaying from side to side, his cadence as measured and steady as a pendulum's.

"I made decisions long ago, when I was someone else, that I cannot take back. I've made mistakes that I cannot erase. I live with the consequences every day. They're a burden. One I deserve, I'm sure. But I'm tired, and I've been tired for so long. For so long tired of being tired."

It's happening again. That thing with his accent.

He laughs. Not his nerd laugh. A tricky laugh. "And then last night, when I saw you, I felt . . . if I could articulate it, I promise I would."

He smiles sweetly at me, looking at me that way he does, with sincere affection. I do believe him. I do trust that he's being honest.

I wish he weren't.

"Last night?" I ask, a tremor I can't disguise in my voice. "You were at the bar?"

I remember now. The man in the corner. Half in shadow, half in the red glow of the neon sign. The man I thought might be watching me.

"Yes, I was at the bar," he says, his big eyes getting bigger. "And . . . and at your window."

A bomb goes off in the dark pit of my gut.

He must be joking. How could he know about my nightmare? That I dreamt of a figure outside the cottage, two stories up? That I woke to find a handprint on the glass? How could he possibly know?

I clear my throat. "Right. Watching me sleep. How brooding."

"You weren't asleep," he says, and my body goes numb, and I feel like I'm floating, like I'm a loose astronaut tumbling around in an inescapable doom.

"What?" I ask, hoping he'll say something to reel me back in. That he'll laugh. Admit he's not serious.

"You weren't asleep," he repeats. "I want you to trust me. To know I will be honest with you. Always tell you the truth, even if that truth sounds like fiction. It is a cruel misfortune that I cannot hope to see you again without revealing what will almost certainly make you never want to see me again."

"Right." I look around the room. There's the collection of sad, dying plants, the musty furniture, the magazines. *The Power Broker.* I clear my throat again. "Whose house is this?"

Henry sighs. "This house belongs to someone who calls himself Roger McLaren. Though that was not always his name."

"Okay. And where is Roger now?"

Henry rubs his jaw, gives a hollow laugh, then says, "If there was a right way to go about this, this wasn't it."

"Where is he?"

"If you stay, I'll explain it all. You told me your story. Your secrets. Only fair that I tell you mine. Every last one," he says.

I thought the part of me that was susceptible to the charms of danger died when I hit the pavement on St. Marks, when I was still young. But I guess not, because I consider what it would be like to ignore every waving bright red flag and welcome Henry back to the love seat. Let him kiss my neck and pretend nothing else exists. Fall back into that vacuum of euphoria.

Admire the view before the zeppelin catches fire. Smile before screaming.

Instead, I ask again, "Where is he?"

"Sloane."

"Where?"

He takes a deep breath. "If you leave, you cannot speak of this. You must swear it. Or they won't let you leave."

"Wha—what?"

"I didn't lie to you, Sloane. I'll never lie to you. Everything I've said has been true." He hangs a hand on the back of his neck. "The cellar really is drafty."

It takes me a second.

Why bring up the cellar? I wonder, assuming for a bittersweet moment that he dodged my question instead of answering it.

But then it clicks into place, and the horror of it sends bile bubbling up my throat. My hands cover my mouth and I'm stumbling off the love seat, over to the stairs, swallowing down acidic, gin-flavored vomit.

"Sloane," Henry says. "Sloane, wait. Please."

I don't stop to see if he's following me. My heel slips on the winding stairs, and I land hard at the bottom. I crawl forward until I gain enough momentum to get to my feet. I scramble past the cellar door, still rattling, the groaning louder now. If I were stupid, or kind, I'd stop to open it, try to help the man behind it being held captive in his own house. But the danger here is real and I'm not taking any risks.

The danger is real.

I sprint down the hall, yelling for Naomi.

"Nay? Nay!"

I trip over myself as I make it to the living room, where there's a pile of naked bodies writhing around on the floor. I avert my eyes.

"Naomi. Naomi!"

It's too late to be subtle, to make a quiet exit.

"Sloane?" Naomi says, out of breath.

"Naomi, we need to go. Now. Hurry. Get your clothes." I'm winded, too. For a very different reason.

"What is it? What's wrong?"

"Don't go," I hear Ilie say. "The night is young!"

"Sloane . . ." It's Henry. He calls my name from down the hall.

"Please, stay," Elisa says. I look over and see she's grabbing at Naomi, who stands in front of the fireplace, slipping on her lace thong. Naomi's hot tip for random hookups was always to tie your underwear around your wrist so you wouldn't lose it. Elisa tugs Naomi's arm, nearly pulling her down.

"Hey!" I bark. Feeling like cornered prey has turned me into an animal. I leap forward, and suddenly the fire poker is in my clammy hands. I'm holding it up like a weapon, like a goddamn lightsaber. "Let go of her! Everyone, get back. We're leaving. We're going."

"Sloane!" Naomi shrieks. "What are you doing?"

"This isn't their house! I—I think they've got the owner locked in the fucking basement!"

"What? Sloane, just calm down. I'm sure it's a misunderstanding," she says, picking up her bra and clasping it behind her back.

"Don't! Don't you dare! We're in real trouble, Nay, so don't tell me to calm down! I need you to listen to me for once. Get your shit and let's go!"

There's stunned silence.

Tatiana, who was in the middle of blowing Costel, lets his dick fall out of her mouth, which is wide with shock or maybe just frozen in position. Miri is spread-eagle on the floor, Ilie's fingers still inside her.

It is very, *very* awkward to interrupt group sex, and for a split second I forget the menace of the situation and have to stifle a laugh.

But then there's a lurid *bang* in the hall. The sound of a door breaking open.

14

Footsteps. Slow, heavy footsteps.

I turn to see Henry. He's already made it out of the hall; he's not too far from me. He's looking at me. Everyone else is looking beyond me, toward the hall, toward the noise, the smack of bare feet coming down hard.

I take a step forward, holding the fire poker tightly though I'm sure it makes me seem more pathetic than intimidating. I move to get a better look at whoever is coming down the hall. Naomi, now wearing her thong, her bra, and her Penny Lane jacket, follows closely behind me.

Before I can even process what I'm seeing, she's screaming.

From the murky darkness emerges a pale, jagged shape. A creature. A skeletal frame.

Its movements are tortured, agonizing just to witness. Its labored approach is accompanied by the groaning I heard earlier, and wheezing. Gruesome wheezing. The sound of absolute suffering.

The closer it gets, the more I can see it, and the more human, the more horrific it becomes. It's got these long, spindly limbs. It's spidering toward us on all fours. It's got a bald head, skin like cellophane, eyes like boiled eggs out of the shell. Its nose is narrow, nostrils gaping. It has no lips, but it has a mouth, a void, a giant hole filled with brown, rotten teeth. A desiccated tongue the color of ash juts out as the thing makes a new noise. A wordless howl.

"What the fuck!" Naomi screams. "What the fuck!"

The thing—the pale man—slows to a complete stop. He goes on howling as he begins to roll up, his bones cracking with repulsive intensity. He wears nothing except a pair of stained, stretched-out tighty-whities that slump from his hip bones. All of his bones are visible. I can count every rib. He's been starved.

He lifts his emaciated arms and lurches forward, but he's too eager. He falls face-first on the floor.

Naomi screams again.

I can't look at her. I can't take my eyes off the man. He's splayed out; one of his arms is broken. I can see the fracture through his gauzy skin. His legs twitch, but other than that, he's not moving. I know he's alive because I can still hear him breathing. Wheezing.

I reach over for Naomi's hand, silently begging her to take mine so we can turn and run out of here.

Then I remember the snow. I remember the gate.

I remember that I don't have my phone, but she must have hers.

"We need to go," I say, taking a step to the side, bringing Naomi with me. We pass directly in front of the man.

"He's gonna die," Naomi whisper-yells at me. "He's about to die."

"We need to *go*," I repeat.

There's resistance. She's resisting. She pulls free from my grip. I turn toward her, and she's fixated on the dying skeleton man. For as freewheeling and oblivious and inconsiderate as she can be, Naomi is also profoundly empathetic.

She drops to her knees in front of the man, compelled by his suffering, undeterred by his monstrousness.

"Okay," she says, reaching a hand over his back. "Okay. It's okay."

There she is. Once, back in high school, we were at her house and a bird flew into her bedroom window and broke its wing. She went out to help it, put it in a shoebox, rehabilitate it. I warned against doing this, telling her birds carry diseases and mites. She ignored me. She doesn't listen to reason. She doesn't listen.

I scan the room. No one's moved. Tatiana is still holding Costel's dick. With the exception of Henry, they're all naked, which should make them seem less threatening, but it doesn't. Because they're the ones who did this. How long has this man been locked away? How long have they lived here letting him suffer and starve beneath their feet?

Did they break in? Take the house by force?

What the hell is going on?

"It's okay. We're gonna get you help." Naomi reaches into her pocket. Her brows pinch together. She reaches deeper. Deeper. She tries the other pocket.

"Where is it?" she mumbles. "Where's my phone?"

"You shouldn't get too close," Henry says. "This isn't what you think it is."

"Sloane. I don't have it. I don't have my phone. We need to get him help."

She's not thinking clearly.

"You shouldn't touch him." Henry's tone has gone harsh. "You're too close."

The man stirs. The movement is subtle at first, but then his head lifts, neck reels back, and with his good arm he grabs Naomi by the hair. His frailty must be only in appearance, because Naomi fails to get away. He has her.

It happens so fast.

He bashes her head to the floor. Once. Twice.

Then he flips her over onto her back and he climbs on top of her, pinning her down with his revolting living-corpse body. He lets out another pained howl before he flops forward and sinks his teeth into her neck.

He bites her. He's biting her. *He's fucking biting her.*

I forgot I was holding the poker until it nearly slips through my hand as I lose control of myself, as I scream like I've never screamed, like no one has ever screamed. I see blood on the man's face, around his rotten mouth. Blood splattering onto his pale, pale skin. Naomi's blood.

My horror turns to fury and my grip tightens on the poker and I lift it over my head, and I dive forward, and I swing it as hard as I can, which turns out to be pretty hard, because when it lands it cracks the man's skull, and the hook gets stuck in it.

And yet he continues to attack Naomi, slurping at her neck.

"Get off her!" I scream, yanking the poker. I put my foot on the man's shoulder for leverage and manage to free the poker from his skull, and I bring it down again, this time on his back. His skin rips open, exposing his bones. I hit him a third time, on the neck, and the hook gets stuck again. I lean down and pull it across, opening a deep gash.

Now I've got his attention.

He pushes himself up on his functioning arm, the other dangling awkwardly at his side. He turns to face me, hissing like a cat. And before I know what I'm doing, I shove the poker into his eye. It makes a wet, squishing sound.

He doesn't react. He doesn't even bleed.

I pull the poker out and try again.

"Die!" I hear myself say. "Why won't you die?"

He lunges toward me, wrapping his bone fingers around my

ankle. The move is so unexpected, and I'm so shocked by it, that I don't have time to ward it off, to kick him away. His hold is so tight it hurts.

It hurts even before he pulls me down and I drop the poker. Even before he brings my leg to his mouth, my calf to his decayed teeth, and clamps on.

He doesn't have all his teeth, but there are enough. It's torment. The destruction of my leg is quick and vicious.

It's so horrifying. I'm looking down, watching it happen, what's being done to me, and I feel completely helpless.

And then I look over at Naomi, and she's holding her neck, trying to stop the bleeding, and her eyes glaze over, and I feel completely hopeless.

And the others, only a few feet away from us, just stand there. Doing nothing. Nothing but watching.

"Help!" I say, though I know no one's coming to our rescue. "Help us!"

My vision goes spotty, and I might lose consciousness, and all of a sudden Henry is standing over me. Stepping over me. He digs his fingers into the gash in the pale man's neck and starts to pull. It looks like it requires some effort, but not as much as it should to separate a man's head from his body. Like untwisting the lid of a stubborn jar.

It takes seconds. It makes a disgusting noise, a sort of vile ripping.

The man's head spirals toward me, landing right in front of my face. There's still some of me between his teeth. Flesh and blood and chunky red something . . . I don't even know. He's so much more human up close; I can see the man he was before he became whatever this is. His eyelids remain open, and I have this terrible feeling that he's looking back at me with the one eye still intact. This terrible feeling that he's still not dead.

The skin of his neck hangs loose and he leaks this treacly substance that I don't think is blood. It's too dark and putrid, and it
drip, drip, drip, drips. Whatever it is, there isn't a lot of it.

Henry nudges the head with his foot and it whirls away. He
kneels in front of me, pushing my hair out of my face with a cold
hand.

"I hope you can forgive me," he says.

I look down at my leg, at the wound that's even worse than
anticipated.

I look over at Naomi, and her eyes have rolled back.

"Help her! You have to help her!" My voice is shrill with panic,
and it sounds so far away, like it's coming from another reality,
another universe. "Please!"

I crawl to her on my elbows, dragging my legs behind me, leaving a trail of blood. Her neck is a mess, a fountain spewing red
through her fingers. It's too much.

"Naomi? Nay. It's me. Stay with me, okay?"

She whimpers, the only response she's capable of. I press my
hand over hers, over the gash.

"Please!" I scream. "Please! Help!"

"Drago?" I hear Ilie say. "What do you want to do?"

Tatiana mutters something in French. Then, in English, "Fool-
ish to have guests here. Did I not say this?"

"Please, please, please, please . . ." I can't watch her die. I can't,
I can't.

"Sloane," Henry says. "Listen to me. You need to make a choice."

"Please . . . She's my life. Please, help. I won't say anything about
the man. Please. Call nine-one-one."

"You need to listen. You need to believe me."

"I am listening. Please!" I look at Naomi, her eyelids fluttering. I hover my free hand over her mouth and feel that she is still
breathing, but her breath is weak.

"Do you hear me? We are offering a choice to you, and to Naomi."

"Are we?" Tatiana asks. "What happened to democracy?"

"It is good with me," Ilie says. "They are fun. Beautiful. Elisa?"

"Yes, I agree. I love them. Both of them," Elisa says. "Real American girls."

"It's time," Costel says. "It's been, what? A hundred years?"

"We haven't encountered anyone else nearly as amenable," Miri says.

"They will cause problems," Tatiana says. "Mark my words."

I'm too desperate to care about their conversation, whatever it's about. "Please! I'm begging you. Please. She's losing so much blood."

"I say we drain them and move on," Tatiana says. She inhales. "Don't you smell it? They are sweet."

"No," Henry says, picking up the fire iron and swinging it over his shoulder. "We let Sloane decide their fate."

He looks at me with that damn fox grin spread across his face. "How would you like to live forever?"

15

W h-what?"
        "Eternal life. Eternal youth."
    "What are you talking about? Are you—are you really not going to help us? What's wrong with you? Fuck you!"
    "It's a simple choice," Henry says. "To live forever or to die as you are."
    "Easy-peasy," Ilie says. "We party, have good time."
    Naomi gasps for breath. My hand is slippery with her blood, and it keeps sliding out of position. I can't believe this is happening. I can't believe this is real. It must be a dream. I must be dreaming. I . . .
    I'm back in the hospital after my fall, slowly sobering up, thinking, *This must be a dream.*
    I'm thinking about Patsy Cline. *Don't worry about me, hoss. When it's my time to go, it's my time.*
    Is this it? Am I about to watch Naomi bleed out on the floor of this dirty lake house? What are these psychos going to do to me afterward? They're not going to let me go, let me leave.
    If I could accept any of this, maybe I'd be afraid. But it's impos-

sible to accept, so I'm not scared, just angry. Really, really angry. And tired. I'm so tired of fighting for a life that's mind-numbingly dull when it's not punching me in the face.

"I don't care!" I say. "I don't care what happens to me. Just do something. Call an ambulance!"

Henry stands, circles us. "You won't leave her, and she can't leave you. The decision needs to be made for both. And she will die if you do nothing."

He's so matter-of-fact about it. It's brutal, and I'm tempted to tell him to fuck off just to spite him, but Naomi's going cold in my hands.

"Fine! I'll do it. Whatever you want. Anything. Just help her. Please."

Elisa jumps up and down. "Oh, so exciting! New friends!"

"Finally," Costel says.

Tatiana huffs. "You will see."

"Good choice," Henry says. He reaches up to his neck and pulls the chain out from under his sweater. At the end is something long and silver. It looks kind of like a whistle.

Whatever's about to happen, I wish I didn't have to be here for it. I rest my head on Naomi's chest. "I'm sorry."

"Don't . . ." she says.

"Nay?"

"Don't . . . forget to say *I told you so.*" She smiles, and there's blood in her mouth, all over her teeth.

The men carry us outside. If I could walk, maybe I would run.

It's probably for the best that I can't, because it's dark and we're surrounded by woods, and who knows how far we are from the nearest house? I'd have to jump the fence, or the gate. Not freeze to death. I think about the Carolean Death March, all those bodies in the snow. Hundreds of soldiers frozen on the Tydal mountains, retreating from a war they couldn't win.

Naomi was wrong. I'm not obsessed with tragedy. I'm obsessed with choice. How one decision can lead to catastrophe.

What if the Carolean general had decided to go a different route? Not travel through the mountains.

What if Buddy Holly had decided to tough it out on the tour bus, not charter that plane?

What if the engineers never ran that safety test at Chernobyl? What if the plant was never built in the first place?

What if I never fell off that curb sixteen years ago?

What if I never got into the car tonight?

I'm sure it's cold out, but I feel nothing. Not even when Henry and Ilie drop us in the snow.

They form a circle around us. Ilie, Costel, Miri, and Tatiana are all still naked. Aren't they cold?

What is their *deal*?

Elisa holds two cups. Wooden goblets.

At the sight of them, I turn to the side and get sick.

What are they doing with those?

What did I agree to?

What choice did I make?

"Don't worry," Ilie says. "Just relax. This part will be over soon. In some years, you won't remember."

Is this a sex thing? A torture fetish in action? That would be my assumption had I not just witnessed Henry decapitating that skeleton man with his bare hands. There's no logic here.

"I would tell you that it doesn't hurt," Henry says, pulling me upright, "but I swore I'd never lie to you."

He holds the silver whistle. Only it's not a whistle. It's a spile. Like what Canadians use to harvest sap from a tree.

"Be still," he says, leaning close to me. "You may not trust me yet, but someday you might. I have no illusions. I know I'm not saving you, but I'm giving you all the time in the world to save yourself."

With that, he gently sweeps the hair from my neck and shoves the spile in under my ear.

The sound is merciless, but my shock must protect me from feeling the insertion. There's no pain. Only an uncomfortable warmth.

Henry gestures for Elisa, and she brings the cups. They fill one of them with my blood.

I think I've done this before. Not exactly in this way, but there's some recognition as I sit here. This is what it is to surrender. To be bled dry. You hold still and you let it happen, because the harder you fight, the harder you lose.

Out of the corner of my eye I see Elisa press the other wooden cup to Naomi's neck. Elisa doesn't need a spile, because Naomi's already open, already bleeding, but Ilie holds Nay upside down so it happens faster.

I want to ask her if she'll wait for me in the dream mall. If we can finally meet there.

If that's where she goes, that's where I'll go. I'll follow her. I'll follow her anywhere.

Just wait for me. Wherever you are, wait for me. I'll be there. I'm coming.

She says, *Only Jersey girls would think heaven is a mall.*

But she doesn't really say it, because I'm pretty sure she's dead.

I'm woozy. The scene dissolves; everything fades away.

When it comes back the cup is gone, and I feel Henry pull the spile out. And then he kisses me. He kisses my neck.

Not kissing.

Biting. Licking. Sucking.

Because that's what he does, because that's what he is. What they all are.

Vampires.

Fucking wild, Naomi says, but only in my head.

Ilie and Elisa and Tatiana take turns at her wound. I look down, and Miri and Costel have my leg, my blood smeared all over their faces.

There's a faint sensation at my wrist. It's Henry. He's chewing through it. Down to the bone. Down to the . . .

There's darkness, and then there's Henry holding metal between his teeth. The plate from my wrist surgery.

He spits it into the crimson snow.

"This one's sweet but the other one's sweeter," Tatiana says, having switched places with Costel. She glances up at me. "Don't give me that look, *ma chérie.* It's too soon for me to regret you."

"We're close," Henry says. "Sloane, I promise this is a favor."

He wraps his hand around my chewed-up wrist, and he squeezes, snapping the bone.

When I scream, a geyser of blood shoots from my mouth.

"There's more," Miri says. "Should we ration?"

"No. No more," Henry says. "We're done."

"But—" Tatiana starts.

"I won't risk them being weak for the sake of gluttony. It's done. It's time to finish."

He presses his face to my neck and takes a final lick. Then he speaks directly into my ear.

"See you in another life."

I fade out again, and when I come back, it's with the taste of blood in my mouth. My eyelids are too heavy to lift. I can't see anything.

I can't feel anything. I can't hear anything—not voices, not the wind, not the beat of my heart or the whir of blood swimming through my veins. I can't smell the snow. I can't smell the lingering of incense in my hair or sweat on my skin. I can't smell Naomi, her signature vanilla perfume.

There's nothing except taste.

It's all there is.

The taste of blood.

I recognize the flavor. It's familiar but it's new. The texture silky. Light on my tongue. Warm as whiskey in my throat.

It's all there is and that's okay because it's all I need.

And then it goes away. The taste is gone.

I open my eyes.

Tatiana holds the wooden cup to my lips. That's what I've been drinking. My own blood. The blood Henry siphoned from me.

But I'm not horror-struck. Not sickened or afraid. I'm not at all upset.

I'm thirsty.

As soon as I understand this, the thirst becomes excruciating. It's louder than a fire alarm, sharper than knives. My skin is bubbling off; my bones are splitting, scraping, grinding my insides; my teeth are exploding, my brain shuddering, and it's going to rocket out of my skull, seep through my ears and my nostrils, push my eyes out. I know it is. I know. This is unrelenting, to the point where nothing else matters. I'm trapped in the agony.

I'm hot. I'm burning. I'm not imagining it. The snow melts around me. I'd scream if my throat weren't so dry.

"Let her sweat," I hear Henry say. "It's going to be a long night."

"This one is still cold," Costel says.

I struggle to keep my eyes open; it's like I'm pressing them into sand. But I see Naomi half-submerged in snow. She looks hollow, like a deflated balloon. She's not moving. Not drinking. Elisa's got the cup and she's trying to help Naomi drink, but the blood is just spilling out the sides of her limp mouth.

"Careful. Don't waste it," Tatiana says.

"Keep trying," Henry says. "Put her head back. Pour it down."

My guts are seething, and my skin can't contain it. I start convulsing, clawing at my throat. My left hand flops loose, my wrist barely held together by whatever remains since Henry destroyed it.

Am I most attracted to the people who are destined to do me the most harm?

I'd forgive him for it, for all of it, forgive anyone for anything, for everything, if I could just get a drink. Just one drink.

I need it.

"I still remember how it felt," Henry says.

"She's fiending," Miri says. "Sweet baby."

"Look," says Tatiana.

I can barely see, my eyes too dry to focus, but I can feel the fresh misery of my wrist re-forming. Splintered bone stitching back together. It's so inexplicably terrible that I'm screaming despite the fact that the screaming is almost as painful.

"I'm not listening to this," Tatiana says. "I'm giving her another sip."

She doesn't wait for Henry's permission.

It's just a drop, but it's enough.

It goes beyond satiating; it unleashes stars. A pleasure and a peace like I've never known, so pure, I could cry but I laugh instead.

"She's prettier when she smiles," Tatiana says.

I consider saying thank you, but the dumb-happy feeling doesn't last, and the blood in my system has granted me enough clarity to realize that Naomi still isn't moving.

She's slouched against Ilie's leg, and he holds her head back as Elisa drips blood between her lips.

"Nay?" I croak. Naomi!"

Her eyes pop open.

I've never been so grateful to hear her scream.

16

I wake up in a strange bed, in a strange room. There's a single window, a quilt hung on a curtain rod. I can see light peeking in at the sides. It's daytime.

Naomi's tucked in next to me, and the red crust at the corners of her mouth reminds me of what happened last night. I sit straight up, kick the covers off my legs. For a second I worry that I'm wearing no pants, just my underwear and the big T-shirt, but then I realize my leggings are on, just ripped to oblivion, and I can see immediately that where my calf was bitten, desecrated—there's nothing. No trace of any injury. No mark.

I look down at my wrist. It looks fine, considering, except . . .

There's a tiny shard of metal poking through my skin. I pluck it out like a splinter and flick it across the room. There's a slight hole where it was. It doesn't hurt. It doesn't bleed.

I twist my hand, circle it around, and my wrist doesn't click. Doesn't ache. But I refuse myself the hope, the possibility, that something good has happened here, because I can't reconcile it with all the bad, horrific, fucked-up things.

"Naomi," I whisper, nudging her shoulder. "Naomi, you have to get up. We need to go."

She mumbles something and reaches up to her neck, which, like my calf, bears no proof of injury.

"Naomi. We're still in the house. We need to get out."

"I'm tired," she says, her voice hoarse. The last thing I remember is her screaming.

"We'll sleep when we're dead," I say, because that's what she used to tell me at sleepovers, coercing me to stay awake, stay up late, participate in her insomnia. Only now it might not apply, because for all I know, we are dead. "Get up."

I rip the covers away and she groans.

"We're not safe here. We need to . . ."

I trail off, not sure what we need to do. Go to the police? Tell them we were unwilling participants in a blood ritual? Tell them we encountered a group of vampires squatting in a lake house? That we were attacked by the starved owner of said house who was being held captive in the basement. That something was done to us.

My heart plunges into the pit of my stomach.

What are we now?

"Naomi . . ."

"What?" she says, yawning. Her breath is so bad, we both wince. "Yikes."

It smells like rot.

"Do you remember what happened last night?"

She turns over and smashes her face into her pillow. "Did we drop acid?"

"No. We got mauled by a skeleton man and then attacked by vampires."

A minute goes by in silence. Then she lifts her head, opens one eye, and says, "That sucks."

"Are you being quippy right now?"

"The pun wasn't intentional, but . . ." She sighs and flips onto her back, stares up at the ceiling. We're both quiet for a long time. "Are you sure we didn't drop acid?"

"Yes," I say, with such confidence that I start to doubt myself.

"Fuck me," she says. "*Fuck!* A shared delusion, then. Maybe?"

"We need to leave," I say. "I don't know where they are, but . . ."

She hugs her knees to her chest and pulls a face.

"What?" I ask.

"I'm thirsty."

"Okay . . . ?"

"I'm thirsty," she repeats.

"We can get you some water. . . ."

"Sloane. I'm not thirsty for water."

My hand comes to my throat, and I start pinching at my skin as I realize what she's telling me. As I come to the grim understanding. "Right."

"Right."

It's easy to forget that the brave aren't immune to fear. There's nothing more terrifying than sitting across from the bravest person you know and watching fear slowly take them, drag them under, bully them, break them until they're as scared as the rest of us.

"I don't know if leaving is the best idea," she says.

"Come again?"

"Whatever happened last night, we don't understand it. We need answers. They're the only ones who can give them to us."

"Naomi. They're monsters. Literally."

She gets out of bed and scoops her jacket off the floor, puts it on. It's got bloodstains on the collar. "We don't know that for sure. Not yet."

She opens the door to the bedroom and marches out into the hall.

"This is a nightmare," I say to myself. "This is an actual living nightmare."

"Hello?" Naomi says. "Hello!"

I follow her into the hall. The house is dark, all the candles burned out, the fire snuffed. But my eyes adjust. They adjust pretty fast, and I can see fine. Better than fine.

Naomi squeaks.

"Oh! Oh fuck. Oops. I just kicked it. I kicked his head. I didn't see it."

The skeleton man's body is in the same spot as it was the night before; no one bothered to move it. His head is now rolling across the floor. It makes a bad sound.

Naomi gags. "Oh God."

"See?" I whisper. "This is why we need to get out of here."

"Look who is awake." Ilie comes sauntering down the hall. He wears a silk robe with nothing underneath. "I will make you coffee. It will taste different but still good."

He's so casual. He steps over the severed head like it's a soccer ball in the yard.

I'm shell-shocked.

"Come, loves. It is early. Or late." He hangs his arms around us and guides us into a big yellow kitchen. There are towels hung over the windows, empty cups in the sink, the wooden goblets left out on the counter. "Sit, sit."

He gestures to the built-in table and benches in the far corner, a breakfast nook. He takes out a French press. Naomi shoots me a look.

"You probably are thinking, *Ilie, we are not thirsty for coffee.* I know. But it will be good. I put a little something in it for you. Quench your thirst. We sit, have coffee, we talk. I have feeling you might be"—he pauses, searching for the right word—"confused."

"I think we're more than confused," Naomi says, sliding onto a bench.

Why is she sitting down? Is she really planning on staying for coffee?

She's either ignoring my signals or not getting them.

"I explain. Drago insists he do it, but he is very serious. Too serious. I tell him, he will make you scared. It is not scary, to live this way. It is good. We are happy."

"And we are leaving," I say. "Okay?"

"Okay," Ilie says, plugging in an electric kettle. "After coffee."

I look at Naomi, and she shrugs. "Things are what they are. What's the difference if we stay for coffee?"

"Can't wait to find out," I say, stomping over to the table and sitting down next to her. "What are you thinking?"

"I'm not," she says. "I'm just . . . I'm thirsty. Aren't you?"

"No. Not really. No." There's an alien tickle in my throat. A weird wriggling. It's not thirst, not exactly. It's more like a craving. A bratty insistence.

"I get special coffee for you," Ilie says. "We don't put milk in our coffee, you know."

He winks at us.

"Christ." I put my head down on the table. Whenever I would wallow about getting older, or occasionally lament the monotony of my life, I would take at least some solace in thinking that my worst mistakes were behind me. That I would never again have to wake up in a stranger's house with a headache and the most potent strain of regret, wearing last night's clothes and a heavy crown of shame.

Ilie measures out some coffee grounds for the French press, and I think about the morning after I lost my virginity, in that random guy's apartment, when he made me coffee and it tasted like possibility. I think about all the mornings after that followed, the taste diluting over time.

Ilie opens the fridge, which is moldy and dirty and mostly empty, and he retrieves a bag of blood, and I wonder, *How will the coffee taste this morning?*

"How is it?" Ilie asks.

I push my mug away, but Naomi downs hers.

"Careful. It is hot. You will burn your tongue," he says.

"Very kind of you to show concern for our well-being," I say.

"You are being sarcastic, yes?" he asks me.

"You brought us here to—to . . . to hurt us! To drink our blood!"

"No, no. That is not true. We did not intend for things to happen like that. It was supposed to be fun party; that is all. You come, we have good time, then you go or stay. You do what you like. But, sometimes, you know, things get crazy. The drama. Drink. Try the coffee."

"I don't want it," I say. "I don't want any of this."

"I gave you the choice, and you said yes." Henry is at the counter pouring himself a cup of coffee. I didn't notice him come in. His presence makes all my muscles tense, and I realize that before this second, the painful, persistent knot in my neck wasn't bothering me, for the first time in years. "Last night. You chose this."

"Under duress. What was I supposed to do? Let my best friend die?"

"You don't need to worry about death anymore. Not a natural death."

"I was fine to die," I say, out loud, by accident.

"Why would you say that?" Naomi asks, grabbing my arm. "Why would you say something like that?"

"Things are what they are, right? What difference does it make? Now we're . . . we're . . ."

"Are we vampires?" Naomi asks.

Henry squeezes a few drops of blood into his coffee and sits down at the table. "Yes."

I burst out laughing, surprising everyone, including myself.

Ilie joins me. "Oh yeah! It is crazy."

"You're right, guy. It *is* crazy."

"I'd think you were fucking with us if I didn't feel so funky," Naomi says. "My body doesn't feel like my body. It's like it's lighter or something."

"It feels good," Ilie says. "Much better. Most people, they feel very bad in their body. Their bodies get old, get sick. Not us."

"You feel good at the expense of others," I say, standing. "You hurt people."

"It's complicated," Henry says.

"It's not," I say. "Whatever mental gymnastics you do to justify violence, that's what's complicated. The truth is very simple."

"You eat meat?" he asks, and takes a slow sip of his coffee. "That's violence."

"Is that your argument? A chicken or a cow isn't the same as a human being."

"You're right. Humans are evil."

"Wait. Can we just drink cow blood? Animal blood?" Naomi asks, licking her lips. "Is that a thing?"

"You could but it is not the same," Ilie says. "Tastes like piss. Look. We are not bad guys."

"I'm sure the owner of this house felt differently."

"*He* was bad guy," Ilie says. "Very, very bad. We know him many years. We come see him, and it was bad, so we put him in cellar."

"Hold up. He was a vampire, too?" Naomi asks.

"Yes. But also no," Ilie says. "Not like us."

"A feeder," Henry says.

"Right," I say. I don't think I want to know any more. "Naomi, please. Let's just go."

"Go where? We need blood, don't we?" She looks to Henry. "Don't we?"

"You need to manage your thirst. It will get easier over time, but in the next two, three days, it will be a challenge. Some struggle to resist their bloodlust. Others suffer denying it."

"We can deny it, though?" I ask.

He shakes his head. "You can. But deny yourself for too long, and you will essentially die of thirst."

"I thought you said we didn't need to worry about death."

"Theoretically, no. Not of natural causes. But there are fates worse than death," he says. "If you don't satisfy your thirst you will wither away, quite like the man you saw last night. Not alive, but not dead. In a state of eternal torment, with enough awareness to be present in your pain but without the strength to end it."

I reach across the table, pick up my mug, and throw it at the wall. Blood-laced coffee and slices of porcelain splatter everywhere.

"Great. Looking forward to it," I say, turning on my heel and walking out of the kitchen into the main hall. My little outburst wasn't as cathartic as I'd hoped, maybe because now there's a scent in the air, faint but bright and inviting, a scent I don't know how I can identify as that of blood, but I can, and I do, and it has me salivating. It exacerbates this peculiar tickle in my throat.

I get my coat off the rack. My shoes are by the door, next to Naomi's. I slip them on.

"Sloane?" Naomi calls from the kitchen. "Where are you going?"

I wish I knew.

17

I stand in the hallway in my shoes and coat with no phone, no ride. No clue. Naomi trots in from the kitchen.

I put my hand up. "Don't say anything."

"Wasn't gonna," she says.

"This—whatever is happening to us right now, whatever was done to us last night—is serious. This is bad. And you don't seem to understand that. Or care."

"I do care. I feel some responsibility to handle it, since I'm the one who brought us here."

"How are you handling it? I'm not shacking up with these people, Nay. This is because of them." I stop short of saying what I really mean, which is *because of you.*

"You heard them. We need to get our thirst under control. I don't want to stay here forever either. Just until we can manage on our own. I'm trying to make the smart decision here. Be cautious."

Where was all this caution last night? I wonder.

"No," I say.

"No?"

"No. I'm done. How do we know if anything they say is true? We don't."

"Do you not feel it? Do you not feel . . . different?"

I won't answer her question. I won't confirm it out loud. "Doesn't matter. I'm not waiting around for another surprise zombie or for them to serve us lunch with blood as a condiment. Because whenever I think my luck can't get any worse, it does! It always does."

"But what if . . ." She shakes her head.

"What?" I ask.

"What if this wasn't bad luck?"

Behind her there's a painting of a sailboat that looks like it could be either in a museum or at a garage sale; I don't have an eye for art. The walls are sooty from the candles, which have burned to stubs.

"I watched you get your neck ripped open. I thought you were going to die in my arms. I appreciate that you always search for the silver lining, but there's none here."

"If we never came here, if this didn't happen, then what? You'd go back to Joel and keep going through the motions? I'd go back on the road with Lee and get caught up in his shit. I've spent the last decade in service of someone else's dream. Decade, Sloane. That time gone. Those years gone, like that." She snaps. "What was our future, before this? Neither of us ever wanted babies. So, what? We get old and no one likes to look at us anymore; no one wants to listen. There's a window for women in this world, Sloane. And once it closes—"

"You told me that it wasn't too late. Last night in the bathroom, before this happened. Now you're saying our lives were hopeless. You're trying to sell me a lie."

"I'm not. It wasn't too late. Just, now the choice was made for us, the change. A change who knows if either of us would have made on our own. Chances are, we would have gone back to our lives, to what was familiar, at the expense of what we really want. But there's no going back now."

"I don't know what I want," I say. "But I know it isn't this."

"If you want to leave, Ilie will take you back to your place," Henry says, walking over with Naomi's dress, neatly folded. She's in only her coat and underwear. He gives the dress to her, then turns to me. "We won't force you to stay."

"We hoped you would stay," Elisa says. She stands at the end of the hall in a crushed-velvet nightgown, a sleep mask on her forehead. "You're welcome to come back. We should be here for another few days. Maybe longer. Oh, are you sure you want to leave? We'd love to have you."

Naomi steps into her dress, which I take as a sign that she's agreed to leave with me. "Thank you, Elisa. That's very generous."

Ilie appears in a fur coat and snow boots and with enormous sunglasses over a balaclava. He slips on a pair of winter gloves. "I will clear the driveway. We have snowblower, goes quick."

"Um, okay. Thanks," I say.

"Not a problem! I like to do it," he says, going out the front door.

I experience the hot crush of shame I get anytime I've been mean to someone and then they're nice to me. Even after I remind myself of the circumstances, the guilt lingers. I stare at the sailboat painting. The longer I look at it, the more beautiful it becomes.

"I'd offer to help him, but he enjoys it," Henry says, coming up beside me. His arm brushes against mine, and the sensation in my throat intensifies to an itch, to this bizarre, fast-mutating ache. I have a split-second fantasy of grabbing his hand and pulling him closer to me, certain his skin on my skin would kill any other craving.

"Just admit you're lazy," I say.

He laughs. The good laugh. The cute, endearing one. "You'll see. He'll be so proud when he's done."

It's him on top of me in the conservatory. It's him chewing my wrist open, ripping the metal out.

I clear my throat, attempting to rid it of the tickle, the itch that I won't scratch. But it doesn't work. I take a step back, a step away from him.

Down the hall, Naomi huddles with Elisa. They whisper to each other like schoolgirls swapping secrets. Does Naomi have any recollection of just how gruesome it all was? Or was she unconscious for the worst of it? Was she spared what I had to witness? Does she not realize the magnitude of this? Do I?

"Your friend is right. It's too soon to be out in the world," Henry says. "Especially for her. She's reckless."

She is, but I don't like him saying it. "You don't know her."

"You do. Is she disciplined? Can she practice self-restraint?"

The answer is no, but I'm too mad to give him the satisfaction of being right, so I change the subject. "You killed someone last night."

"There's more to that story. I hope you'll give me the chance to tell you someday. Maybe then you'll think better of me."

"Don't you have any remorse for what happened? For what you did to us?"

He gets out a cigarette, lights it as he looks at me. "More than you'll ever know. Too much and still not enough."

He ashes his cigarette on the floor, then hunches over so his mouth is at my ear. "But also, not at all. Because I want you."

The tickle in my throat becomes a storm. This immense, raging, urgent thing that makes it impossible to breathe.

He leans back. Takes a long drag. "It's beyond attraction, isn't it? What's between us."

I can't answer him. I can't look him in the eye.

"Goodbye, Sloane." He turns around and walks down the hall, past Naomi and Elisa, who are both staring at me in a way that feels invasive and embarrassing. Henry goes left, and then he's gone from view.

Ilie bursts through the front door. "Okay, we are ready! Come see. It is clear."

"Coming," I say, so relieved to be getting out of this house—this awful, awful house. I hurry out the door, inhaling fresh air.

It's cloudy, but it's bright. Too bright. I wince at the daylight.

"We are sensitive," Ilie says, pointing to the sky. "We don't catch fire; that is just rumor. But it is not the best."

His car is where we left it, now covered in snow.

He opens the passenger-side door for me. I turn around to make sure Naomi's coming. She is, but she doesn't look happy about it. Or maybe she's just recoiling at the light.

"After you," I say, letting her sit first. I squeeze in next to her.

"Sloane," she whispers to me. "I'm still thirsty."

"Just . . . try not to think about it."

Ilie wipes the snow off the car, then hops into the driver's seat. He backs up too fast and the tires skid. "Whoa, whoa."

He pulls up to the gate, and as it opens, he strokes Naomi's hair. "It is too bad you are leaving. We like you. Drago likes you, Sloane. He never likes anybody."

"Who's Drago? Henry?"

"Oh, yes, yes. He changes his name. He is my great uncle, you know. Good guy. But very moody."

"Ilie," Naomi says, shielding her eyes from the light, "how often do we need to drink?"

On the short drive back to the cottage, Ilie attempts to explain to us the logistics of vampirism. I struggle to concentrate—exhausted and overwhelmed and distracted by the light incinerating my eyeballs, melting my brain.

He tells us we can eat and drink whatever, but it won't be the same as it was. He tells us nothing will satisfy us like the taste of blood. He tells us we can survive without it for weeks, even months at a time, but we will want it, and the want will consume us if we don't give in. He tells us we don't need permission to enter places, but it is polite to ask. He tells us we don't get fangs. We don't have any particular aversion to garlic, or crucifixes, and being impaled with a wooden stake wouldn't feel great but also wouldn't necessarily kill us. He tells us, with regret, that we do not turn into bats.

"I do not know who started that," he says. "Too bad. It would be cool. But we can float. Not too high, for not too long."

I think about the shadow at my window. I think about Henry.

I don't know if I'm flattered or horrified.

I'm not special enough to hold my own husband's interest, but an ancient vampire will watch me sleep.

Ilie turns onto the winding road that leads to the Waterfront. "It is your choice, I know. You do what you like, but if you change your mind, you have my number. We can help you. If you do not get blood from us, you will have to . . . you know."

"We're all set," I say.

"Okay, boss," he says, throwing a hand up. "If you say *all set*, all set. If you change your mind, you call me anytime. Who knows? Maybe our paths will cross again."

He winks.

We pull up to the cottage and I'm out of the car in two seconds, but Naomi idles.

"We'll go inside and make a plan," I tell her.

"Yeah, okay," she says. She takes a breath, then leans over and kisses Ilie on the cheek. "Bye."

"Goodbye, my loves," he says. "But maybe this is not goodbye."

He gives another wink before Naomi closes the car door; then he zooms off, spraying us with snow.

We stand in place for a minute, watching him drive away. His car disappears beyond the trees and the world is quiet, snowy and still, and everything seems perfectly ordinary. I'd swear it was all a bad dream if not for the tickle in my throat and the heaviness in my chest and the harshness of the light.

Naomi takes my hand.

"I'm sorry," she says.

I'm not ready to accept her apology, and I can't tell her that everything's going to be okay, because we'd both know that was a lie. I pull my hand away, too sullen to be touched.

"Let's go in before someone sees us," I say. We look a mess. Our clothes ripped and bloodstained, our hair tangled nests.

We look like victims, and maybe that's what we are. Or were.

I don't think I know what we are anymore.

18

The cottage is hot and stuffy, too bright with all the windows. Naomi staggers into the bathroom. "I really don't feel well. I feel so . . . so weird . . . like . . . Oh shit."

"What?" I ask, poking my head in.

She stands in front of the mirror. "Look."

It takes longer than it should for me to realize that we don't have reflections. That we don't appear in the mirror.

My lip starts to quiver, and my eyes go wet. One, because it's further proof of something I don't want to accept. And two, because I've been so frustrated and upset by my reflection lately, and I never thought I'd ache for it like this. I've never wanted to see myself more. To stress over a forehead wrinkle, over crow's-feet, over beautifully perfect drooping eyelids. It's the worst feeling in the world, knowing you've taken the sight of your own face for granted. Knowing you'd give anything for yesterday's problems.

Naomi sniffles. She's crying, too.

"This is really happening, huh?" she says. "This is . . . really happening."

I can't stand watching her cry, so I leave the bathroom before we both lose it. I go upstairs to the loft. I plug my phone in, turn it on, anticipating at least one missed call or message from Joel checking in, but there's none. There's nothing.

I find the present he gave me and rip off the bow, tear the pretty paper. Underneath is a plain cardboard gift box, taped shut. I get a nail under some puckered tape and pull.

The box is stuffed with glittery tissue paper. Did he pick this out for me? I'm not glittery. I never wear sequins, or shimmery eye shadow. Not even on New Year's Eve. At no point ever in my life have I been a sparkle person. We've been together for so many years. Shouldn't he know this about me?

I flip the box over onto the bed, shake it so the paper falls out. Somehow this is just as terrifying as anything that went down last night. I'd almost prefer getting my leg gnawed by the skeleton man to this. Discovering what the person I chose to waste the last fourteen years of my life with got me for my birthday.

It's AirPods. A pair of AirPods. No card.

"What?" I ask, picking them up. I rack my brain. Did I ever mention wanting AirPods, or any wireless earbuds?

If I'd opened this box two days ago, I would have thought they were a good, considerate, practical gift. Because I would have needed to think that. Because if I allowed myself to think it was impersonal, to be disappointed, that would have meant acknowledging my unhappiness, pulling out a block in the Jenga tower and risking the collapse of everything.

A few days ago, I would have opened this gift and said *Thank you.* I would have plugged these stupid things into my ears and listened to podcasts about horrific shit happening to other people, or music—art made by other people—and I would have gone on being grateful for the AirPods, until they inevitably broke or were lost within a year or two, and I had to get new ones. Maybe I would have asked for them for my birthday. And I don't know anymore if that's the saddest fucking thing, or if I wish that were still my future.

I repeat Naomi's ridiculous question in my head. *What if this wasn't bad luck?*

I run my tongue across my teeth, which are no sharper than usual, I don't think, and I call Joel.

He picks up on the fourth ring. "Hey! Happy birthday."

Right. It's my birthday. Some birthday. "Thanks."

"How's the place?"

I'm quiet, waiting for some magical clarity. Do I bring up the woman, admit what I know, what I saw on that camera? Admit what I did last night, my own indiscretion? Or do I sweep it all under the rug? Does any of it really matter now?

"Sloane?"

"Thanks for the AirPods."

"You're welcome. Everything okay?"

Needing to fidget, my fingers stroke my neck. They find a silky patch of raised skin just below my ear. Where Henry stuck the spile in.

I'm tempted to say nothing. To keep the peace. It's easier this way. So much easier to pretend. But here's Naomi again, in my head. *The choice was made for us.*

"Joel. We have a doorbell camera." I sound angry. Am angry. When did this happen? When did I wake this beast?

I get a flash of me beating the shit out of the skeleton man with a fire poker.

Where did she come from?

"What—what do you mean?" he asks.

"Denial? Really?"

"I'm not . . . I don't . . . I—I . . ." he stutters. "What are you . . ."

"I saw a woman show up to our house Thursday night. Our

house. *My* house. Hours after I left, after you sent me on this trip that you had the gall to pretend was a gift for me."

"Sloane—"

"No, I get it. I've let a lot slide over the years because I genuinely didn't want to know, didn't want to deal with it. I think I checked out somewhere along the line. I know I'm not blameless in this situation, in our marriage. Which I used to tell myself was happy, despite the bullshit, but . . . it's hollow. I'm hollow. And I'm . . . I think I'm done. Yeah. I'm done."

"Sloane, slow down. I've made mistakes. I'm sorry. I am. But I love you. I've always loved you. I like our life. Our marriage . . . we can work on it."

"Can we?"

"I can work on it," he says, with such resolve. No one in his family has ever gotten a divorce. He has no divorced friends. Then there's the issue of alimony. The house. That's what he cares about, mostly, I bet. He doesn't like hassle. To be fair, neither do I. "We should sit down and have a conversation when you get back and figure out a way forward. Together."

I would have. And I would have been grateful, to go home and keep on pretending. To keep up the charade, to move through life as docile and unflinching as a rag doll until I died. Never feeling too much of anything. Thinking the emptiness was what I deserved.

But that's no longer an option.

"I'm not coming back."

"Sloane."

I open the AirPods, pop one out of the packaging, twirl it between my fingers.

"Sloane? Please. I'm sorry. You know I am."

"Are you?" I ask. "If you're so sorry, why is this the third time? That I know of."

"I—I've made some bad decisions. I don't know why I . . . I don't want to lose you. I just . . . I have these . . . urges. These needs." It's very evident that he wasn't prepared to have this conversation. To explain himself. I can't blame only him for that. "I've tried to figure out how to communicate them to you. My needs. I just . . . I don't know."

What I think he's saying is, I didn't fuck him enough. I wasn't wild enough. Could be true. Could be that those of us who are ashamed of our needs inevitably become slaves to them.

He was too ashamed to ask me for more, and I, a reformed slut, was too ashamed to give it to him. Or maybe I just never loved him enough. He stirred such little want in me, and I thought it was my fault, that I was incapable. Until last night.

"Needs," I repeat.

"Yeah. And then—then I go and do things, and then I regret it and then I do it again. Maybe it's because of my dad. I just—it just happens."

"Well, we all make mistakes," I say.

"I'm human."

"Right," I say, failing to stifle a laugh, because he might be, but I don't know if I am anymore. "Exactly."

"We can work on it," he says. "Work it out. We can go to therapy or something. We can figure something out, right? Together. We can fix this. I can fix it. It won't happen again."

That's what he said the last time. This time, whether he means it or not, it's true.

I walk over to the window. I can still see it on the glass. The handprint.

"Joel?"

"Yeah?"

"I hope you have a nice life," I say, pressing my own hand to the windowpane. "Take care of the peach tree, okay?"

"The peach tree? Sloane, what—"

Just as I hang up, I hear a door slam.

"Naomi?" I call down the stairs.

No answer.

I repeat her name. I go check the bathroom. Check her room. She's not there. She's not anywhere.

She left. She's gone.

Her suitcase is still in her room. Her purse is here. Her phone.

Where did she go? Why would she leave?

Then I remember what she said to me in the car, not half an hour ago.

I'm still thirsty.

I grab my key and step outside.

I want to believe she's not lurking around the grounds of the Waterfront, trying to find someone who she can—I don't know. Drink from? I'm not sure what we do or how we do it. There's a vague tug in my throat, so I swallow my spit, wanting to wash it away, drown it out. Banish it.

The sensation isn't unbearable, not acutely painful. It's like the early hours of strep throat, when there's still hope that if you ignore it, it'll go away on its own.

My nerves pinch, stomach knots, because I don't see Naomi anywhere. I should be running after her, but I don't know which direction to go. I'm allowing too much time for things to happen. For our situation to get worse.

It's inevitable, though. Things are going to get worse.

"Naomi?" There's a rasp to my voice that's strange and new. The tug in my throat isn't relenting. I cough. My lungs are tight, tongue sits heavy in my mouth. It's getting harder to breathe, like there's a damp cloth over my face.

She's reckless, Henry said. Where is she?

It's still overcast. A doggedly gray, cloudy day. But it doesn't matter. I squint at the light like I'm coming out of the eye doctor with my pupils dilated.

I spin around, back toward the cottage. There are icicles dripping, long and sharp, winter's teeth. These are the kind that kill people. The kind that leave death in the snow.

I look down. I don't see any dead bodies in the snow, but I do see footprints. I follow them down the slippery drive to the road, then toward the main building. The sun emerges from behind a cloud, and my eyes white out, skin prickles like I've broken out in hives. I *hate* the light, this horrible, hideous, belligerent daylight. I cover my eyes and wait and hope for them to adjust, or to be spared by the clouds.

It's hard to see, my vision distorted as if I'm looking through a lava lamp. It's dizzying, and I lose my footing, slip and fall into the snow.

Then I see. The footprints veer into the woods.

There are two of them now. Two sets of footprints.

Is she disciplined? Can she practice self-restraint?

No. No.

No no no no no no no.

I get back up, spitting snow from my mouth that tastes like sour milk, and I run, following the footprints into the woods. The trees are naked, but there are so many of them that it doesn't make it any easier to navigate through them, and the steep incline of the hill doesn't help either.

I'm out of breath, but it's not because of physical exertion, or because I've been calling for Naomi. It's because of what's lingering in my throat. The strange sensation. The thirst. It's dry but it's gluey. It's steady but it's growing. I force myself to cough again.

I can fight through it. I can ignore it until it goes away.

No, you can't, says a voice in my head that sounds like me but also like Henry.

I remember blood in the snow.

There's blood in the snow, coloring the footprints.

No no no no no no no.

What did you think was going to happen next? says the voice. *Don't you understand? This is your life now.*

The ground flattens and I come to a small clearing, where I find Naomi, crouched in red snow. Her back is to me. She doesn't turn around when I call her. She's in the middle of something. I hear it. A slurping, a sucking. The ugliest sound.

I'm afraid to approach her. I didn't think I was in denial; I thought I'd accepted the circumstances, but how could I possibly? How could I digest the death of my humanness? The death of Naomi's. How could I grieve what I didn't fully understand?

The pang in my throat goes nuclear.

I want to fall to the ground and lap up the blood from the snow.

But I won't. I won't. I bury the want, and I take a step toward Naomi.

I pause. If I don't move, if I just keep myself in a sort of stasis, if I don't look, maybe I won't have to confront it. Maybe I'm past pretending, but I'm not ready to submit to what's next. It's too big and too scary.

A violent gurgling echoes through the trees. It's Naomi. Her shoulders jut up past her ears, and she starts to shake, to twitch.

I run to her.

Her long, dark hair curtains her face. Blood drips down, through her fingers. She's holding something. Something I'm relieved isn't a person, or from a person.

The relief is fleeting.

It's a rabbit.

She's got a dead rabbit in her mouth. She's not looking at me. She might not even be able to see me. Her eyes are glazed over, staring raptly at nothing.

She gurgles again, and then spits, spraying the ground with little grayish bits floating in viscous red globs.

Bones. Inedible parts.

All of a sudden, she lets the rabbit drop and she keels over, landing hard on her side. She starts groaning, and it reminds me of the skeleton man, of what he sounded like. She doesn't sound good. She sounds sick.

I fall in front of her. "Naomi?"

"I didn't mean to," she says, her eyes still glass. "I couldn't help it. I needed it. I thought I would die. I would die without it."

"It's okay. It's just a rabbit," I say.

"It was so disgusting," she says, retching. "It tasted awful. Rancid. But I couldn't stop. I couldn't stop myself."

Her eyes finally find mine, and there's something feral in them that turns my stomach. She shoots up, clutching my arm, sinking her nails in.

"I couldn't help it," she says. "I was thirsty. I'm still thirsty. Still so thirsty."

19

Naomi collapses back into the snow, wheezing. I shift to my knees, staring at the rabbit carcass, at the tiny pile of innards beside it.

"I'm sorry," she says. She wipes her mouth with her sleeve, then cries out, "I ruined my favorite jacket."

She's serious about the jacket. She's had it since high school. She loves that thing.

"You can get it dry-cleaned," I say.

"It's your birthday. I ruined your birthday."

"Honestly, I was dreading my birthday. I was freaking out about getting older," I say. "Now it doesn't seem so bad. I'd be so lucky to grow old."

She doesn't have anything to say to that. She gets on all fours and takes a shallow breath.

"You need help getting up?" I ask her.

Somewhere behind me, a twig snaps.

Her eyes dart over my shoulder, and she's on her feet.

"What?" I ask, turning around just in time to see someone slip behind a tree, too slow to hide, and too smelly to be discreet. Whoever it is, they reek of weed.

I remember the second set of footprints.

I turn back to Naomi. She's covered in blood. There's a dead animal between us, in plain sight. What a scene to happen upon. I don't blame the person for hiding.

Do we run? Hope they didn't get a good enough look at us? Is it illegal to eat live rabbits in the woods? Would we get in trouble? Kicked out of our cottage? Reported to the police or to the wildlife authorities? I don't know. I don't know.

Naomi's expression alerts me to the fact that I'm asking the wrong questions, worrying about the wrong things.

She's past me; she's at the tree; she's pulling the person out.

It's the porter. Michael. No, Matthew. He wears his dorky uniform under a North Face fleece. Naomi's got him pinned to the tree, with her hand clamped over his mouth. She bounces his head off the trunk, and it hits with a loud *crack*. He's out.

"Naomi! Stop!"

I know she won't. Naomi always gets what she wants. She doesn't ask for permission or consider the consequences. She reaches out and takes it.

I watch her eyes go wild again—chillingly savage. I watch her jaw open wide, too wide. I watch her push up the boy's sleeve and bite down on his wrist.

I clench my jaw tight, so tight that I might grind my teeth to dust.

I watch her drink. I watch the ferocity fade, replaced with satisfaction.

I watch his other arm hang limp. Available.

I know I won't. Because I don't let myself get what I want. Because I'd rather starve than feast. Because I'm scared. I'm too scared.

"Stop! You'll kill him!"

Naomi lets her head back, coming up for air, letting the porter crumple. He's a heap of limbs. There's a crescent moon of crimson holes on his wrist. Naomi's tooth marks. He's bleeding out of them. He's going to keep bleeding. Keep spilling.

"Damn," Naomi says, licking her lips. "It tastes so fucking good."

I can't keep looking at the blood. I can't keep smelling it.

It smells briny. Like the sweat on the back of a lover's neck. Like your shoulder when you come out of the ocean, which you lick when no one's looking. Like the lightning-charred air from a summer storm. Like the quiet moments when you feel most alive. An elusive aroma.

And he's at my feet now. I'm above him.

If he'd bothered to look at me when he met me, would he have thought I was capable of this? I was so preoccupied lamenting my invisibility as a woman getting older, I didn't realize it could be weaponized. I didn't realize it's part of our power, no one thinking we have any.

I'm in the snow, coiled up next to him. I'm thirsty.

Another decision. Another thing I can't come back from.

His bleeding wrist so close to my lips. My teeth. My tongue.

"Have some," Naomi says. "You don't need much. Just enough. Just enough . . ."

I take my first sip. It's even better than I remembered, than I imagined it would be. It's better than anything. My tongue starts to dance, now fluent in joy. I flood my throat with gold and my head with sweet emptiness. There are tiny stars where my worries once were. Pretty colors in place of bad memories. I'm brand-new.

And I might stay this way forever, silly with bliss, if I couldn't hear his heart beating. If I couldn't hear it getting weaker as I steal what's most precious.

Before I can change my mind, I pull away. I rip the sleeve of his uniform and wrap the scrap of fabric tightly around his wrist to stop the bleeding. I prop him up against the tree, his arm up above his head.

He looks a little pale, but it's not dire.

"Do you think we could leave him here?" I ask Naomi. I check the pockets of his fleece. "He has his phone. He might be concussed, but . . ."

Naomi stands in the middle of the clearing, continuously licking her lips, breathing heavily. She's a mess.

"Should we go get our stuff and leave and then call nine-one-one anonymously?" I ask. "Are there anonymous calls anymore? Should one of us stay with him in case he wakes up, to . . . I don't know. Shit. We're going to need the valet for my car. I think he's the valet."

"I'll watch him. I'll stay," she says, with a zealousness that stomps out the remaining glimmers of my blood-sipping serenity. "I'll stay with him."

"Look at me."

"I can stay with him. I can stay. . . ."

"Naomi." I snap my fingers at her like an asshole. "Look at me."

She struggles to make eye contact. She's not breathing right.

I walk over to her and put my hands on her shoulders. "Hey! You're not thinking straight."

Her tongue sneaks out to the corner of her mouth, where there's the tiniest speck of blood. "But he's seen us. He knows. We can't leave him alive."

"Do you hear yourself right now?"

"I . . ."

"You love people, right? This isn't you. You aren't a killer."

"I . . . Fuck," Naomi says, sounding like herself again. "Ah, *fuck*. He's still out?"

"Yeah," I say. "You . . ."

"What?"

"You hit him pretty hard."

She puts her head in her hands. "He was stoned."

143

"Yeah. So?"

"I think . . . I think we're high."

"I'm not high," I say. Only it's been so long since I've been high, I don't really remember what it's like.

"Your eyes look funny."

"Stop. Let me think."

I almost suggest that she go inside and get our stuff and call reception for a valet, if there even is one who isn't currently bleeding in the snow. Except I don't trust her to be on her own. But I can't leave her with Matthew. I also don't want to risk leaving him alone, because what if he comes to and tells someone what he saw, what happened? What will we do then?

What if we're arrested? What if Naomi's bloodlust takes over and she attacks the police?

What if they shoot us? Will we die? And if we don't die, will they turn us over to the government? Put us with the aliens?

And what if . . . what if I *am* high?

"We could get your car, and then, like . . . go," she says.

"What about him?"

"He didn't lose that much blood. He's already making more," she says. "Can't you feel it? I can feel it. Like a . . . sixth sense. You know, I could—*we* could—probably have a little more. One for the road."

"No," I say.

"One sip."

"No sips," I say, sidestepping the rabbit corpse to grab her by the arm and drag her through the snow. I snap a branch off a tree and pull it behind us, covering our tracks.

"Look at you, Nature Lady," Naomi says. I prefer her being stoned and goofy to her being bloodthirsty, but none of this is ideal.

And I can't shake the sense that we're being watched. That the trees have eyes, or that there are eyes peering out from behind them, or from above. We're being spied on. There are witnesses to our crimes.

I look up, searching the sky for drones.

Does the Waterfront have cameras? Will they have security footage of us going into the woods, coming out? Will they be able to zoom in, see how bloody we are?

Am I being paranoid because I'm high, or am I justified in all this worry?

"We need to change before we leave," I say. "No one can see us like this. We need to hurry."

When we get to the edge of the woods, I ditch the branch and start walking backward, swiping my feet from side to side to disturb our footprints in the stretch from the woods to the cottage.

"This would be easier without all this fucking snow," I mutter to myself. Naomi shuffles beside me, her mind elsewhere, on another planet.

"The taste," she says. "Remember making lemonade? Hot summer day, cold lemonade. Pink. The pink kind. The pink taste . . ."

We make it to the cottage, and I nervously fumble the key twice before finally managing to get the door open.

"Go," I tell Naomi. "Hurry."

I lock the door behind us, like we're being chased by monsters, which is stupid, because we are the monsters.

20

I put on clean clothes, throw the dirty ones in my suitcase, zip it up. I check to make sure I have everything. My wallet. My phone. The AirPods.

"You ready? I'll call for my car. What do you think? We get my car, get away from here, and then stop somewhere to figure out what's next? I still don't feel great about just leaving him in the woods. Naomi?"

She sits on her bed, just staring out the window, still in her bloody clothes.

"Get changed!"

"Don't yell at me," she says, pouting.

"Help me out here," I say.

She stands up and undresses, pausing to examine her jacket, a mournful look on her face.

I call the number on the Waterfront website, press one for reception, and someone too friendly answers. They assure me that the valet will have my car outside in ten minutes. I thank them multiple times, hoping they can't tell the difference between gratitude and guilt.

I drank someone's blood. I drank someone's blood. Manners won't make up for that. Nothing will.

Naomi now wears a tie-dyed sweat suit. I open my mouth to ask her if she has a matching neon sign, to tell her to change, to tell her we need to lie low, that she needs to use her head. But there's no time to argue.

"They'll be outside in five," I lie, knowing that if I tell her five minutes, she'll take ten, and if I tell her ten, she'll take fifteen.

"Okay," she says, sitting on her suitcase so she can zip it up.

"Do you need help?"

"I got it," she says. "I'm a pro."

"How are you feeling?" I ask her, leaning against the bedroom doorframe.

"Like I just ripped a bong."

"That's not what I meant. We're about to interact with a human. Can you handle that?"

"Can you?" she asks. I can't tell if she's being defensive or not. I wonder if she's embarrassed about the rabbit, about her lack of self-control. She's never been the type to feel guilty for indulging her whims. If she wanted chocolate cake, she'd eat chocolate cake. If she wanted to get railed by someone, she'd take them home. If she wanted the Gucci shoes, she'd swipe her card and not worry. But this is different.

"Yeah. I think so." If I ever wanted chocolate cake, I'd do calorie math and ruin it.

"Well, then, we'll just have to see what happens," she says, hopping up. "Why are we in such a rush to leave, again? It's not like we have a destination or any plan of action here."

"Because we left an employee bleeding in the woods," I whisper.

"Oh, right."

We move our suitcases next to the front door. Wait there.

147

"Let me do the talking. Why don't you stay at a safe distance?"

"Fine," she says. She looks nervous, and it's making me nervous. "What?"

"Can I drive? I need something to focus on."

"Are you good to drive?"

"Yeah," she says. "The high is wearing off. Which is kind of a bummer."

I don't believe her but I'm too tired to argue. "Okay, well, let me get the keys from the valet. Don't get too close."

"Okay, hoss." She chews her lip for a moment, contemplating something. She punctuates her thought by blowing a raspberry. "Let's just go back to the house. It's somewhere to stay. No one will know we're there. They have blood, Sloane. They said the first few days are the hardest. We can wait out the worst of our thirst there. See if that guy in the woods reports us or not."

I know what she's suggesting is likely smarter than just taking off without a plan, but I'm reluctant to go back to that place, return to the site of such horror. To seek shelter from monsters. Monsters I don't trust not to fuck up our lives more than they already have. And going back would be giving them too much power over us. It'd be dangerous to set ourselves up for that dynamic, to put ourselves in a position where we need these strangers. These vampires.

We can't go back. Even if part of me wants to see Henry again. Especially because of that.

The sound of an engine interrupts my thoughts. I go to the window, watch my car pull up in front of the cottage.

"No," I say.

She shakes her head. "I don't like it."

"Need I remind you, the last time we went to that house it didn't end too well for us?" I say, opening the door to meet the valet. Luckily, the sun has sunk behind the trees, twilight mild, making it more tolerable to be outside. "Wait here."

Todd steps out of my car. "Hello."

"Hi," I say, the word catching in my throat. There's that tickle, that itch, and I can hear his heart beating. I can hear the blood sailing through his veins. I can smell it. Pungent.

"Here are your keys," he says, coming toward me, passing me the fob. I bristle on contact, pull away as fast as possible. Take two big steps back.

"Thank—thank—" A cough interrupts me. "Thank you."

He narrows his eyes, maybe sensing something is amiss. But then he shrugs. "Okey dokey. Well! You drive safe. Slippery out there."

He starts down the drive toward the road, but then—

"Hi, Todd."

I stop breathing as he stops walking, turns back toward the cottage, where Naomi stands in the doorway. I can hear her wheezing. From the look on Todd's face, he can, too.

"Naomi," I say, failing to disguise the panic in my voice.

She takes a step forward, making eyes at him. Flirty eyes. Not her feral, thirst-crazed eyes.

He bows his head to her, which might just save his life, because his neck sinks into his collar and there's no exposed skin for her to lunge at, to sink her teeth into.

Though I guess if she wanted blood badly enough, she could go after his face.

"Hope you have a great day, Todd. Stay warm," she says. She looks at me, giving a smug grin, proving a point. In this moment, her desire to show me that she's capable of restraint is stronger than her bloodlust.

Whatever works. I give her a thumbs-up, and she beams.

149

"All right, then. Bye, girls," Todd says, walking away. I can only hope he goes straight back to the mansion and doesn't take any detours through the woods.

Once he's out of sight, I open the trunk of my car and we throw our bags in. I slam it shut and toss her my keys. "Go on."

She catches them and does a spin, then hurries toward the driver's side. I climb into the passenger seat of my own car, despondent. Naomi throws it into drive, accelerates. I'm surprised to find there's some relief in movement. A false sense of freedom. It feels like we're escaping something, though I know there's no putting this weekend in the rearview. The things that happened here can't be undone. I'm keenly aware. We left Matthew bleeding in the woods.

There's no putting space between us and the problem, because we are the problem.

But for now, it's just us in the car, like old times, and we can listen to some music, and we can fake normality for a little while, for as long as we can. Fantasize that this is enough to sustain us.

Naomi speeds. She's got a lead foot—she's told me on multiple occasions that she believes speed limits are "suggestions for people who can't drive."

"Slow down. We don't want to get pulled over," I tell her.

"I never get pulled over," she says. "Besides, I'm not going that fast."

I know for a fact that she does get pulled over, because she often brags about being a pro at talking herself out of tickets.

Her phone buzzes, and she picks it up to look at it. I cringe. Why did I let her drive?

"It's Lee," she says, sighing, dropping her phone back into the cup holder.

She turns up the music, signaling that she doesn't want to talk about him, or how, whether she likes it or not, their relationship is now over. I'm tempted to ask if we can put on my Chernobyl podcast, just to hear about other people having an exceptionally bad time, but I know she'll veto it.

And I doubt it would help, be of any comfort.

I stop myself from chewing on the inside of my cheek, my bad habit now off-limits, too hazardous. What if I bleed? Would I drink myself dry? I don't understand the ways my body is different now, and it's so frustrating, I could scream. Yet at the same time . . . my wrist, my joints—they're all so quiet. Everything destroyed by my fall or corroded by age doesn't hurt or bother. I'm hesitant to call it healing, reluctant to be grateful, because it cost me too much.

I can't see myself in the car's mirrors. I can't say this was a good trade. It certainly wasn't a fair one.

I know I'm not saving you, Henry said last night, *but I'm giving you all the time in the world to save yourself.*

Was that romantic? Or was it deeply messed up?

Actually, the same questions apply to our entire time together.

He said he was giving me a choice, but I didn't have a choice. Why does it always feel like this? Like every open door is a trapdoor.

Naomi's phone buzzes again, and she curses, lets her head back. She tries to shake it off, drums her fingers on the steering wheel. There's no ghosting Lee, and I know she doesn't want to ghost him.

He's going to be a problem.

I should be coming up with next steps, because I know she isn't. But I've always had an easier time running away from something than running toward anything, and it's so hard to think right now. My throat . . .

"Do your parents still have that"—my words chafe against the burgeoning need—"that summer house? It's in North Carolina, right?"

"Uh-huh," she says, craning her neck to look at road signs, as if we have a destination.

"Maybe we stay there until we acclimate to our thirst? Until we figure out if we're in trouble for . . . for what happened at the Waterfront."

She doesn't say anything. She should be on board; she basically pitched the same idea, just at the vampire house instead of her parents'.

Except her idea would solve our thirst, assuming the vampires would continue to share their supply. On our own we'll have to . . . to pay for our own meals.

How is this happening? How is any of this real?

I pinch my throat. Clear it. Cough. It's thirst; it feels close enough to ordinary thirst, just for something so specific. I think about how in cartoons or movies, when someone's wandering in the desert and they're delirious from their thirst, they hallucinate finding water. An oasis. They're splashing around in it, elated, and there's a palm tree overhead providing shade. I imagine us pulling over somewhere, stepping out to find a spring with blood bubbling up from the ground. And we could sip from it, and no one would be hurt, no one would suffer, and I wouldn't have to feel any guilt or doubt over my satisfaction.

I must manifest the idea, because now she's pulling over. Only I don't want it. The fantasy wasn't real. Is never real. Those cartoons and movies always cut away from the hallucination to show them writhing around in the sand.

"What are you doing?"

"I have to talk to Lee or he's going to freak out. And I'm so dizzy, I can barely see."

"I can drive," I say. "We shouldn't stop."

"I need a minute," she says, parking.

We're at a basic rest stop with some vending machines, picnic tables, bathrooms. There's a path down to a vista of the lake and surrounding woods, coated in fluffy white marshmallow snow that glows in the moonlight. There's a plaque that I'm sure details the historic significance of this spot, who lived here once upon a time. Who died here.

There's no oasis.

Naomi grabs her phone and gets out of the car. I know "a minute" is never just a minute, so I get out, too. I walk down the path and sit on a snow-covered bench, staring out at a beautiful view while trying not to hyperventilate. Time liquefies, leaks away.

The feeling in my throat is getting harder to ignore, morphing from discomfort to pain. It's taking over. I'm in danger of its monopolizing my body, my thoughts.

The onset of panic makes me feel like I'm trying to breathe inside of a plastic bag. I can't do anything about it except resist. Pretend the resistance isn't futile.

I push myself to stand, walk over to the ledge where the hill drops off. There's no fence. One misstep and it'd be a long, long fall. A hard landing.

I brace myself, bend my knees, lean forward, prepare for a scream I'm too shy for. I swallow it down and bury my head in my hands.

And I wonder . . . if I'm not screaming . . . then who is?

21

I run up the path and discover there's now another car in the parking lot of the rest stop. A truck. There's no one inside it. There's no one around. There's no more screaming. No more sound. I don't know exactly what situation I'm about to stumble upon, but I have a pretty good idea.

I try the women's room. There's a smear of blood on one of the sinks, spatter on the mirror above it. I walk up to the sink, run my finger through the blood, and put it in my mouth, just to taste it, as if it's frosting on a cake and I'm an impatient child. I hate myself for it.

There are a few drips leading out of the bathroom, like bread-crumbs into a wicked forest. I follow them around the side of the building, to the back, where I find Naomi on top of this mountain of a man, annihilating his neck.

She picks her head up only after I call her name for the third time.

"Sloane," she says, her voice tremulous and thin. "Where were you? Where *were* you? He came . . . he followed me into the bathroom. I didn't mean for this to happen. I didn't want it. He tried to . . . he gave me no choice."

The man lets out a gurgled cry.

I'm not totally convinced she's telling me the truth, but the truth is irrelevant at the moment; there's a man bleeding.

"Um . . ."

"Didn't you see? Didn't you see him pull up?"

"I . . . I didn't. I was over . . . What did you do, Nay?"

"Do you not believe me?" she says, vexed. "It was self-defense."

"Okay," I say, getting closer so I can see the wound. It's a red abyss. There are distinct teeth marks, ribbons of skin. He had a neck tattoo, but there's no telling what of. He's a puzzle with warped pieces. It's brutal, and I know in the dark of my heart, we're not leaving this one alive. "What did you do to him?"

"What I had to! You're not listening."

She's wrong. I am listening. Blood gushes from his wound onto the ground, going to waste, and I hear it whispering to me. Calling me to it.

"He's going to die, isn't he?" I ask, closing my eyes and holding my own neck, as if my weak little hands can contain the thirst.

Naomi spits skin out of her mouth. "I fucking hope so."

The man's lips flap. He convulses, blood spewing from his maw as he attempts to speak. I lean over, attempting to listen.

"Cu—" he says. "Cunt."

With that, I'm on him. I'm drinking. Chugging. Jubilant. He kicks his feet at first. He breathes until he doesn't. And the taste is heaven—better and better and better and better, the blood so deliciously warm until suddenly it goes cold because he's gone cold.

"They taste a little different when they're dead," I hear myself say. "But still good. There's plenty left, if you want it."

Naomi takes me up on the offer, takes my place at his neck, and I lean against the back wall of the restroom, gawk at the world's soft edges. I feel so light, so magnificently untethered. I wonder if I might float away.

"Woof," Naomi says, wiping her mouth on the man's shirt. "I think I have brain freeze."

I'm not sure how much time passes, but eventually I come back down to earth, and the edges are sharp, and I've killed someone.

I've got some of his skin stuck in my teeth.

I claw at my mouth, trying to get it out as fast as I can. I scrape my gums.

"Hey, hey," Naomi says, taking my hands. "Stop."

"I killed him. I killed him." I keep saying it, so I understand that it's true, that it happened. The repeated admission my immediate punishment for something I know I can never ever atone for.

"No, you didn't. I did," she says. "He followed me into the bathroom and waited for me outside the stall. He grabbed me by the hair and covered my mouth so I wouldn't scream."

She lets me go and reaches for the man, flips his hand over, showing me deep gashes. Bite marks.

"He saw a woman alone at a rest stop at night. He saw an opportunity," she says. "He's dead because he deserves to be dead. It's not your fault. It's not mine. It's his."

"Please don't lie to me," I say, sobbing into my knees. "Please."

"I'm not lying!" she says. "Why would you even say that?"

"Because . . ."

"Because why?"

"Because you're thirsty."

She scoffs. "What are you saying?"

"Nothing." I wipe my face. "Never mind."

"You think I was the aggressor?"

"I don't know."

"Wow." Her indignation doesn't exonerate her, but it does make me feel worse. If she is lying, I'd rather believe the lie than live with the truth, if the truth is that we're murderers.

"His last word was 'cunt,'" she says, shaking her head. "Since when do you not trust me?"

Since last night, I think but don't say. "It doesn't matter. He's dead."

"It does matter. It matters to me that you believe me."

"I believe you," I say, unconvincingly. "Now, what are we going to do?"

"Last time I had to dispose of a dead body, I had a vat of acid at the ready, so . . ."

I can't tell if she's sassing me, or if she can see how distraught I am and is trying to save me from a total spiral of despair by making me laugh. If it's the latter, it fails.

"This is a crime. We're criminals. We maybe could have gotten away with assaulting the porter, but this? How are we supposed to get away with murder?" I ask, standing. I don't want to look at the body, but I can't look away. We chewed so far into his neck.

"You're the one who's always listening to those podcasts and watching serial-killer documentaries. Pick up any hot tips?"

"Yeah. Don't kill people."

"Let's just leave him. By the time anyone finds him, we'll be long gone. And there's nothing to connect us to him." She steps back, looks around. "There are no cameras. It's a rest stop in the fucking Finger Lakes."

"There are cameras everywhere. There are trackers in our phones, our cars."

"We stay on back roads. We ditch our phones. The car. We get new identities. Change our hair," she says.

"You're romanticizing."

"So?" she asks, throwing her hands up. "You say that like it's a bad thing. Don't you know me? That's how I live, Sloane. How I survive."

"And it works for you. It doesn't work for me."

"What does work for you? Settling and playing it safe and telling yourself that living, actually living, isn't worth the risk? You let one mistake, one bad judgment call, scare or shame you into permanent inaction. You're so afraid of doing the wrong thing that—"

"This isn't actually living," I say. "We're vampires. Don't you get it? This is what we do now."

I point to the dead man.

"It *is* living, Sloane. Living is complicated and messy. To live is to fuck up and make mistakes—"

"This is more than a mistake!"

"Oh, whatever! Fine! Then go back to your air fryer and fucking Dyson stick vacuum and suburban delusion. Go back to Joel."

Surprisingly, I'm more upset that she'd bring up the Dyson than that she'd bring up Joel. I knew I never should have told her how much I love that vacuum.

"We don't have time for this." I lift the man's feet. "We should at least drag him into the woods."

"Sure," she says, scooping her arms under his. "Shit. He's heavy."

"How did you get him back here in the first place?"

"I don't remember," she says. "It was a blur."

We carry him to the woods beyond the picnic tables. There's a slope, and we drop him at the edge and let him roll. I wince as it happens, at the sounds of his lifeless body tumbling down the hill until he smacks against a tree.

"I'm sorry," Naomi says, snapping off a branch to cover our footprints. At this point, why bother? "I'm sorry I said that thing about Joel. And the vacuum. That was low."

"If you cleaned, you'd understand."

"It hurts me that you think I'd lie to you about this. About him," she says.

SO THIRSTY

"I'm sorry," I say, walking ahead of her so I don't leave any
more tracks.

"Did you really not see him? Didn't hear him pull up?"

I shake my head, too ashamed to admit that I was preoccupied
attempting to fight the pull of my thirst. And for what? Just to turn
around and let it overtake me.

We make it back to the rest stop. There's blood in the snow, so
we scoop it up, treat it like a snow cone. The blood tastes good but
the snow tastes sour. I'm realizing that everything that isn't blood
tastes sour.

We go into the women's room, clean the blood off the sink, the
mirror, and the floor with toilet paper, then flush the paper.

"Good enough?" she asks me. "If anyone finds his body, they'll
probably assume it was an animal."

"They'd be half-right," I mumble, washing my hands in the sink.
There's blood crusted on my cuticles, under my fingernails. "There's
no soap."

"It's almost eight now," she says. "We could drive all night. Even
if we take back roads, we could probably still make it to Pittsburgh."

"Pittsburgh?"

"I need to see Lee," she says, staring down at her phone screen.
"Then we can head to North Carolina. Or, I don't know. Mexico."

"It's a *terrible* idea to see Lee. One, because if anyone's looking
for us, they'll go to Lee. Two, because it would put him in danger.
Serious danger. Think about what just happened. What we just
did. Are you insane?"

"Sloane. Please," she says, looking me in the eye. In the soul, if
I still have one. "I need to see him."

"Naomi . . ."

"I know. But . . . please? If we're going to start over, I need to
say goodbye. Face-to-face. And he'll hound me if I don't. If I just
disappear, he'll make noise. You know he will."

159

"Okay," I say, doing what I do best. Giving up. "Okay."

She offers to drive again, and I acquiesce. She slips a lollipop into her mouth out of habit, and she promptly gags.

"Tastes like ass," she says, throwing it in the garbage can in front of the rest stop as we pass by.

"Good. Be sure to leave your DNA all over the crime scene."

"The cops aren't gonna look in the trash for incriminating candy," she says as we climb into the car.

"Go the speed limit," I say, and she rolls her eyes. "I'm serious."

"I know," she says as she speeds out of the parking lot.

If she has any remorse for what happened here, she's doing a stellar job of hiding it. But I don't think she does. I really don't think she does.

And that just might be my biggest problem.

"Music?" she asks.

"Yeah. Okay."

She puts on some old-school Arctic Monkeys, and I lean against the window and close my eyes. All I can think about is what it felt like to have that man's blood go cold in my mouth. The weight of him. The sound he made as he fell down the hill.

"You shouldn't sleep," she says. "We'll sleep tomorrow. During the day. When it's light out. Otherwise we'll just be bored, cooped up in some motel room."

"Right," I say, yawning. "Right."

But I don't take her advice. I allow myself to drift off, to disappear into a gentler consciousness.

22

When I wake up, it's in the parking lot of the seediest motel I've ever seen in my life.

"Good morning," Naomi says. "I forgot you have the cutest little whistle snore."

"Where are we?"

"Somewhere outside of Pittsburgh, Pennsylvania," she says. "At the Quality Star Motel."

The exterior is either brown or that dirty. The doors to the rooms are powder blue, scuffed, and dented. There's a death trap of a playground in a weedy patch of land on the other side of the parking lot, which crumbles beneath us.

"It's cheap enough that I can pay cash," she says, putting on a pair of sunglasses and a black beanie. She tucks her hair into the hat, then pulls down the driver's-side sun visor to check the mirror. "Goddamn it. I keep forgetting. How do I look? Inconspicuous?"

"Hard for me to say. I'd recognize you anywhere."

"Aw," she says, opening the car door. "I'm gonna go get us a room. Two nights? Just in case?"

"Yeah," I say, queasy at the idea of spending two nights in this place.

"Cool," she says, stepping out.

I stop her before she closes the door. "Wait. Are you okay to talk to someone?"

"Why wouldn't I be?"

I raise an eyebrow.

"I'm not super thirsty," she says. "We drank enough last night. I think."

"Naomi."

"I'm fine! I can do it," she says, then shuts the door before I can talk her out of it.

"Yeah, let's just roll the dice, see what happens. Maybe someone else will end up dead or injured or a vampire or a skeletal zombie," I mutter to myself, rubbing the sleep from my eyes. "Wouldn't that just be a trip?"

I watch her go into the office, and I consider running after her so I can babysit, but by the time I talk myself out of it, she's already coming back, dangling a room key over her head.

I get out of the car. "Nice."

"Room six," she says. "Right here."

She goes in, leaving me to unload our bags from the car, drag them into room six.

The room is as expected. Wood-paneled walls. Matted carpet. An ancient TV. Furniture that looks like it's held together with chewing gum. There are two double beds made up with paisley bedspreads, though I can't distinguish between the pattern and the stains. There are several lamps, with their shades all covered in dust. There's a ceiling fan that's hanging loose, the wires visible. The room is stuffy, and it smells like mustard.

Naomi comes out of the bathroom, walks over to one of the beds, and lifts the covers to check the mattress for bedbugs.

"See any?"

"Surprisingly, no," she says.

"Some bloodsuckers have higher standards."

She waves me off. "It's not that bad. I think it's charming."

I lock the door, secure the dead bolt, the chain. I pull the curtains across, releasing a dense cloud of filth and making the room go dark.

"How's the bathroom?" I ask.

"It's pretty clean."

I see for myself. She's not wrong. It is pretty clean. At least, cleaner than the rest of the place. There are two small spiders in the corner near the toilet. I let them be.

I stare at the toilet. I haven't used one since before . . .

I sit down and wait for something to happen. Nothing does. I flush the toilet anyway. I wash my hands, splash some water on my face. Avoid the mirror not because of my reflection, but because of the absence of it.

Naomi lounges on one of the beds, shoeless. There's blood on her tie-dyed sweat suit. I hadn't noticed until now. Maybe it was a smart outfit choice after all.

"So . . . what did you say to Lee when you called him?" I ask, taking the other bed, the one closer to the window.

"Nothing about our exploits, if that's what you're getting at," she says. "Obviously."

"Obviously."

"He flies in today."

"Okay."

"I'll see him tonight. I know where he's staying."

"Do you know what you're going to say to him?"

She slips under the covers, then turns on her side to face me. "Thanks for the memories. I'm about to fall off the face of the earth."

"I'm serious."

"I don't know yet. I'm sad and I'm—I'm not entirely, like, processing any of this as reality. I know what needs to happen tonight, and I'm not ready. I love him. But at the same time . . ."

"At the same time what?"

"I've been with him since I was twenty-four years old. How do you even know if you still love someone for who they are, or if you love them out of habit?"

I don't have an answer for her.

"We've always been touch and go; you know that. Sometimes I'll look at him and think he's my soul mate, and other times I wonder if he's the worst thing to ever happen to me. If I'd be better off if I never met him. He takes so much energy, so much air. Things get bad and we fight, and I get resentful. Then, when things are good, it's almost like we're regressing or something. Like we keep each other from changing because we fell in love with the versions of who we used to be, who we were when we were younger, in our twenties. It's this weird codependent arrested development. I know it isn't healthy. I've tried to change the dynamic, but . . . Eh, whatever. Doesn't matter anymore, right?"

"Why haven't you talked to me about any of this?"

"I wanted to figure it out on my own before I dragged you into it," she says, breaking eye contact and fluffing her pillow. Lying.

"The real reason."

"I've tried. But . . ."

"But . . . ?"

"I worried you'd encourage me to stay."

"Why would you think that?" I ask, realizing it's a stupid question as soon as it crosses my lips.

"Have you spoken to him?" she asks, pausing to yawn. "To Joel?"

"Um, yeah. I did. It's done."

"What do you mean? What did he say? What did *you* say?"

"I told him I wasn't coming home."

"Did you give a reason?"

"He gave me one." I exhale, shake my head. "We have a door-bell camera. He had someone over Thursday night."

"He did *what*? That motherfucker. That piece of—"

I cut her off. "It's fine. It's over now. He's not expecting me. Good timing, I guess."

"How do you feel about it?"

"Numb," I say, debating whether it's grosser to lie on top of the bedspread or underneath it. I kick my shoes off and get under. "I feel completely numb. About him. About everything. Like you said, how are we supposed to process any of this?"

She doesn't respond. When I look over at her, I see that her eyes are closed. She's out.

Naomi has a long battery life, but when she goes down, she goes down hard and fast. She'll wake up in eight hours fully charged.

She was right. I should have powered through my exhaustion last night, because now I'm bored cooped up in a motel room, with only my thoughts to keep me company, and my thoughts suck.

I get my phone out. It's dead, and I let it stay dead. Better that I don't check my messages—generic *Happy birthdays* from friends and coworkers, from my family—whom I'm not particularly close to. I wonder how long it will take them to notice I'm gone. When I don't log in to work on Monday, will anyone clock my absence? Will it make any difference at all?

It's too soon to miss anyone, to miss any of it. I wonder if any-one will miss me. The vanilla version I'd been living as for so long, anyway—mild mannered, true neutral. I filed down all my rough edges to fit in wherever, appease whoever, and maybe I made my-self entirely forgettable in the process.

I look around this seedy motel room, and I wonder if the life I have to leave behind is that much better than the one I'm stuck with now.

Then I remember that I'm a killer.

I doze off eventually. When I wake up, I'm thirsty.

My skin is dry and flaky, my lips splitting.

"You're fine," I whisper to myself. "You're fine."

Naomi's in the shower. I can hear the water running, and she's singing to herself. *"'Another night, another dream, but always you . . .'"*

I bury my face in my pillow. I get a musty whiff and remember that the case maybe hasn't been washed ever.

It's motivation for me to get out of bed. I check the alarm clock on the nightstand, but it's broken. I shuffle over to the window and cautiously peel back the curtain. It's dark out. It was dark when we checked in, but that was early-morning dark. This must be night dark.

For once I'm grateful it's winter.

I look around the parking lot. There's a blue hatchback, but it was there this morning, so no new cars. No new people. Nothing amiss. Except . . .

There's a handprint on the window. Outside, on the other side of the glass. An outline in the grime.

Maybe it was there before? And even if it wasn't, we're at ground level, not like at the cottage. Anyone could have left it. That's the rational explanation. The one that makes the most sense. Not that Henry followed us here all the way from New York to leave me a cryptic message in the form of a handprint.

"Hey," Naomi says cheerily, catching me off guard.

I clap a hand over my heart. From my limited knowledge of vampire lore, I thought vampires didn't have heartbeats, but I have one. There's just enough of me that still feels human, feels normal, until the thirst asserts itself.

I clear my throat. "You startled me."

"Sorry," she says. She wears a fluffy white hotel robe.

"Where's that from?"

"The Waterfront," she says.

"You stole it?"

"They'll charge the room," she says. "Joel will pay for it. Don't worry—I took one for you, too."

"Thanks?"

"You're welcome," she says. "How am I supposed to do my makeup if I can't look in the mirror?"

"I can do it," I say. I pull the curtain closed and turn my back to the window, to the handprint.

"What's wrong?" Naomi asks. "You're not upset about the robes, are you?"

"You don't think they'd come after us, do you?"

"Who?"

"The vampires."

She lugs her suitcase onto the bed and opens it. "Why would they do that?"

"I don't know. They're vampires?"

"So are we."

It's strange how matter-of-fact this is. But we're already past blood sucking and murder, so why wring our hands over it now?

"Did something happen?" she asks.

"No," I say. "Just . . . paranoid, I guess."

She gets out her makeup bag and waves me over to her.

"What was the deal with you and that guy?" she says, passing me a liquid liner.

"What guy?"

"The hot, weird one."

"They're all hot and weird," I say, taking the cap off the liner. "Hold still."

"Did you hook up?"

"No," I say. "Look straight. We just kissed."

She gasps. "Really?"

"I said, hold still."

"Tell me, tell me," she says, not holding still.

"It doesn't matter. Everything that happened after is what matters." Not wanting to talk or think about Henry, I change the subject. "Does Lee know you're coming? Are you meeting him somewhere?"

"He rented a house," she says. "For him and the band. We'll go by. I'll talk to him. Try to leave things in a place where he won't ask too many questions. Won't report me fucking missing or anything like that. Hey, you think he'll notice if I repurpose Bogart's goodbye dialogue from *Casablanca*? If I go full *Here's lookin' at you, kid?*"

"Probably not. As long as you don't do the voice."

"Eh. Too bad. My Bogart impression is top-tier. Uncanny."

As I finish her winged liner, check to make sure it's even, I notice her skin is dry like mine.

"Naomi?"

"Yeah?"

"Are you thirsty?"

She waits a long time to respond.

23

The house is in a quiet neighborhood just outside of downtown, about a half-hour drive from the motel. On the way over, I continuously checked the rearview for Ilie's obnoxious sports car. For cops. There was a shady-looking van that trailed us for a few miles, but it went straight when we turned into the neighborhood.

We park on the street. We sit in the car, staring at the house, saying nothing. We still haven't solved the problem of our thirst. If we get out of the car, there's no telling what will happen. When Naomi tries to break up with Lee, she might end up killing him instead.

I know she needs this goodbye, that she's after closure. I also don't doubt that Lee would react poorly if Naomi up and vanished into the night. If she tried to do this over the phone, he'd be suspect. He'd come looking for her. For us. He'd start digging around.

There's no right move here.

She takes a deep breath. "I can do this."

"Naomi, it's too risky to go out there." I'm struggling with my thirst, to think of anything other than the taste of blood, the euphoria of having it in my mouth, in my throat. And if the thirst is bad for me, it must be bad for her, too.

"I can do this," she repeats. "Right? I can say goodbye?"

I wish I could reassure her. The truth is, staying with Lee isn't an option anymore. Even if she got her thirst under control, I'm not sure how that would work. I don't think we age anymore, something he'd be sure to notice eventually. We've been so preoccupied with the immediate logistics, we haven't had time to confront the long term—the long term being immortality, I guess. But I don't want to bring any of that up right now. I'm a little jarred by Naomi's fragility.

"I've thought about this before. About leaving him. When I know what I want, I go after it. Easy as pie. It's when I don't know— that's what fucks me up."

"Don't you always know?"

"I used to. I feel like the older I get, the less sure I am about anything. It's annoying. Is it like that for you?"

"I've never been sure about anything. Just careful about everything."

"Mm," she says. I wonder if she's procrastinating.

"I could play 'Kitchen Floor' if you think it'd help."

She laughs. "Don't."

She takes her phone out of her pocket. She calls him. It rings twice; then he answers.

"Hey, babe. You here?"

"Yeah," she says, unbuckling her seat belt. "Come outside."

The front door of the house opens, and Lee steps out. He's in gray sweatpants, combat boots, and a Sherpa jacket. He lights a cigarette.

He didn't quit when Naomi quit. Not a fan of lollipops.

I'd asked her at the time, "Does it bother you that he still smokes?"

"Does it bother me that he's a fucking asshole?" she'd said. "Nah, not really."

Whenever I spent time with Lee he always went out of his way to be nice to me, but I never got a real sense of who he was. He grew up in Pittsburgh. Started playing guitar in the seventh grade. Went to SUNY Purchase. Moved to Brooklyn after graduating and started his band. Met Naomi at a show, asked her out. They split a pitcher of cheap beer and were living together a week later. He doesn't care about sports, pretends to care about politics. He can be funny and loud and can hold his liquor. He loves Naomi. That I never doubted. It's obvious.

I trusted Naomi to pick her own partner, as she did with me. Maybe we both picked wrong. Or maybe there is no picking right, just getting lucky.

Naomi unlocks the car.

"What if you just roll the window down?" I say. "Crack it. We stay in here. Use the glass as a buffer."

"Sloane. I'm not gonna hurt him," she says, opening her door and stepping out onto the street. She meets him halfway down the driveway.

"What's going on?" Lee asks. It's hard for me to hear them at this distance, their voices muffled. "Is that Sloane? Why are you with Sloane?"

He goes to embrace her, hug her, but she jumps back.

"Can you just . . . stay over there?" Naomi says, holding a hand up. "Don't come any closer."

"Uh, okay? Is this some kind of game?"

"No, Lee. I need to talk to you. I need you to listen to me."

"It's fucking freezing out," Lee says. "Can we go inside? What's going on? Why are you acting like this? Did somebody die?"

I shift in my seat.

"No," she says. A lie. "I . . ."

RACHEL HARRISON

She looks down at her feet, struggling for words. Or with her thirst.

"What?" he says. "You're freaking me out."

"I've done a lot of thinking. For the both of us."

Oh Christ, is she really going to go full *Casablanca*?

"If we stay together, keep going like this, we'll regret it. We've had a good run, Lee. But I've been feeling for a while now that—"

"Wait. What are you saying? Are you quitting?"

Her head snaps up. "Quitting?"

"This isn't a good time, Naomi. We start recording this week. I need you. The band needs you."

I can feel her anger from here. See it radiating off her, a red glow. "Fucking really? I wasn't quitting. I was breaking up with you!"

"What?" he says, putting out his cigarette.

"I'm leaving. I'm going away for a while and you're not going to hear from me, and I don't want to hear from you."

"Hold on. Slow down. This is crazy. What are you talking about?"

"And yeah, technically I am quitting. Goodbye, Lee. We'll always have Paris."

"You're not making any sense right now. What are you saying?" He takes a step toward her, and I cringe. He's too close.

She backs away. "I'm saying what I should have said a long time ago. What you should have said. I love you, but . . ."

Her voice breaks, and it hits me like a crowbar, the immensity of years spent together, all the memories created coexisting with someone for so long, the mutual witnessing of the world they share.

I think of all the stupid little things. One time Joel and I saw a kid in the Wegmans parking lot attempt to shove a Popsicle up his nose, and he said it smelled "cold good," and now every once in a while we'll describe scents to each other as "cold good" and laugh. Maybe we'll be better off without each other, and maybe so will

172

Naomi and Lee, but what about all of the cold good? The shared experiences we now have to crack in half and live alone with?

"You can have the apartment. The stuff. I don't care," she says, walking backward toward the street. "You won't be able to reach me. That's by design. That's how I need it to be."

"Babe, are you serious? Are you high right now?"

"No, I'm not high, and yes, I'm serious. And I need you to take me seriously for fucking once. Please." That she has to ask for this makes me furious. Why do women always need to ask, to beg, not to be dismissed? "I mean, this can't be a total surprise."

He follows her into the street. "You show up here and tell me you're leaving and I can have the apartment? I know we fight, and shit gets intense with the band, but this is crazy. It's crazy."

"You say that so I can't argue. No point I make will be valid from here on out. Everything I say will just be crazy. You know what? I should be thanking you. Any doubt I had that this was the right thing is now gone."

"Where is this coming from?" he asks. "Is this about what happened in Budapest? Because—"

"No! It's not about Budapest. It's about you and me. I'm grateful for the time we had, but it's over now. It's done," she says, turning around and reaching for the car door. She looks at me through the window, and she's crying, but she's also got that wildness in her eyes. The bloodlust.

She gets the door open, but Lee darts forward, shoving his arm in front of her to stop her, to slam the door. His jacket sleeves are too short, exposing a sliver of wrist.

She bites him.

He screams. He tries to rip his arm away, but her teeth have sunk in too deep.

"Naomi! Stop!" I don't know if she can hear me—if I'm louder than her thirst.

I don't know what makes her let him go.

"What the *fuck*?" Lee yells, and I see lights flick on around the neighborhood. "What is wrong with you?"

"I'm . . . I'm sorry," Naomi says.

I reach over and open the door for her, and she climbs into the car. She hits the locks and looks at me. There's blood around her mouth. She grabs me by the back of the neck and pulls me in like she's kissing me, only she's not. She's sharing.

Lee bangs on the driver's-side window.

"Naomi! Naomi, what is going on? Are you leaving me for *Sloane*?" he says. "You bit me. You fucking bit me! Jesus. I'm still bleeding."

At that, Naomi pulls away from me and starts the car.

"I really am sorry," she tells him.

"Naomi. Naomi, wait! Babe!"

He's still banging on the window as we drive away. He chases the car, running after us until we turn onto the main road.

Naomi's crying so hard that I suggest she pull over.

"Let me drive," I say.

"I can drive," she says, cracking the windows. "I'm driving. I can drive."

"I know. But why don't you let me get us back to the motel?"

Her phone rings. It's Lee.

"Can you silence it?" she asks, putting the driver's-side window all the way down, allowing the bitter night to spill in.

I do what she asks. He texts two seconds later.

"He's messaging you."

"What's he saying?"

"Um . . ." He sends message after message. Telling her she's fucking crazy. She's a psycho. That he might have to go to the hospital. That if she doesn't come back right now, she shouldn't bother coming back at all. Then his tone shifts. He says Please come back. please. just come back.

"Fuck it." She takes her right hand off the steering wheel and shoves her palm at me. I give her the phone, and she casually tosses it out the window.

My mouth falls open.

She puts her window up and puts mine down.

"Your turn," she says, digging into her pocket and pulling out my engagement and wedding rings. "Give me your hand."

"Are you serious?"

"As a heart attack."

"I . . . um . . ."

She sighs, drops the rings into the center console, among my collection of loose change—oxidized pennies, worn nickels and dimes.

"I mean, you can hang on to them if you want," she says. "I just figured maybe you'd want to throw them out the window in a symbolic gesture of newfound freedom. Leaving the past behind. Letting go."

"Right."

"You could also flush them down the toilet. Pawn them." She's not crying anymore. She bounces back pretty quickly.

"I have options, is what you're saying."

"Exactly."

I pick up the rings. Examine them, rub them between my fingers. I've never really cared about jewelry; I have no sentimental attachment to the rings themselves. But if I toss them, what do I have left of Joel? Of that life?

The AirPods?

"I'm not ready yet," I say, slipping them into my pocket and fumbling for the button to put my window up.

She frowns. "I wasn't ready either. But I was never gonna be ready."

"Are you okay?"

She laughs. "Fuck no. Are you?"

I press the button down. The window whirs. I dig one of the rings out of my pocket and toss it out the window. A symbolic gesture, not of freedom or release, but of solidarity.

"Nope," I say.

I look out at the side-view mirror as if I might be able to see where my ring landed, its resting place until someone else happens upon it, or it sinks so deep into the earth that it's lost forever.

I don't see the ring, but I do see the shady van. It's behind us.

"There's that van again."

"What van?"

"It was behind us earlier. I think it's following us."

Her eyes flick up to the rearview. "I don't think it's the same van."

"It's definitely the same van." It's black, and there's a distinctive dent in the side.

We pull up to an intersection. Red light. The van breaks about a car length away from us, so we can't see who's driving.

"Might be a guy," Naomi says, squinting. "What do you think? Slam on the gas?"

"Easy, Steve McQueen. Just take a right."

"Who would be trailing us? That's not Ilie's car. Do cops drive unmarked vans? Also, I didn't see anything in the news."

"You checked the news?"

"Yeah, I checked," she says. "Nothing at the Waterfront, which tracks. I was thinking about it, and do you really think they'd let it get out that one of their employees was attacked while getting high in the woods? His story would be too ridiculous. And they have to protect their reputation. Imagine the pearl clutching."

"The light's green."

She puts her signal on and makes a quick turn.

"What about . . ." I can't finish the sentence.

"Nothing about a missing man in the Finger Lakes."

"I wish that made me feel better," I say as I look out the back window for the van. It goes straight.

"See? Not being followed," she says.

"I wish that made me feel better," I repeat.

"We should stop at an ATM. Get cash out."

"If we're not suspected of being criminals, should we maybe stop acting like criminals?" I ask. "Won't it look suspicious if we withdraw a bunch of cash?"

"Not a bunch," she says, pulling up to a Chase. "Enough for gas. I mean, what else do we need?"

Nothing money can buy.

24

The van reappears on our way back to the motel.

"Maybe it's just driving around?" Naomi says, pulling into the parking lot. The van goes past, and we hold our breath until it's out of sight.

"Wait," I say. "You have a little . . ."

She still has some of Levi's blood at the edge of her mouth. She licks it up. "Probably shouldn't have bitten him."

"At least you didn't kill him."

"Are you being a dick?"

"No. I'm just saying."

"Right. I mean, maybe it's good that I bit him," she says. "He definitely won't come after me now. He'll be fine. He'll rebound with some groupies. He'll be just fine."

"I'm sorry, Nay."

She sighs. "I know. Me, too."

She opens the door and steps out into the lot. I follow her.

"Van's back," she says, peering over her shoulder as she unlocks our room. "Don't look."

She ushers me inside, closes the door, and locks the dead bolt, secures the chain.

I pull the curtain back just enough for a single eyeball. "It's turning in here."

"Really? Shit."

The van parks on the far side of the lot, near the rusty playground.

"Maybe we'll get abducted on this trip after all," she says.

"It's them," I say, the handprint on the window reaching into the corner of my eye.

"Who?"

"The vampires," I say.

"Why are you so convinced?"

"Because . . ." I say, waving her in to show her the handprint.

"So?"

"It's a long story."

"Someone's getting out," she says, and I yank the curtain closed. "Hold on. Let's see who it is. They already know we're in here."

She peeks behind the curtain. "Hmm. I can't really tell."

I poke my head over. It's a man. His back is to us. He stands under a sputtering streetlamp. One second, he's drenched in bright orangey light; another, he's in the dark.

"Is he alone?" Naomi asks.

My heart thrums.

"What's he doing just standing there? Should we go out?"

"No," I say, pushing her back and closing the curtain. "Absolutely not."

"Should I call Ilie?"

"Do you have his number, or was it in the phone that you threw out the car window?"

She opens the curtain. "There's a chance I didn't think that through."

The man has moved closer to the motel, but he's keeping his back to us. He wears a sweatshirt, hood up.

"Why is he walking backward?" Naomi asks.

I close the curtain. "They like games. What if they're playing some weird cat-and-mouse game? What if they let us go so they could chase after us?"

Truth or dare.

"They had that guy locked in the basement. What if they torture people? What if that's their thing?"

"Let's not get ahead of ourselves," she says, opening the curtain. She screams.

He's at the window. He's right outside.

He turns around.

It's Ilie.

"Hello, loves."

I close the curtain, check the dead bolt.

"What do you want?" I ask him through the door.

"We thought you might be thirsty," he says.

Naomi and I look at each other. We are thirsty. *So* thirsty. But this doesn't sit right with me.

"Why did you follow us?" With the aching in my throat it's difficult to shout through the door.

"You don't want to stay, but it is not good for you to be on your own," he says. "You get those guys."

"What?"

"Those guys. You get three guys. Second one very bad."

"You've been watching us," I say, clutching Naomi's arm. Her expression is unreadable.

"Not the whole time," he says.

Naomi laughs, and I smack her leg.

What? she mouths. *That's kind of funny.*

They watched us murder, I mouth back.

She cocks her head.

"They saw us murder that guy," I whisper.

"May I come in?" he asks. "I have a drink for you. To share. We got from hospital, not from human. Well, originally it came from human. They gave it on purpose. Not for this, but . . ."

"Leave it at the door," I say, pinching my throat.

"You don't want to hang out?" he asks.

"No."

"That's mean," Naomi says.

I can't with either of them.

"Leave it at the door. Then turn around, get back in the van, and drive away. Go home."

"I will leave it," he says. "But you are our responsibility. We look after you, like we look after each other. You want to do your own thing, that is okay. But we watch."

He knocks on the door twice.

Naomi peeks behind the curtain. "He's going back to the van. He left a cup."

I undo the chain, unlock the door, open it just enough for me to stick my arm out and grab the cup—an ordinary travel tumbler with an extraordinary substance sloshing inside. I pull it into the room, barely get the door closed before I start drinking, sucking through the hard plastic straw.

It's like my body rises to meet it. It's so good. I soak it up. Succumb to the indulgence.

Naomi's hands clamp over mine as she pulls the tumbler away from my mouth and toward hers. I don't want to let it go. I don't want to share.

"Sloane!" Naomi says, trying to pry it out of my hands. "Sloane! Save some for me! Please."

Do I let it go? Or does she successfully wrestle it from me?

She unscrews the lid and tips the cup back. There isn't much left. A sip at most.

Naomi sticks her tongue out, licks the inner rim of the cup.

I'm buzzing with the taste. Otherwise I might feel guilty for being greedy. Though why should I? We're this way because of her. Because of her poor judgment, not mine. Why should I be punished? I've been so thirsty for so long. Why should I go on depriving myself?

"What was that?" she asks me.

Her voice sobers me up. And there's the guilt, waiting for me in my right mind. "I'm sorry. I got carried away."

"All right . . ." she says, giving me some legendary side-eye.

"I'm sorry," I repeat. "I'm sorry."

"It's fine," she says, setting the tumbler on the nightstand. "But for the record, can you acknowledge that your thirst is just as intense as mine?"

"What?" I say, pulling back the curtain to see if the van is still there. It is.

"You make it seem like I'm the only one who's out of control. It's bad for you, too."

She is out of control. She's never been in control. She lets her emotions drive, acts on impulse, on whims. That's why her thirst is more dangerous than mine. I'm right about this. I know I am. But it's not worth the argument.

"Yeah," I say, and run my tongue over my teeth, searching for lingering flavor. "What are we going to do about that?"

I tap on the window.

"Why would we do anything about it? He brought us blood. They're looking out for us."

"You don't find it creepy that they're following us? That they know about what happened at the Waterfront? At the rest stop."

I have a vision of the man we left in the woods, his body blue and ruined. Frost in his hair, in his eyelashes. If it snows again, will it cover him? Will it preserve him in the frightful state he's in?

When spring comes, will he thaw like meat? Will it be the smell that leads to his discovery? Will the cops find him before the animals do? Before something else in the woods helps itself to our leftovers?

The remorse should be consuming me, but it isn't. His murder is the worst thing I've ever done, by far, and it just melts into the rest of my shame, my regret. Sinks into the tar pit that I slog through every day, that's constantly rising, that will overtake me eventually. I can barely function with the calamities of this lifetime, the last thirty-six years. How am I supposed to go on existing forever?

Aging isn't just about our bodies decaying while we're still inside them. It's about living with the accumulation of experiences. The heavy burden of the ugly ones, the longing for the beautiful.

"They could have stopped us from doing it, but they didn't," I say. "From killing that man."

"Maybe because they saw he deserved it," she says.

"Or maybe because they're killers and they get off on this stuff," I say. "What now, Nay? It's nine o'clock. Do we pack up and go? Try to lose them? How did they find us in the first place? Did you notice the van at all last night?"

"No," she says, picking up the tumbler and staring inside it, as if it will have magically refilled. "Do you think they have more?"

"Don't you see what they're doing? They're making it so we rely on them."

"Or they're being nice."

"I was awake while they changed us. You weren't."

"Can we not fight? This night is shitty enough already."

I sit down on my unmade bed. "I think we should leave. Drive until morning. We're sitting ducks here."

"Whatever you want," she says, tossing me the car keys. "You can drive. I don't feel up to it, probably because I'm thirsty, and because, if you recall, I just cut ties with the person I spent the last twelve years of my life with, which was pretty fucking hard and ended pretty fucking poorly."

"I told you seeing Lee was a terrible idea," I say, because I'm not done fighting. Because I have the energy, because I'm full of blood and resentment.

"You did. But you know what? If you'd asked me to take you to see Joel, I wouldn't have said anything. Not a word. I would have taken you. And when you were done with your goodbyes, I would have kicked him in the balls so hard that he'd see God."

Now I remember why I don't pick fights with Naomi. She has a way of winning.

She takes her sweet time packing up, getting her suitcase ready. I compulsively check behind the curtain. The van hasn't moved. I wonder why Henry wasn't the one to come to the door. I know he's here, and that he wants me to know he's here. He left me the handprint. He's not finished with his playground games.

When she's done packing, she pulls up her suitcase handle and opens the door, heads out to the car.

"I need you to unlock it," she calls from the parking lot.

I take one last look around the motel room, and suddenly I wish we weren't leaving. It's grimy and ugly and the perfect place for us, for the versions of us we are right now. I know that wherever we find ourselves next, we'll be different once we get there. I'm afraid of meeting our future selves. Afraid of what they'll be capable of.

Naomi left the tumbler on the nightstand, so I go pick it up, then get my suitcase and walk out of the room, letting the door shut itself behind me.

I unlock the car.

"I'm dropping off the room key," Naomi says, leaving her suitcase for me to put in the trunk. It weighs fifty tons.

She comes back and hops into the passenger seat. "The roads are icy."

"Got it." I start the car to a fun surprise. "Nay. It's on Empty."

"Yeah. We need gas. So?"

"Nothing," I say, backing up, watching the van in the rearview. I fully expect it to follow us out of the parking lot, but it doesn't. It stays parked there.

And I'm reluctant to admit that part of me is disappointed. That maybe part of me, some part I've either long forgotten or just discovered, likes being chased.

25

Naomi doesn't know the exact address of her parents' vacation house.

"It's in Wilmington. North Carolina."

"Yeah. That's not specific enough."

"I've only ever been there twice," she says. "But I'll know how to get to it once we're in the area."

"Will you?"

"I'll have to. Can't exactly call them up and ask, can I? *Hey, Mom and Dad, it's your not-doctor-or-lawyer daughter that you're so disappointed in. Can you drop a pin for the place you call a real estate investment, which I called an egregious display of wealth, which led to a shouting match that resulted in me and Lee getting a hotel?*"

"You've made your point," I say, plugging Wilmington into the GPS. It's nine and a half hours away. Even if we drive all night, we won't make it before sunrise. Meaning we'll have to find somewhere else to stay. Another fleabag motel.

"My parents only go down in the summer, so we can stay there until then. But we're going to have to figure something out for, like, the rest."

She says "we," but it's going to fall on me to figure out what's next. I've spent so much of my life grounding myself in logic, in practicality, convincing myself that if I didn't allow want to warp my reasoning, I'd make the right decisions. I'd be in control. But these rules no longer apply—if they ever did—because I need the thing I want. There's no denying it. There are fresh logistics that can't be ignored. There's Naomi's voice, which can't be ignored. It's drying out. She's thirsty.

I should have shared.

I look over at her. She stares out the window, and I can't remember the last time I saw her sad like this. But it's not her sadness that's startling. It's her weakness. I barely recognize her as she idly taps a nail to the glass. Her lights are off. She's dim.

It doesn't take us long to find gas. There's a dilapidated Sunoco a few minutes down the road, with a little convenience store at the back.

I pull up to a pump.

"Should I use my credit card?" I ask.

"I don't think it matters," she says.

I pop the gas hatch and get out of the car. "I miss New Jersey. Full service."

"In New Jersey you'd have to talk to someone," she says. "Better this way."

"Good point." I identify as an introvert, so avoiding people is fine by me. But I worry about Naomi, about what it will do to her if she can't be around people.

I get out my wallet. My credit card. I hesitate.

Maybe Naomi is right and no one's looking for us. Maybe we got away with what happened at the Waterfront, at the rest stop. Maybe we got away with murder, but we won't get away with murders.

It's inevitable that something else will happen. We crave blood.

I don't want to leave behind any breadcrumbs for law enforcement. It's bad enough that the vampires are on our tail. Or were, at least. I haven't seen the van since we left the motel.

"I think I'm going to pay cash."

"Whatever you say, hoss." She barely gets the words out before breaking into a coughing fit. She holds her throat.

"Are you okay?"

"No, I'm not okay," she snaps. "I'm fucking thirsty."

She's angry with me, blames me for not sharing the tumbler. Naomi doesn't typically hold grudges. But I do. And I hope she understands that she's the one who got us dragged into this nightmare. We're this way because of her. I'm this way because of her.

I leave her in the car and go into the convenience store. I wince at the fluorescent lights. Hot and yellow and relentlessly bright. There's no clerk behind the register, so I just stand there and wait, squinting. Minutes pass. I look around at all the glorious junk that I used to deprive myself of. Combos and Twizzlers and Reese's cups and Doritos. And in the fridges against the wall, Coca-Cola and Dr Pepper and AriZona iced tea. I walk over to one of the fridges and get out a bottle of Schweppes. Normally I wouldn't open something in a store without paying first, but I'm too curious, and it seems a small crime, considering what else I'm guilty of. I unscrew the cap and take a small sip.

It's like drinking hydrogen peroxide. It burns.

I start to gag so hard, I double over. "Ugh!"

It stings to breathe. I'd cut out my tongue if it meant I could exorcise the taste.

There's a rustling somewhere. In the back?

"Hello?" I caw.

"Yeah, just a minute," says a disinterested voice.

"Okay, thanks." I shuffle toward the front of the store, toward the glass window, to check on Naomi. She's still in the car, leaning against the window.

I'm about to turn around when I see another car pull in, pull over to the pump next to ours. I watch Naomi perk up as a woman gets out of the other car. She could be about our age. She wears a purple knit hat, a matching peacoat. No scarf. Her neck is exposed.

"Hey, uh, what'd ya need?" There's a guy behind the register. A twentysomething who reminds me of Matthew in how he barely looks at me.

"Um . . ." I say, distracted by what's happening outside. By the woman who has started to pump her gas. Who looks over her shoulder to find herself being watched by two wide, wild eyes.

She turns back toward the pump with a puzzled look on her face.

Does she know she's in danger? Can she sense it?

"Ma'am?"

"Sorry," I say, fumbling with my wallet. "I need, um, fifty dollars of gas on pump one."

He grunts as I get out two twenties, as I search for a ten. I don't have time for this.

"I guess forty," I say, anxiously looking through the window, my view obstructed by a sign advertising two Monster Energy drinks for the price of one. "Just forty dollars."

He grunts again as I shove the bills across the counter. I step back so I can get a better look at what's going on outside.

Naomi's got her window rolled down, her elbow hanging out. She's talking to the woman, whose back is now to me, so I can't see her expression. Naomi's smiling, but it's not a genuine smile. It's too big. Too toothy.

The woman begins walking toward her.

"Do you want a receipt?"

Panic has me glued in place. Whatever code-red urgency had me springing into action two nights ago, wielding a fire iron, it's failing me now. I need to run out there, but nothing's working. Not my legs. Not my lungs. Not my hands.

"Ma'am?"

Take a step. Grab the door handle. Run. Do something.

The woman stops, but Naomi beckons her forward. I don't know what she's saying to draw this woman in, but it's working. It's working.

It worked.

Naomi grabs the woman by the back of the head. It happens fast. From here, Naomi's hand looks strangely nasty—like a scorpion clenched on the woman's skull. The woman goes limp, and since her head is in front of Naomi's, I have no idea what's happening.

Well. I have some idea. An awful, devastating idea.

I hear a chime and turn around to find the clerk walking into a back room, staring down at his phone, unaware of the attack happening on the other side of the glass, and I've never felt luckier or more grateful to be ignored.

But then the woman screams. A bloodcurdling, night-shattering scream. The clerk pivots, and he looks at me, and I look at him, and his eyes narrow. His gaze shifts out through the window, out to the pumps.

"Holy shit!" he says.

He raises his phone, and I expect him to dial 9-1-1, but he doesn't. He opens his camera. He's taking a video. He's filming.

I don't make the decision. It just happens. Next thing I know, I'm snatching the phone out of his hands, pushing him hard into the wall.

"You didn't see anything," I say, in a voice much more menacing than my own. "And if you say anything, we'll come back for you. We'll drink your insides until you're nothing but bones and skin."

I slam his phone onto the floor and stomp on it until it breaks apart, and then I walk calmly away, noticing the security camera in the corner.

Whatever hope I might've held for avoiding further violence is now gone. Any and all hope I had is gone, forever silenced by this woman's screaming.

Naomi must have lost her grip. The woman is now thrashing around on the pavement, holding her face, blood pouring through her fingers. Naomi bit her face.

She *bit* her *face*.

Would I bite someone's face? Will I? Will I ever be that thirsty?

Am I that thirsty now, looking at the puddle of blood forming underneath the woman's head?

Naomi remains in the passenger seat, licking her lips in a stupor of satisfaction.

I run out of the store, past the woman, and get into the car, slamming the door, which wakes Naomi from her bliss coma. She shakes her head, then leans out the window and sees the woman on the ground.

She doesn't flinch. She doesn't recoil in horror at what she's done. She just says, "Drive."

I start the car and hit the gas. There's oncoming traffic, so I can't pull out onto the road.

"Go!" Naomi yells.

"I can't! Someone's coming! What were you thinking, Nay? You can't tell me that was self-defense. I saw you attack her."

"I was too thirsty! You drank all the blood Ilie gave us. What are you waiting for? Just go!"

The woman is up. She stumbles to her car, gets something out of her bag. Her phone? She must be calling the cops. She must be taking a picture of my car, the license plate.

She must be—

There's a *pop*.

It sounds like a bottle rocket. It doesn't sound like a gunshot, but it is. The woman has a gun—so small it looks like a toy—and she's shooting at us. She's shooting at the car.

"Goddamn motherfucking shit! Drive, Sloane! Fucking go!"

I take my foot off the brake and lay my hand on the horn, and I go. I don't look. I just go.

There are headlights, bright as twin suns, and they're coming toward us. I swerve to narrowly avoid a sedan, but I lose control of the car. The road is covered in black ice, and we're spinning, and spinning, and there are brakes screeching and horns honking, and Naomi screams, and she's trying to grab the wheel, and I'm remembering what it felt like to wake up broken and hungover in a hospital bed, what it was like to learn how quickly it all can get so ugly, and I see another set of headlights approaching, and the two white orbs merge into one, and I don't wonder what this will be like, because I've lived through it once before, only this time my body isn't colliding with the pavement; it's colliding with an enormous pickup truck. Head-on.

There's an earsplitting *crunch*, like we're between the teeth of a great beast. The pickup truck at the front and a hatchback from the rear. *Crunch, crunch.* My airbag goes off, punching me square in the face. I hear glass breaking, and then I feel broken glass pelting me like a hailstorm.

The air smells of smoke, and there's a troubling heat coming from somewhere.

"Naomi?" I blink through the fog and see she's climbing into the back seat. "Naomi, what are you doing?"

"I need it," she says, reaching. The trunk is smashed in. There's broken glass everywhere. She crawls on top of it, but she doesn't cut herself. Maybe her skin is too thick. I look down at my hands, my arms. I touch my face. I'm not cut either.

Is this immortality? The body surviving horror unscathed, the mind taking all the damage? The heart? The interior to sag and spot, to bruise, to be wounded and wither, while the exterior betrays nothing?

Naomi clambers out through the broken back window.

"Nay!" What is she doing? Where is she going? Why is she leaving me?

26

The scene comes into focus.

The driver of the hatchback has gone through her windshield. She's alive—she's moving—but she's bleeding. The driver of the truck is also bleeding. I don't need to look, because I can smell it. Smell his blood, and cheap cologne, and whiskey. He's been drinking. I know the accident wasn't his fault—it was mine—but part of me wonders if a sip would be justified.

I open my door and drop out onto the road.

The pickup-truck driver is there, already in my face. He's an older man, probably in his fifties.

"What the hell happened?" he asks. He slurs his words. "Weren't you paying attention?"

He bleeds from his forehead, from his nose, from his knuckles.

"Hey!" he says. He's not shouting at me; he's shouting beyond me.

Naomi comes up behind me, and there's blood smeared across her face. I'm too afraid to look back at the other driver, the one laid out on the hood of her hatchback.

"Sloane," Naomi says, possessed. Ghoulish. "Are you thirsty?"

There's another *pop*. The woman at the gas station is still shooting. Still screaming. "Stop them! Stop them!" She runs across the street toward the accident, waving the gun in one hand, her phone in the other.

"I'm calling the police! Don't let them leave!" she says.

I look to Naomi, the fear of consequences taking hold, but Naomi doesn't look back. She's busy salivating over the truck driver, who is now slowly backing away from her.

"Miss," I say to the woman with her cheek chewed through. I clasp my hands behind my back, for her sake and for mine, so I don't neutralize this threat the way I want to. The bad way.

"Stay right there!" she says, pointing the gun at me. "I'm calling the—"

She's gone.

She vanished.

She just vanished into thin air.

Only, I can hear her screaming. The screaming is the worst screaming I've ever heard. Worse than when she was getting her face bitten into.

Where is she? Where did she go?

"Holy shit," the truck driver says as all the lights on the street go out.

I look at him, and he's looking up. Until Naomi's on him. She sweeps his legs out from under him, so his head hits the pavement, and his lights go out. She's sipping the blood from his knuckles, cradling his hands to her lips like he's someone precious to her.

I would tell her to stop, but I can't get past this screaming. I spin around and around trying to figure out where it's coming from, to see where the woman went, and how she went so fast.

And then I see.

She's on top of the convenience store. There's someone behind her, veiled in shadow, feeding on her. Her arm is pulled back at a terrible angle, and someone's got it. Someone not letting go.

"Help me! Help!" she screams, until whoever it is reaches forward and twists her head, snaps her neck. Then she's quiet. Then everything's quiet.

Sometime between when we pulled out of the gas station and when we crashed, the van arrived. It's parked on the street right in front.

The woman's broken, bloodless body drops from the roof and lands on the pavement with a sickening *splat*. A second later, Tatiana jumps down. She wears a set of hot pink silk pajamas. Her hair is pulled back, and she unties it, shakes it out as she strides past the pumps toward the van. She waves at me, smirking.

Henry stands at a pump, letting gas spill out everywhere. He's got an unlit cigarette in his mouth.

"Don't!" I'm trying to shout, to be loud, assertive, because the clerk is still inside the store, and enough blood has been shed, but my voice won't cooperate. Because my throat disagrees. There's no such thing as too much blood.

There's movement inside the convenience store, and I see Ilie and Elisa. They're framed by the doorway as they feed on the clerk, Ilie on his leg and Elisa at his neck.

"Sloane," Naomi says. "Have some. He tastes like bourbon."

I turn around to find her sprawled out on the road next to the flattened body of the truck driver. He's covered in puncture wounds. Bite marks.

"I saved you some," she says, with a glint her in eye that might be drunkenness or antagonism. Either way, it doesn't look like there's anything left in the man. And even if there were, I wouldn't touch him.

I'm in the middle of a massacre.

The truck driver starts to wheeze, his chest like a plastic bag in the wind. He inflates and deflates. I step toward him, the soles of my boots crunching on bits of broken glass. His eyes have sunk into his head. He's too close to death to live. He's dying, and there's nothing I can do about it.

"Go on, Sloane," Naomi says.

Would it be a mercy?

"No. No! I'm not . . ."

"Not what?" Naomi asks. "Not bad like me?"

The door to the convenience store opens. Ilie and Elisa walk around the far side of the lot to avoid the gasoline.

"Are we almost done?" Tatiana asks, exasperated.

"In a rush?" Elisa says, stroking Tatiana's hair as she passes her by. She crosses the street, coming to us. She opens the gas tank on the hatchback.

"Bring your trunks, loves," Ilie says, getting into the van.

I shake my head. "No . . ."

Elisa helps Naomi off the ground, kisses her on the mouth, and then goes to the pickup truck. Climbs in. Pops open the gas hatch. Unscrews the cap. She rips some fabric from the hem of her dress and stuffs it into the tank.

"Don't worry," Elisa says, swiping my neck with a cold, soft hand. "We'll take care of you."

Elisa and Naomi get our suitcases, pull them toward the van.

I look down at the truck driver. He's still breathing. They'll burn him alive.

"Stop!" I say, my voice infuriatingly weak. "What are you do-ing? What have you done?"

"What have *you* done?" Tatiana says. She clicks her tongue. "I knew you two would cause problems."

She carries on muttering in French as she gets into the van. Elisa puts our suitcases in the back, then climbs into the passenger seat.

"Come on," Naomi says, reaching toward me. "We should go."

This is her getting what she wants. She's wanted to be back with them ever since we left. Ever since she met Ilie. She's under their influence. Their guilt-free, free-love, "take what you like; leave what you don't" lifestyle. They don't care about consequence. They don't have remorse. And neither does she.

But I do.

"No," I say. "I won't do it."

The distant sirens quickly change my mind, my fear leveling the moral high ground I like to believe I have. That I need to believe I have, to hold on to whatever's left of my humanity. The smell of gasoline is so strong now that I can barely think straight.

I walk toward the van. Naomi's already in the back, where there are two rows of seats and a pile of suitcases and duffel bags and a giant cooler.

"We should hurry," Ilie says. "We will need to go fast."

"Sloane," Naomi says, curling up next to Tatiana in the back seat. "Get in."

The sirens are loud. Getting closer.

And there's a flickering in my peripheral vision. I turn toward the convenience store, and through the windows I can see the fire burning inside.

"Okay, fine!" I say, jumping into the van. I go to the middle row, because it's empty.

"Leave the door open for Henry," Elisa says.

Ilie slaps the side of the van. He calls out to Henry in a language I don't understand. Henry nods, letting the gas pump drop. When he gets to the van, he lights his cigarette, takes a drag, then flicks it, at the exact moment the convenience store windows burst.

Everything goes up. Flames come hurtling toward us. Henry closes the door, and Ilie puts the van in reverse. The road is blocked by a fallen power line, and there's a queue of cars on the other side of it. Ilie pulls a U-turn and drives onto the curb, past the car wreck right as it catches fire, then cuts across an empty lot.

"Just relax," Ilie says as he picks up speed. I close my eyes so I can't see the explosion, but I can hear it. I'll be hearing it forever, ringing in my ears, echoing in my fucking soul.

"All done," Elisa says, clapping twice. She turns around and looks at me. "Behind us. Literally and figuratively."

I'm nauseous, but I don't know if I can puke with only blood in my system. I want to expel whatever's inside me, be rid of it all. Eradicate this horror. This guilt. This fear.

"Such brats. You should be thanking us," Tatiana says. She whispers in my ear, "We cleaned up your mess."

"You just set a gas station on fire," I say. "I wouldn't call that cleaning up a mess."

Naomi giggles in the back seat, still buzzing on that guy's bourbon-laced blood.

"No evidence, only ash," Henry says.

I won't look at him. I won't look at any of them. I stare down at my hands, shaking in my lap. There's a second explosion, and I think of the Texas City disaster, the worst industrial accident in US history. In 1947, two ships carrying ammonium nitrate exploded at the port, first the SS *Grandcamp* and later the SS *High Flyer*. The damage leveled almost a thousand buildings, killed more than four hundred people, injured many more. The second explosion was caused by the first, which was caused—historians think—by a discarded cigarette.

"It was an accident," I say to myself. "It was an accident."

"Don't be sad," Ilie says. "These things, they come up. We get in pickle; we get out. We move on. It is life."

"What just happened was always going to happen," Elisa says, again turning around, this time putting her hand on my knee. I pull away. "When you've lived as long as we have, you come to understand there are greater forces in the universe. Someday you will look back on this night and be grateful, know it was necessary."

"If I'm ever grateful for tonight, I hope someone kills me," I say.

"Sloane likes to think about death," Naomi says, hiccuping. "Because she came so close. She took the rejection pretty hard."

It's the meanest thing she's ever said to me, and I doubt she'll even remember in the morning.

"What do you think, Drago?" Ilie says. "We go to the castle and get the bus?"

"Yes," Henry says. "To the castle."

"The castle," Naomi sings. "Sounds fucking magical."

"Yeah," I say to the van door. "Happily ever after."

27

The castle isn't really a castle. It's a Renaissance fair, closed for the season. The entrance to the fairgrounds was made to look like a castle gate, and through the gate there's a fake medieval village. The snow lends the place some legitimacy, concealing the modern, like utility boxes and signs for restrooms.

Naomi snores in the back seat. She passed out shortly after the second explosion and slept through the forty-five-minute drive, slept through Ilie putting the van in park, getting out, floating over the gate, and opening it for us so we could drive in. She slept through Elisa closing the gate behind us. She slept through us pulling up to the King's Tavern, a large Tudor-style building.

I envy her. I'd love to be asleep. To be unconscious.

"Home," Elisa says. "For now."

"Wake up, terrible creature," Tatiana says, tugging on Naomi's hair.

"Wha-what? Where are we?" Naomi says, blearily.

Everyone gets out of the van, stepping into a few inches of wet, slushy snow. Elisa goes up to the tavern door and picks the padlock. I'd be impressed by how fast she does it if I weren't so preoccupied with horror and hopelessness.

Elisa goes inside, her footsteps echoing. "Barely any cobwebs."
The rest of us follow her in.

I'd expected the building to be only a pretty shell, but the interior is just as detailed as the exterior. There's a giant stone hearth at the back, a built-in bar with decorative molding, crests hung up on the walls—intricately carved and painted. Of course, none of it is authentic, but it looks good enough. There are exposed beams overhead. Elisa was wrong about the cobwebs. They're everywhere. And dust. There are tables and chairs and benches pushed up against the walls, all covered in a thick layer of dust.

Tatiana strolls in with a blanket tucked under her arm. She unrolls it on the floor and lies on it, stretching her arms, her legs wide. Making herself right at home.

It's cold in here, but it's manageable. There are no windows. I couldn't think of a better hangout for a bunch of unhinged ancient vampires.

Ilie pulls out the chairs and benches, and I look for a place where I can be alone. I go behind the bar and sit on the floor, pulling my knees to my chest.

I shut my eyes, and they're all waiting for me in the dark. Matthew, slumped against a tree trunk, neck slack, sleeve pushed up, the vicious array of teeth marks on his wrist. The man at the rest stop, his neck butchered, his lack of pulse. The woman at the gas station, the gaping hole across her cheek. The convenience-store clerk. The woman thrown from her hatchback. The truck driver with his hollow eyes, wheezing his last breaths.

Naomi's right. I do think about death a lot, but in the abstract. Numbers on a Wikipedia page, in a news article. I never thought I'd be the cause.

"What do you think? We play cards?" Ilie says. "We play game?"
"Not cards," Tatiana says. "I'm so bored of cards."

"You're bored of everything," Elisa says.

"Of course I am," she says. "It's a miracle you're not."

"Naomi, you play cards?" Ilie asks.

"Where are we?" She yawns.

"Disneyland," Henry says, and I kill my smile right before it hatches. I won't be charmed by him. By any of them.

"I have actually been there once," Ilie says, his excitement challenging my will. "It is very fun, but a little bit hard to be around so many people. Also, very expensive. But I ride roller coaster. As a boy, I could never imagine. So cool."

I remind myself that an hour ago he was sipping from someone's leg. The vampires' ability to perpetrate and be so unfazed by such violence scares the hell out of me.

"What is the matter?" Elisa asks. "Our Naomi is very worried about something."

"Not worried," Naomi says. Must be nice. "Are we—do we, like, live here now?"

"Oh, no!" Elisa says, laughing. "We do not live anywhere. We live *everywhere.*"

"We like to travel. Keep it moving," Ilie says. "It is part of the lifestyle."

"We find new places," Elisa says. "The castle is one of our winter places in America."

"America is all McDonald's and parking lots," Tatiana says, sighing.

"It is not," Elisa says. "I love it here."

"Sloane and I were headed to North Carolina," Naomi says. "My parents have a vacation house that'll be empty 'til May. We could all stay there for a while."

"Great," I mumble to myself. "Sure. Why not? Invite them. Who cares?"

"Vacation house sounds nice!" Ilie says. "We go there."

"No, no. We've been in this horrible country far too long," Tatiana says. "Let's go overseas."

Ilie and Tatiana start to argue back and forth, and I push myself to stand. "I'm going for a walk."

Naomi moves to follow me.

"Alone," I say.

I trudge through the snow, past a maypole, down Storybook Lane, with little kiosks that look like enchanted mushrooms. My socks are soaked through, and I shiver against a cold that can't harm me beyond mild discomfort.

There are stocks to my left, a silly photo op. There's a fairy-tale tower, covered in painted vines. There's an elaborate stage, the backdrop tall, with stairs up to a Juliet balcony. There's a giant chessboard, mostly covered in snow. There's a large pond, frozen over, with a Loch Ness–esque serpent in it, covered in iridescent green scales, its long body sinking under and rising up out of the ice. Its face is more adorable than ferocious. Icicles hang from its chin like whiskers.

As I stare out at the serpent, I become aware that I, too, am under observation. That I'm being watched. I whip around and see no one, but that doesn't eliminate my suspicion.

I keep walking, and my footsteps are clumsy, sloshing around in the wet snow. I hear none other than my own, but that doesn't change my mind either. If a threat is quiet, that doesn't mean it isn't a threat.

My body knows a threat.

I walk faster, slipping as I approach the bridge over the pond. There's a heart-shaped arch over the entrance with a sign that reads THE KISSING BRIDGE.

"Don't you dare follow me onto this bridge," I say. The smell of tobacco and bergamot identifies the presence. It's Henry. "I don't want to be followed. Stop following me."

If I say it enough, maybe I'll convince myself that it's true. That I'm not flattered by the chase.

I forgot how good it feels to be wanted.

But I don't deserve to feel good. And neither does he.

"Your friend asked me to check on you," he says, appearing first as a floating ember. Out of the inky darkness, he materializes on the chessboard, moving across it like a rook. "She's concerned."

"She needs to get her priorities straight," I say, stepping backward onto the bridge. I realize I'm now directly under the heart arch and take another step.

"I warned you it was too soon to be out in the world. I warned you she was reckless."

"This isn't my fault. I didn't ask for any of this."

"Mm," he says, pissing me off.

"Why did you let us go? If you were just going to hunt us down."

"'Hunt'? That's a strong word."

"Is it?"

"What would you have done if we hadn't shown up?"

"I . . . we wouldn't have been there. We left the motel because you were parked outside like creeps."

"Creeps?"

"Yeah."

"We gave you a gift."

"This isn't a gift."

"I meant the blood. Not the thirst."

"Okay."

"If we didn't turn you, Naomi would have died."

"If you'd told me about the man in the basement the first time

RACHEL HARRISON

I asked, we would have left, and Naomi would have been fine, and I would have been fine, and we wouldn't be here right now, and those people would still be alive."

"Speculating about alternate fates is a waste of time," Henry says, reaching a corner of the board.

"I'm painfully aware of that. You don't need to tell me."

"Then why resist?"

"Resist what? You?"

"Your thirst."

"Because it's savage—that's why. It's wrong."

"It's survival."

"It's murder."

"Not always," he says. "We're of a different mind, the rest of us. We come from another time. Lived through plagues. Fought in wars. Death is nothing to us."

"I'm not talking about death. I'm talking about killing."

"You didn't kill anyone tonight, did you?"

"I was involved."

"To exist is to participate in destruction."

"You're full of shit!" I say, so infuriated by the conversation that I scoop some snow off the bridge and throw it at him.

It lands at his feet. He's amused by it. He does his goofy grin.

"Don't," I say. I turn to continue crossing the bridge, but there's ice under the snow, and I lose my footing and fall, landing hard on my ass. The embarrassment and the frustration are too much. I lie back in the snow, roll around so I'm covered in it. I want to bury myself. I want to disappear.

"Am I allowed to come onto the bridge?"

"No!"

"Not even if I answer a riddle?"

"Hey," I say, sitting up and looking back. He's at the other end of the bridge. He lowers himself to the ground, stretches his legs out, props himself up on his arms.

"What if I dared you to let me cross the bridge?" he asks.

"I'm not playing games with you. It didn't end well for me last time."

"It didn't?" he asks, giving me his fox grin.

"I wish I never went to that house," I say, unconvincingly. "I wish we did anything else that night."

I'm surprised by how little I mean it. Ashamed, and yet maybe—maybe—exhilarated.

He hangs his head. "Another regret?"

"If you could be . . . be normal again, would you?"

"No," he answers, too fast. "I've been this way for so long, I've forgotten how to be any other way. It's this or nothing."

"Nothing?"

He draws a finger across his neck.

"Is that possible?"

"There are ways," he says. "But I told you, I am a coward. There have been times when I have wished for the forever sleep, the release of death. Not now. Not when things have just gotten interesting."

"What's interesting?"

"You."

"Me?" I can't help it; I laugh. "You just met me! Two nights ago. Maybe. Three? I don't know."

It feels like another life. I guess it was.

He runs his fingers through his hair, pushing it out of his face. "It's been a long time since I was young. Since I experienced anything new. The longer you live, the more everything has context. You relate it all to what's happened before, what you've already experienced. Look at the moon tonight; it reminds me of that time in Istanbul, when it was so low, you could almost touch it. These hills are like Tuscany. This hotel is like the one we stayed in in Paris. These people coming over to us in the bar—they look so familiar. But every face is familiar. Every place is familiar. Every conversation. Every emotion . . . But then I saw you. Your face. That freckle, right there, under your eye. I watched you move. I—"

"Watched me sleep," I say, interrupting him.

I wait for him to apologize, admit it was weird. But instead he says, very matter-of-factly, "I wanted to see you again. I thought I might never get the chance."

"Well, you did."

"I did. You came to that house, and I listened to you speak, to the sound of your voice and your laugh, how you chose your words, expressed your thoughts. We kissed and I tasted you, and I felt you, the warmth of you. All this is to say, yes, we just met. But I've never met you before. You're new."

"I'm . . ." Should I tell him the truth? That I'm not new? That I'm sure there are hundreds of thousands of bored, suburban thirtysomething wives just like me? Who got married for a sense of stability, to tether themselves to someone because they were terrified of being alone, because they were terrified of themselves. Who gave up on their dreams before they could fail. Should I save him the disappointment? Or should I just shut up? I think about how good it felt to be touched by him. How caught up I was in it.

The only feeling that compares is that of the spilling of blood down my throat. Nothing else comes close.

I think about the blood on the pavement, the accident at the gas station. The broken glass. The smell of gasoline. The bodies. I think about the tumbler that I held so tightly, that I would have drained to the last drop. I think about the fiendish selfishness that overtook me in that moment. The possession of bloodlust, like at

208

the rest stop, in the woods behind the cottage, as the wooden cup was brought to my lips at the lake house.

I think about when he first kissed me. That wasn't possession; it was surrendering to myself, to my desire, to pleasure.

I look up and there he is, on the other side of the bridge, perfectly framed by the heart-shaped arch, and it's a cruelty. Does satisfaction always come at such a high cost? Does its pursuit always leave such ruin?

If I give in to this want, I betray everything else.

If there is a happy medium between being a resigned, mildly depressed thirty-six-year-old woman with a thankless job and cheating husband, and being an immortal vampire indulging her lust for blood and sex and her desire for love and excitement, it sure would be nice to find it.

"What if I can't get past it?" I say. "What I am now. What you made me. What if I can't live like this?"

"It's early days," he says.

"That doesn't make me feel better."

"What about Naomi? Will she get past it?"

"Naomi is past it," I say, drawing spirals in the snow with my finger. "She's maybe been a little more erratic than usual, and a lot less empathetic, but overall, she seems to be adjusting to blood sucking just fine."

Normally I wouldn't vent about Naomi to anyone other than Naomi. I've always kept my frustrations to myself out of love and loyalty. I refused to give anyone else the opportunity to agree with whatever I was annoyed about, because they didn't know her like I did, or love her like I did. Whatever conclusions they would draw from my complaints would be wrong, and I couldn't risk misrepresenting the most important person in my life, the only person who ever really saw me. That would be treason.

But right now, treason doesn't seem like such a crime.

"Naomi grew up with money. She's always had something to fall back on. She doesn't understand what it is to lose," I say. "She hasn't had it easy, but she's had a safety net. I never did. I understand there are consequences. I'm not sure that's a lesson she ever learned."

Why am I telling him all this? Because he's easy to talk to or because I need for someone to listen? Because there's too much on my chest and I'm being crushed under the weight.

"I don't know her like you do. She said you think of death, and yet she strikes me as someone afraid of dying. She lives as though she's running out of time. There's a desperation about her. Even now, when the long shadow of death is gone, she fears it. And you're the opposite. You fear living. A pity. You'd be so good at it."

It's too much effort to feel insulted. Besides, I suspect he's right. About me, at least. I'm not so sure about Naomi. "Why do you think she's desperate?"

"You don't see it?"

The way he asks—something about his tone—makes me feel oblivious, like I've missed something obvious to everyone but me. I hate it.

I stand up and brush the snow off. "You can cross the bridge now. I don't know any riddles."

"No riddles? No truth or dare?"

"No. Definitely not."

He laughs. He stands, bows, and crosses the bridge to me. He stops about three-quarters of the way over.

"No chance you'll meet me on it?" he asks, pointing at the arch.

"Nope," I say, turning my back to him.

"Do I have permission to follow you?"

"You've never needed it before," I say, walking to the other side of the pond, toward a shipwreck. Another photo op, maybe. Or a big prop for kids to climb all over with their greasy turkey-leg fingers.

"Will you forgive me?" he asks.

"For what?"

"Following," he says, walking a few steps behind me.

"You don't care about forgiveness."

"Yes, I do."

We reach the ship. Its name is carved in the side in big, bold script. Unfortunately, appropriately, the *Demeter*.

There are stairs up to the deck. I climb them cautiously, afraid there's ice hiding under the snow. I don't want to fall in front of him again. I listen for his footsteps, but he doesn't make any sound. He's stealthy.

From the deck of the ship there's a solid view of the fairgrounds. The kingdom. It's a clear night, and the moon is out, the stars. They reflect off the frozen surface of the pond, make everything shimmer.

"Have you thought about what you want to do next?" he asks.

"Well, Naomi so generously shared our plan to go to Wilmington," I say. "But I don't know what after that. It's hard to make plans when you don't know if you're a fugitive or not."

"We took care of that for you," he says.

"What about traffic cameras? What about other witnesses? What if the convenience-store camera footage uploaded to the cloud? It's not so easy to get away with things these days."

"I know," he says. "Not like it used to be."

I remember something he said to me in the conservatory. Something I'd initially dismissed as a joke. "Are you really five hundred years old?"

"Five hundred and ninety-two. But who's counting?" he asks, leaning back against the mast of the ship.

He's too old for me. Way too old. "How old were you when you were . . . ?"

"When was I turned? Twenty-seven."

He's too young for me.

If this had to be my fate, couldn't it have at least happened when I was twenty-seven? Before the mercilessness of collagen loss. I was insecure then, of course, but now I aspire to those insecurities.

"I thought it might bring me glory," he says. "But we never know where the paths we take will lead us until we get there."

"Didn't lead you to glory?"

"It did. Until it didn't."

"You won't go into detail?"

"Another night," he says, staring out across the pond. "This one is too pretty to spoil with sad songs."

"I love a sad song. All the best songs are sad."

"No," he says, coming toward me. "You can't believe that."

He takes my hand and spins me around. He's dancing with me. We're dancing, gliding across this fake ship deck. My clothes are soaked from the snow, and I can't remember the last time I showered. I don't know how I look, since I can't check my reflection, but I can't imagine it's beautiful. It's been a long time since I felt beautiful. Desirable.

I'd given up on romance. I'd already settled. I figured the only women over thirty-five who get to be swept off their feet are the ones in books and movies. In fiction.

But I'd thought vampires were fictional, too, so who the hell knows?

I get so dizzy spinning that I forget all the bloodshed of the last forty-eight hours and press myself against him. I squeeze his hand, his skin against my skin the answer to a prayer I was too shy or too jaded to ever conceive, ever utter, ever whisper into my pillow at night.

He holds my waist. He leans down and presses his forehead into mine, our noses almost touching.

"You should come with me," he says. "I'll take you wherever you want to go."

"I . . . I don't know where I want to go."

"Somewhere warm? Somewhere cold? The mountains? The desert?"

"I still don't know how to live like this. With the thirst."

"You wouldn't need to worry. I would make sure your throat was never dry. You'd never crave anything. You'd have whatever you needed. Whatever you wanted."

I wish I could stay in the fantasy. I wish I could believe him. "That sounds too good to be true. You can't promise me all that. You can't promise me that you wouldn't get bored of me eventually. When I'm not new anymore."

He tilts his head back, looking at me with a strange face.

"What?" I ask.

"You could be right. There's no way for me to disprove that in this moment. But why would I promise you something with no intention of following through?"

I can't tell if he's being serious or cheeky. It's an innocent question, and he's not innocent.

"To use me."

He furrows his brow. "Why would I do that?"

"I don't know. Because you like to play games. Because you're a—"

"A monster?"

"*A man* was what I was going to say."

He laughs. "Even worse!"

He spins me again, then pulls me in. "If I'd had any doubt about you, I would have drained you and let you die. And if I'd wanted to use you, I wouldn't have let your first taste of blood be your own. You would have been forever bound to me, the one who turned you. Now you are bound to no one but yourself. And whoever you may choose."

The wind blows, rattling the mast, my bones.

He reaches out and takes my face in his hands. Gently. Almost too gently. He traces the outline of my lips with his fingers.

"You're beautiful," he tells me, and somehow I believe it. I know it. I feel it. My skin sparks at his touch. Maybe he was right, what he said as we stood in the hallway of that terrible house. Maybe whatever this is between us is more than attraction. It feels like more.

There's a gravity to it. To us. But it isn't heavy, or constricting. It's almost like walking with the wind at your back, a confirmation from nature that you're going the right way. I let the feeling carry me. Push me toward him.

I kiss his fingers. His hands. His wrists.

He kisses mine. My left hand. My left wrist. He kisses the exact spot where he ripped the metal out with his teeth, extracting the painful remnants of my greatest shame.

He takes my hand and pins it behind my back. He nestles his face in my neck. He lets his teeth scrape the place where he turned me, and then he presses his lips there. His lips. His lips. His tongue.

My free hand reaches for his jeans, for his belt loop. I pull him closer to me and it still isn't close enough. He lets my other hand go. He shifts my face so he can kiss me on the mouth. I wrap my arms around him, grab his back. Closer. Closer.

He slides his knee against my inner thigh, lifting up my leg, lifting me up onto him. His hand is on my hip, his fingers pressing down hard enough that I release a breath, a sound—one I've never heard myself make before—and it sets me off; it's like gunpowder. The sound of me getting off gets me off. Discovering I'm capable of this kind of hedonism.

My back hits the mast, and I reach behind me for it, slip around to the other side of it.

"Where are you going?" he asks, circling.

He gets to me, and moves to kiss me, and I slip away again.

"I thought you didn't like to play games?" he asks, darting after me as I swing around the mast. I smash into him, burrowing my head into his chest. He puts his hands on me, sails them up from my hips to my waist, to my ribs, chest, neck, jaw, hair.

"If it's me," I say. "It's only me."

"It's only you."

On our walk back from the ship, however much later, I try to remember the last time I talked about sex with Naomi, or with any friend. The day after I lost my virginity, she took me out to her favorite tapas restaurant and I gave her a play-by-play as we split a pitcher of sangria that we were legally too young to drink, but Naomi flirted with the waiter, so he served us anyway.

She'd already lost hers and had been giving me explicit details for years. It was silly fun to sit there and giggle and blush. It was novel to us then. But by the time I got with Joel, and she got with Lee, we were past all that.

I'd never seriously considered cheating on Joel. I wasn't motivated, and I wondered who would want me anyway. I thought decent, routine sex once a week was just part of being married, part of what I'd signed up for. I'd made my peace with that, and over the years, sex became an obligation, something I did because it was part of life, like haircuts and taxes. I'd hear pop songs on the radio and wonder why everyone was so obsessed, then think, *Because they're young. Because these pop stars are young, and sex is exciting when you're young.*

But just moments ago, I was on my back on a fake ship in the middle of a deserted Renaissance fair, staring up at the stars as Henry pulled off my jeans and kissed up my thighs. He spread my legs, and I dug my nails into his back as I felt him move inside me, his dirty-blond hair hanging in my face. And I took my hands from his back to his chest, where I could feel his heart beating, alive, *alive*. Then I touched his face, his grinning, magnificent face, and he kissed my hands, dragged his teeth across their flesh, took my fingers into the softness of his mouth. We melted the snow, and we were wet with it, wet with sweat.

And then he bent me over the ship's railing to take me from behind, and I was eye to eye with the sea monster and I bit my lip so I wouldn't laugh, and I bit my lip for other reasons. Hard enough to draw blood, which stung but was worth it just so I could deliver it to him, to his lips, his mouth, his perfect tongue.

My body was new to me, new again. Capable of this new, transcendent satisfaction.

After we both came, we carried on kissing, with our hands in each other's damp, tangled hair, and I realized that wonder isn't reserved for the young. That maybe my best years aren't behind me, after all. Only my human years . . .

I want to share this with Naomi. I want to tell her everything. I want to pull her aside, throw a blanket over our heads so we can gossip and swoon. But what I don't want is for her to think that because this happened I'm fine with the rest. That because I slept with someone, had an incredible night, the ugliness that came before is absolved.

The ugliness I hold her accountable for. Along with the others. Henry included.

Living is complicated and messy, she said to me at the rest stop. "Messy" is an understatement for whatever I feel now, as I subtly slip my wedding band out of my pocket and drop it into the snow.

Henry and I pass by the fairy-tale tower. I can see the tavern up ahead.

"Do we have to go back right now?" I ask him.

"No," he says. "We can keep walking, if you aren't cold."

"I'm not cold," I say. "Or maybe I am, but I don't get cold like I used to."

"That happens." He takes my hand to hold, like we're going steady. Like we're walking through the halls of our high school. Only I doubt he's ever been to high school.

"Do you read books?" I ask him.

"No, I hate reading," he says, and I experience a moment of acute panic before he starts to laugh. "What else would I do with all this time?"

"What your friends do," I say.

"They're more family than friends. Brothers and sisters."

"They don't act like brothers and sisters."

"I meant, to me. Not to one another. There's no enjoyment in food or drink. There's sleep. There's sex. Material things. Books. Films. Art. Fashion. People—though rarely."

"You can be around people without . . ."

"Without draining them? Yes. You'll see."

I pinch my throat, the thirst blossoming.

"We don't do what we did tonight every night," he says, bringing my hand to his lips. "Hardly ever."

"What's 'hardly ever' to someone who's lived hundreds of years?"

"It's been maybe . . ." He pauses to think. "Fifty years since we've had to take measures."

"That's what you call it?"

"Would you prefer I say 'kill'?" he asks, letting my hand down. "We try to get our blood without violence. We take it from hospitals. We buy it in dark alleys. We have our ways."

217

Robbing hospitals and buying black-market blood isn't exactly ethical either, but it's better than leaving a pile of bodies in our wake. Better than murder.

"If you stay with me, I will show you," he says, stepping up to a platform where there's a sword stuck in a stone. He gestures for me, and I go to him. I put my hand on the hilt of the sword; I grip it and I pull, and I break it. I break the hilt clean off.

"Oops."

He laughs. "See? You're strong."

"Now I feel bad."

"I'm sorry," he says.

I attempt to press the hilt back into the stone, because I'm too thick and stubborn to recognize when something broken can't be fixed, can't be unbroken. And I wonder if that means I'm too thick and stubborn to recognize when something broken isn't actually broken. If I've spent my life trying to glue pieces back together when I should have just let them lie. Or set them on fire.

"It's okay," I say, tossing the hilt into the snow.

He takes a breath. "We will take you wherever you want to go. We will not linger if you do not want us to. But you should think about it. What you want. Who you want to do it with. You have time. It's on your side now, isn't it?"

"I guess so," I say, looking back at the swordless stone.

"Though just because you have all the time in the world doesn't mean you can't still waste it."

Sometimes wisdom sounds like a threat.

28

We spend the rest of the night wandering around the fairgrounds, until I get too thirsty. He leads me to the van and goes into the back for the cooler, which is stocked with bags of blood. He reaches to the chain around his neck, pulls it out from under his shirt, revealing the spile. He uses it to puncture a bag. He lets me drink first, and I nearly empty it. He takes the rest.

I watch him drink, watch his neck move as he swallows.

It's almost as satisfying as if I were drinking it myself. I can almost taste it.

When we're done, he tosses the empty blood bag into the back of the van and closes it.

"Is it okay that we just took one? We didn't need to ask?"

"I'd be the one to ask," he says. I already sensed that he was in charge, but I never wondered why until now. "The sun will be up soon. We should go inside."

"I bled. Before. I bit my lip, and I bled a little. I didn't know that was possible."

"We bleed. There is blood in our veins. We have thick skin, but we aren't impenetrable. We need to be careful; we do not have much to spare. It's painful to lose."

"Didn't really notice," I say, cracking a grin. "Preoccupied."

He chomps at me, and I laugh. "Is that how we don't empty ourselves? Because it hurts too badly?"

"Yes, in part. Vampire blood doesn't taste the same as human blood. It tastes like nothing," he says. "As soon as we consume it, it's altered. Before you ask, I don't know why or how. I don't know everything. Not sure I care to."

He opens the tavern door and leads me through it.

Tatiana is where she was when I left, on her blanket. She paints her nails, looking apathetic. Ilie, Elisa, and Naomi sit at a table playing cards, all topless.

"You two were gone for a while," Tatiana says, smirking.

"Get good rest," Henry says. "We have a long drive tomorrow night."

He takes my hand and walks me past the hearth, around the corner to a doorway. There's a small storage room. "We can sleep in here."

"On the floor?" I ask, sounding snotty though I'm really just concerned. I'm too old to sleep on a hard surface. I can barely get comfortable on a mattress.

He points to a stack of cushions in a corner. They're dusty, but they're something. He picks them up and arranges them on the floor and we get on top, and I rest my head on his chest. It's not so bad.

"If you decide you might want to go somewhere with me, they wouldn't have to come with us," he says. "We could go out on our own."

"What do you mean?" I ask. A stupid question. I know what he means.

"The two of us."

"I'm not going to ditch Naomi," I say.

"She'd go with Ilie, or Elisa. Or both. They would look after her. And we'd see them again."

I turn onto my back, look up at the ceiling, where cobwebs cling and flutter as a draft sneaks in from somewhere.

It's not like I see Naomi all the time as it is. We go months without getting together. We lead separate lives. We talk at least once a week, though. And I doubt we'd be able to communicate now, considering she tossed her phone out the car window, and I just realized I left mine in the car after the accident, so it's likely been cremated.

As much as I'm frustrated with her, disappointed, resentful . . . the thought of separation makes me uneasy. After everything we've been through, how could we leave each other now?

Henry slides his arm under me and starts to play with my hair, and somehow it's more intimate than the sex, more intimate than anything I've ever experienced.

My mind empties of everything except one question. *Wouldn't it be nice to stay like this forever?*

It's the best sleep of my life. Deep and dreamless. There's no need to dream when your reality is so surreal. When you get to wake up next to Henry.

"Good evening," he says, nudging me with his nose.

"Hi," I say. "We slept all day?"

He nods, then starts to kiss up and down my neck.

Normally I'd be insecure about how I haven't showered, or brushed my teeth, or applied deodorant, about how my body isn't what it used to be. I'd be thinking about all my flaws, and all the things I'd have to do when it was over. Joel would be on top of me and physically I'd be under him, but mentally I'd be paying the electric bill or sending a work email or cleaning the filters on my beloved Dyson or adding bananas to the grocery list.

But it's impossible not to be present with Henry. Not to be here in my body while he undresses me slowly, while he—

There's a knock on the door.

"Hey." It's Naomi. "Sloane?"

"Yeah?"

"We're getting ready to head out."

"Okay. We're coming."

Henry chuckles and I pinch his side, which only makes him laugh harder.

"Are you?" Naomi asks.

"Can you give us a minute?" For once I'm not the buzzkill.

I get dressed as Henry stacks the cushions back in the corner. He kisses me again before opening the door, where Naomi waits, standing with her arms crossed and her eyebrows raised.

"Hey," I say.

"Hi there."

Henry nods to Naomi, then bows past us, leaving us alone outside the storage room.

"Well, well, well. What's going on here?" she asks. She seems more suspicious than excited, more annoyed than anything else, so I hold back on any girlish divulging.

"Nothing," I say. "Just woke up."

"Where did you go last night?"

"For a walk. You sent Henry to check on me."

"No, I didn't," she says. "I went to go after you, and he said he would."

"Really?"

"I mean, he said to leave you alone like you asked. When I pressed, he said he'd go. Make sure you were all right."

"You say that like it's a bad thing."

She shrugs. "If you're upset about the gas station, we should talk about it. Don't freeze me out."

"*If? If* I'm upset?"

"I get it. It was bad. But—"

"Do you remember what you said to me last night? In the van? Or were you too drunk off that guy's blood?"

She cocks her head. "What'd I say?"

Either it's a great act or she really doesn't remember. If she doesn't remember, I won't repeat it. "Let's just leave it in the past."

"Tell me. You're obviously still mad."

"What else do you not remember about last night? Do you remember what you did to that woman's face?"

"Yes, I remember. What do you want me say? I was out-of-my-mind thirsty because you didn't share. You always find a way to make it my fault."

"Because it—" I cut myself off.

"Because it is? Is that what you were going to say?"

"No," I lie.

She sighs. "I get it. I was the one who made plans with Ilie, and now here we are. It's on me. I own that. But you also have to understand, if I didn't push you, I don't know if you'd ever do anything."

I open my mouth to argue, but I have nothing to counter with.

"You can't put all the blame on me. I didn't know any of this would happen. I was trying to do good by you. To help you because you refuse to help yourself."

"Yeah, thanks. This was so helpful."

She shakes her head. "I'm on your side, you know. We're in this together. And for what it's worth, you're not the only one struggling here."

"Okay," I say.

"Okay?" she says, scoffing. "How come you're mad at me but

are happy to share a bed with him? He doesn't get any of the blame for our little situation here?"

"I . . . I . . ." I hate it when she's right. "It's different."

She raises an eyebrow. "Guess so."

"We don't have time for this," I say, diverting because I'm embarrassed by my hypocrisy. "If we want to get to Wilmington, we need to leave now."

"Fine," she says.

We join the rest of the group in the main room. Tatiana rolls up her blanket. Ilie pushes the tables and chairs back against the wall. Elisa is . . .

"Where's Elisa?" I ask.

"Oh, hello, sleepyhead!" Ilie says. "She went to get the bus. We change cars. I miss my car, but Costel and Miri take it."

"Are they still in New York?" I ask.

"Who knows?" Tatiana says, stretching. "Let's get a hotel tomorrow. Something nice. How much cash did you get out of the register last night?"

"Three hundred something," Ilie says.

I shouldn't be scandalized or surprised, but I am. "You robbed the convenience store?"

"Why burn money?" Ilie asks. "Are we ready to go? Naomi, Sloane, what do you think of the castle? It is nice, yes? Cool place."

Neither of us respond. I'm hung up on the robbery because it reminds me of the gas station and the murders and that whole sick, horrible mess. Naomi just stares out into space.

"I think it is cool," Ilie says to himself.

We shuffle outside as Elisa pulls up in a 1980s camper van. It's brown and beige with an orange stripe across the side. It's in rough shape.

"Where did this come from?" I ask Henry.

"Some guy," Ilie says.

"Wait, what? When?" Why do I ask questions I don't want the answers to?

"Long time ago," Ilie says.

"We keep it here in case we need it," Henry says, opening the camper door for us. "There's an employee parking lot on the other side of the grounds."

The inside of the camper is just as dated as the outside. There's bench seating covered in brown and orange upholstery that wraps around the back of the van in a U shape. The windows are hidden behind burlap curtains. There's also a curtain that separates us from the two seats up front.

Ilie and Henry get into the back with me and Naomi.

I ask about our suitcases.

"Your luggage is on top," Elisa calls from the driver's seat, from the other side of the curtain.

"Do you need something?" Henry asks, sitting beside me.

"It'd be nice to change my clothes eventually," I say, reaching for my seat belt, which goes across just the waist, not the chest. I'm still rattled from yesterday's crash. "When we get to the house."

I look at Naomi, who sits across from me, still with that glassy-eyed stare.

I kick her foot. "You okay?"

"Peachy," she says.

"Is everyone ready to go?" Elisa asks. She doesn't wait for a response. She starts the engine, which stammers before settling into a gruff hum. When we pull up to the fairgrounds gate, Ilie gets out to open and close it because Tatiana refuses. I peer out from behind the curtain, sad to be leaving the only place I've been in the last few days where anything remotely good has happened.

Might have happened.

I'm not sure how I feel about last night anymore. Naomi's point stands. Henry's the one who turned me into this. Why was I so

225

quick to forgive him? To trust him. To fuck him. Am I that desperate? Am I that stupid?

I should be angry with myself, but I'm too fragile for it. So instead I'm angry at her. At Naomi. Why couldn't she just leave it alone?

Elisa puts on the radio, flips through stations, finding mostly static. She gives up eventually, leaving us with only the grunts of the camper. Ilie puts his arm around Naomi. She lets him, but after a few minutes she unbuckles her seat belt and lies down, using his lap as a footrest. She closes her eyes.

"*'Every day, it's a-gettin' closer,'*" she whisper-sings, "*'going faster than a roller coaster. . . .'*"

She opens her eyes and looks at me.

Whatever she's trying to tell me, I don't understand. Our silent vows, our ESP—none of it's working. We're out of sync. She's right in front of me, but she's further from me now than she was when she was on the other side of the world.

When we were seventeen and had just gotten our licenses, Naomi would drive us around in her Jeep and we would listen to curated playlists, writing our favorite lyrics on our arms in pen, contemplating future tattoos that we never ended up getting. Sometimes we'd go to a cemetery for a quiet place to smoke weed. Sometimes we'd go to Hot Dog Johnny's, because it meant driving through Buttzville, which we always got a kick out of. We'd sit at the picnic tables outside and have hot dogs with sweet relish, split some crinkle-cut fries, and drink root beer out of frosty glasses. Once, on a rare Saturday when I didn't have to work, we went down to Seaside Heights, where we wandered the boardwalk, ate giant slices of greasy pizza, and mint soft-serve ice cream in waffle cones. We played Skee-Ball at Lucky Leo's until our arms were sore, until we ran out of money. We pointed out syringes on the beach.

She's not just my best friend. She's my youth. She knew me when

I was young—the purest, truest version of myself, before life got in the way. Before I knew about things like property taxes and deductibles and inflation, about the slow drain of ordinary days and the quick disappearance of ordinary years, about how men I'd never meet, with beliefs I don't share, could make decisions about what I can and can't do with my body. Before I gave in to doing what I had to and never what I wanted. Before all the choices that got me so far from the path I'd dreamt of. Before dreams became impractical.

She holds the best of me, and I think I hold the best of her.

But maybe that doesn't matter. Maybe it's too late to be our best selves. Maybe we've changed too much.

Maybe. Not maybe. I know we have. We're bloodthirsty creatures now. We're killers. We've bitten into a pulse. We've had a taste of something.

Henry reaches for me. I let him take my hand, thread his fingers through mine. He doesn't know who I was before two days ago. He knows me only as this.

I always thought mutual history was something precious, to be coveted. I never understood it could be an anchor. Our shared past won't necessarily help us move forward. It won't answer the question that needs to be answered, and fast.

How do we live now?

29

I t's a long drive, which provides me with the unfortunate opportunity to think. There's an awkward silence in the back of
the camper that everyone else seems to think is a comfortable
one. Nobody attempts to break it.

The van's faint grumble grows increasingly loud, but no one
comments. No one seems to notice except me.

"Is that normal?" I ask when the noise is accompanied by the
reek of exhaust.

Ilie and Henry exchange a look.

"What is it?"

They don't answer. More time passes. Henry turns around,
pulls back the curtain an inch, and peeks out the window.

"Elisa," he says, his tone startling. Urgent.

"I know," she says, making a sudden, sharp turn.

Naomi almost rolls onto the floor. "The fuck!"

"Put your seat belt on," I tell her.

"I thought we were invincible," she says, sitting back and fold-
ing her arms over her chest, annoyed that I scolded her. "What's
happening?"

The tires squeal as we take another tight turn, and the grumbling becomes beastly.

"Is something wrong?" I ask Henry.

He gets up and goes behind the curtain at the front. I hear him and Elisa whispering, but I can't make out what they're saying.

"Ilie," Naomi says, "what's going on?"

"Sounds like problem," he says with a shrug. "It will be okay."

"Has this happened before?" Naomi asks. She ducks her head under the curtain to look out the window. "We're on a bridge."

There's a loud *bang*, and it reminds me of the gunshots, the woman with the bite taken out of her face shooting at us, and I think of what Henry said about how as you get older everything has context—only, what if the context is unwanted? What if the context is composed of experiences you want to scrub from your memory with steel wool?

Elisa pulls the camper over. I join Naomi under the curtain and see train tracks. A short row of brick buildings, of abandoned storefronts. A ghost town.

"Where are we?" I ask.

"When are we?" Naomi says. "It looks like 1915. Do we have the right to vote here?"

"You know something? Everyone says now is bad time, but now is much better," Ilie says, getting up and opening the camper door. "There were worse times to be alive."

Naomi turns to me. "Well, fuck."

Everyone gets out of the camper. Across the tracks there's a coaling tower with a worrying lean, and beyond that nothing but woods. Spiky, winter-bare trees piercing the backs of rolling hills.

Elisa and Henry stand in front of the camper, which is now smoking.

"Wonderful," Tatiana says flatly, and I wonder why she didn't go with Miri and Costel, or anywhere else. She lowers her voice to a whisper, and I think she says, "Not here. Not this place again."

Ilie, who is typically brimming with happy-go-lucky enthusiasm, grows tense. He looks over his shoulder, pivots, looks, pivots, looks. His nervousness is severely unsettling.

"Is there . . ." Naomi starts, pawing at her throat, and suddenly I feel the pinch in my own throat sharpen. I've been thirsty for the last hour or so but have been too shy to ask for the blood that I know is in the cooler.

I imagine some do-gooder at a blood drive thinking they were saving innocent lives. I suppose in a way they were, by satiating our thirst. Still, I doubt this is what they had in mind.

Ilie scales the side of the camper and retrieves the cooler from the storage up top.

"We drink first," Tatiana says, slipping her arm into the cooler and taking out a bag of blood. "The new ones won't be able to stop once they start."

Henry tosses her his spile, and she punctures the bag, then takes only a sip before passing it to Elisa, who also takes just one sip. Naomi pants beside me, shuffling from side to side, forward and backward. She can hardly contain herself. Her thirst.

It is difficult to be patient when it's right there. When you can smell it.

Ilie takes two gulps, then Henry. He watches me while he drinks. Holds eye contact.

He passes it to me, and I want it—I want it badly—but Naomi's practically whimpering, and the last time I drank first, things ended poorly.

So I hand the bag to Naomi. She falls to her knees as she sucks it dry.

"What did I tell you?" Tatiana says, flipping her hair over her shoulder like a high school mean girl.

Elisa, Ilie, and Henry begin speaking to one another in a language I don't understand. Tatiana goes up to one of the storefronts, puts her face to the window. Naomi remains on the ground, clinging to the empty bag of blood. I turn toward the train tracks, which go on and on until they vanish into the night. I start to walk them, gravitating toward something, or to the nothingness. Toward the quiet. Away from the tension orbiting the smoking camper. Away from the cooler. Away from Naomi, the satisfaction of her bloodlust somehow amplifying the denial of mine.

I balance on one rail like I'm walking a tightrope. Focusing on not falling means I'm not focusing on my thirst. On how much I regret passing the bag to Naomi. On how my skin itches because it's dry. Because I'm dry. My insides feel brittle.

The voices and the smell of smoke fade behind me. I keep walking. I hold my arms out to help me balance. I watch my feet.

The rustle of branches catches me off guard and I slip, stumble off the tracks.

I look around. The trees sway. Only some of them, which means the disturbance isn't from the wind. There's something out there.

"Henry?" I say, though I know in my bones it's not him. The night coils around me. My heart plummets. "Naomi?"

She would answer. If it were her, she would say so.

I slowly turn on my heel, prepared to walk fast in the opposite direction, back toward the camper, but I'm met with an obstruction. Way down the track, between me and the ghost town and the vampires and Naomi, there's a pair of red eyes glaring out from the dark. Just floating there.

I go rigid.

For a moment I let myself believe that the eyes are not eyes but something else. For a moment I let myself believe they belong to an owl. For a moment I feel no fear because I remember what I am, but then I realize, if I am what I am, if I exist, what else does?

The eyes move toward me, two floating red orbs coming closer and closer until they belong to a face, until the face belongs to a body. Until there's a very old woman before me.

She smiles, her eyes no longer red but a watery blue. "Are you lost, dear?"

She speaks with a thick Southern accent.

"Um . . ."

"Let's not stand on the tracks. Wouldn't want to tempt fate. Not after we've already spat in her face. Suppose I should introduce myself," the woman says. "I'm Ms. Alice. What's your name, little bird?"

"It's, um, Sloane." My name comes out more like a question than like a statement. I'm not sure how to interact with this woman, if she's friend or foe. "Hi."

She's a little taller than me, though her spine and shoulders curve in at the top like a candy cane. Her hair is white and flossy, and her sweet face is deeply lined. She wears a red flannel shirt tucked into cargo pants, which are tucked into some rugged snow boots.

If it weren't for the red eyes that I watched magically turn blue, I might wonder why she isn't wearing a coat. But I know she's not cold because she's not human. If the eyes didn't give her away, her smell would. She doesn't smell human.

"Are you . . ." I start the question but find it's too ridiculous to finish. And maybe rude?

"I work for the park service," she says in her sugary drawl. "A volunteer. That's what I tell people, anyway. Ordinary people. This land is managed by the National Park Service. It's a historic landmark. Get the occasional visitor. The curious. The adventurous. They come out here, and some of 'em get lost. Some of 'em just don't ever find their way home. Such a shame."

Since she knew what I was getting at, a simple "yes" would have sufficed.

"I'm figuring you're not out here alone, are ya, birdie?"

"No," I say, but the word lodges in my throat. I cough.

"Poor dear," she says, putting her hand on my back as she starts to walk me toward the camper. "I'll take care of you. Always nice to have visitors."

It's bizarre to watch someone who looks so fragile move so nimbly.

The smell of smoke lets me know we're getting close to the camper, and soon I hear Elisa's and Ilie's and Henry's voices.

Ms. Alice clucks. "Now, where are my manners? Would ya like a drink?"

"I—I'm fine," I stutter.

"Come on, now. Ain't nothing to be ashamed of." She points to the coaling tower. "You can go on and help yourself if you don't like an audience."

She starts to rub my back, her bony hand pressing into me.

"I'm not . . ." I start, but my voice won't lie on my behalf. Its allegiance is to my throat, which aches in need.

"But you are, aren't ya, birdie?" she says. "I can tell."

"We have some. At the camper . . . Can we— Let me, um, ask Henry."

She puts her hands on my shoulders and turns me around. "Oh, I'm sure he won't mind. Ilie. Elisa. All of 'em. We're old friends. Besides, whatever you have will only get you so far. Trust me, birdie. If someone's offering, you take it."

I don't resist. If she knows them, then it's okay . . . right?

She leads me to the tower, to a rickety fire escape that she floats up, her boots hovering just above the steps. I cling to the banister, fearful that the whole thing is about to separate from the building and crash down to earth. Or that the building itself will collapse.

"No one thinks to look up here," Ms. Alice says, dipping into a window. "Don't dawdle. Not polite to keep an old lady waiting, and I am very old."

She laughs this horrifying, soul-demolishing cackle. It singes my eardrums, burns into me like acid, makes me want to crawl out of my skin. I'm tempted to jump from the fire escape, just to get as far away from the sound as possible. But I'm thirsty, and I'm a servant to my thirst. It compels me to follow Ms. Alice into the tower, to follow the promise of blood.

The inside of the tower is mostly open, a crumbling shell full of giant machinery, rusty chains and pipes, rotten wood. There's a narrow platform, and all that's beyond it is a three-story fall into industrial guts.

"Over here," Ms. Alice says, disappearing into the dark. I take a cautious step forward. The clang of metal echoes throughout the tower. "Why ya draggin' your feet? You want someone to drink or not?"

Not some*thing*. Some*one*.

I walk slowly in the direction Ms. Alice went, toward the clanging.

"Come closer," she says. "Closer, dear. Closer."

There's a click, followed by the fizz of electricity. She holds up a lantern, illuminating the scene.

There are three bodies chained up in a corner. They're naked, pale, emaciated, but not like the skeletal man. He looked unnatural. These people look like people. They're human. Or they were.

Two of them are silent and still, but the one in the middle is clearly breathing. I can practically see his lungs pulsing through his skin, which is pulled taut across his rib cage. His mouth is open, jaw slack. He's missing teeth and his tongue is shriveled and gray.

"The other two are almost empty. Scraps. Unless you want the marrow. You're welcome to it," she says. "But this one has plenty left. And as I'm sure you know, they taste better alive."

I now notice that all of the bodies are missing parts. The one on the left doesn't have arms. The one on the right has arms, but only one leg. And no foot.

"What's the matter, dear?" Ms. Alice asks me, bending down and snapping a finger off the body on the right. She presents it to me, holding it out on her open palm. "I'm all alone out here. I can't afford to be wasteful. I'm offering you something. Being a gracious host."

"Thank you," I say, my bottom lip trembling. "But I'm not . . . I don't . . ."

"You don't what?"

"No . . . no, thank you. I'm fine."

"Have you ever tried?" she asks, her eyes sparking red. "The taste of flesh? The crunch of bones between your teeth? Blood is one thing, but over time . . . well, I developed other appetites."

She bites into the finger like it's a stalk of celery.

"I think you should," she says, chewing with her mouth open. "I think you'll like it. It'll quench your thirst. Fill ya right up."

I shake my head. I'm thirsty—I'm so thirsty—but seeing what's in front of me, I'd rather starve. I'd rather die. I won't participate in this.

"Have a taste," she says, once again offering me the finger, now half-eaten.

"Alice." Henry appears beside me, his big eyes alert. His expression unmoors me.

"What about you, handsome? So kind of you to join us. Can't interest you in anything?"

235

"What are you doing, Alice?" he says, stepping in front of me, putting himself between me and Alice and the bodies. Shielding me.

"Getting your new bird some sustenance."

"We're not here for that."

"Let me guess. Car trouble again," she says. "And here I thought y'all might have come around to see me. Stopped being so uptight. It's been so long. You promised you'd come visit."

She deposits what remains of the finger between her lips, goes on talking with her mouth full. "You're lucky you weren't turned any later, birdie. I'm out here all by my lonesome in these woods. Can ya blame me for getting myself some company?" She gestures back to the bodies.

"You're alone *because* of the company you keep, Alice," Henry says. "The company you choose. What you do to them."

She clucks. "I like what I like. Why should I apologize for it? Why should I deprive myself? Anyone who sees me, they think nothin' of me. Treat me like I'm fragile, or stupid. Or they're repulsed by me, by this body. This body I'll have forever and ever."

She gets close to me. "So I take *gooooooooood* care of it. Of myself. My body."

She wipes her mouth on her sleeve, then walks past us. "Go on. Cast your stones. But you, birdie—you should know, to live as a woman in this world, you can give and give and get used up, suffer the emptiness, or you can start taking. And I ain't suffering. I already done mine, my fair share. So I fill myself up. *Num num num num num.*"

I wince, and she cackles.

"You're lookin' at me like I'm some kind of monster, but we're the same, you and me. You just ain't ready to admit it to yourself. The sooner you accept what ya are, the better. Because maybe you're fooling yourself, but you ain't fooling me. You want this. You're scared of how bad you want it. Afraid of what would happen if you tried a bite of flesh. Of how much you'd like it."

She steps out of the window onto the fire escape. "Come on, now. Don't try my patience."

30

The journey down the fire escape is even more trying than the journey up. I'm light-headed, and I keep wanting to turn around, to go help those people—or the man who's still alive, at least. But I know I can't save him. And even if I were to go back up those stairs, I'd probably just end up doing something I'd regret. Draining him.

Maybe he'd be relieved to die, would welcome the release.

Maybe that's just what I'd tell myself.

When we get to the bottom of the fire escape, Henry offers me a smoke. The two of us hang back while Ms. Alice heads over to the camper, her hands on her hips.

"You shouldn't wander off, Sloane," he says.

"I . . . She knew all of your names," I whisper, my voice rough. "She knew you."

"We've met before," he says.

"Did you . . . Do you . . . *know* her? Know what goes on here?"

"I'm sorry you had to see that," he says, lighting my cigarette for me.

"I don't know what to say." I take a long drag.

"Some like us don't stop at blood. Once they develop a taste . . ." He pauses, shaking his head. "You've met someone like Alice before. A feeder. The night we met. The man in the cellar. We'd encountered him in passing. When you live as long as us, paths cross. We were in New York and needed a place to stay. When we arrived at the house, we found he'd been . . . he'd broken a rule. That's why he was down there. That's why we deprived him of blood. Retribution."

"What rule?"

"He'd taken a girl. Several girls. Young girls."

"Christ," I say, collapsing onto the bottom step of the fire escape. "This just keeps getting worse."

"But we're not like that," Henry says, sitting next to me. "That's not how we live."

"Okay, but not being cannibals or child murderers is a pretty low bar."

"When you put it that way . . ."

"It's not the phrasing. It's the truth," I say, anxiously pawing at my face. "What I just saw up there—what am I supposed to do with that? With knowing she's out here eating people. I just have to go on with this knowledge? Forever?"

"There are many horrors in this world we have to live with."

"I know. But before, I could be the victim," I say, surprising myself. I hadn't realized it until it came flying out of my mouth. Hadn't realized that part of me liked being cheated on, because it gave me an excuse to feel sorry for myself, and ever since my fall, I've looked for any excuse for self-pity, any opportunity to feel like one mistake cost me everything, like the world was a ruthless and unfair place and there was nothing I could do about it, because admitting defeat felt like it protected me from losing more than I already had. But now I've made more than one mistake, and my whole narrative is fucked. "I'm just overwhelmed. And—and what she said about me. About . . ."

I can't repeat it, the insinuation that I might turn into what she is. That I could ever let my thirst bring me to the point of such depraved overindulgence.

"You can't listen to her," he says.

"It scares me," I say, my voice small and quaky. "The thirst scares me."

"Let me show you," he says, kneeling in front of me.

"Show me what?"

"How we live without killing. Without hurting anyone. How we get our blood," he says. "We'll find a blood bank nearby, a hospital. We've done it countless times before. Not a drop of blood given unwillingly. I promise. Let me do this for you."

"Why?" I ask, my exhaustion giving way to my cynicism. "Why are you trying to be good to me? Is it guilt? Don't you get it? Your words, your promises—they don't mean anything. I don't know how to believe you, how to trust you. I don't even know how to trust myself."

He shakes his head, pushes his hair out of his face. "You ask me why. Do you not see it? Do you not feel it? Am I imagining this? What's between us? If I am, tell me."

I sigh. "No. I . . ."

"How can I earn your trust?" He puts his hands on my knees and pulls them apart, and he leans into the space, into me, and he kisses me. "This way? Will you trust my mouth? Will you allow me to prove myself? Prove that I mean what I say. May I?"

It feels unnatural to release the millstone of cynicism and grant myself permission to be in this moment, not to think of circumstance, of consequence, of fear or shame, the potential of future shame. Unnatural, awkward, wrong. So wrong.

But then, all of a sudden, it isn't anymore. Or it is but I just don't care.

"Go on, then," I say, my throat still dry and the words raspy and hushed. "Prove it."

His hands slide under my shirt, his skin on my skin. He unbuttons my jeans, kisses down my side, and then sinks between my legs. Right out in the open, at the bottom of the fire escape, in the shadow of the coaling tower.

My back arches as the rapture jolts my body, my being, and I look up at the dark velvet sky, manage to clear my mind of everything except this: *How do we know the difference between a curse and a cure?*

By the time we get back to the camper, it's no longer spewing fumes into the atmosphere. Ms. Alice appears to have fixed it. She chats up Naomi, who looks perfectly content to be in conversation with her. Charmed, even. Blissfully ignorant of what I know about Alice. Ilie sits with Elisa on the steps to one of the abandoned stores, and Tatiana is a few feet away, drinking what I assume is blood out of a flask.

"Look who it is. And here I thought you two had gotten lost," Ms. Alice says, turning to me and Henry. "Y'all owe me some thanks. You'll be able to drive on outta here. Though I don't know how far you'll get. The sun won't wait for you, you know."

"Thank you, Ms. Alice," Elisa says, standing and walking toward the camper.

"Yes. Thank you very, very much," Ilie says, following Elisa.

"Aw," Alice says, shuffling over and pulling one of Elisa's curls straight.

"So," Naomi says to me, "where'd you disappear to?"

I just shake my head.

"We're leaving," Henry says, going to open the van's driver's-side door. It's locked.

"Hold on, now. Not so fast," Ms. Alice says, dangling the keys to the camper over her head, unleashing something rank and insidious that permeates the air. "'Cause I ain't do it for nothin'. Last time it was a favor, and I was happy to do it. But you said you'd come back to see me sometime, share a meal. You *lied*. So this time—this time I want something in return. And I want it now."

"What?" Henry says, with a grimness that startles me.

"Well, since I'm such a sweet old lady, I'll give you a choice. You can either give me all the blood you got on ya, and I know ya got some because your little birdie told me," she says, pointing to me, making me instantly queasy, "or . . . I'll take this one."

She sidles up to Naomi, who goes rigid. Alice reaches out and lifts her chin. Gently at first. But then she clamps on, grabbing Naomi's jaw. "I like the look of ya. I reckon you look like I did once upon a time, years and years and years and years ago."

"You can let go of her now," I say, my voice doing that weird thing it did with the gas-station clerk. I sound different. Frightening.

Ms. Alice doesn't budge. She lets her eyes shift to the side, to me. She smiles a syrupy smile, but her eyes flare red. "Oh dear, is that how you speak to your elders? Tsk, tsk, tsk."

Alice releases her grip on Naomi's jaw, begins to stroke her hair. I hadn't noticed until now how long her fingernails are. How sharp. "Was I too rough with ya, sweetheart? I'm sorry. You'll have to forgive me. I ain't used to people. I'm so lonely up here. So lonely, and with so much time to be lonely."

"It's all right, Ms. Alice," Naomi says, instantly forgiving her, granting her the benefit of the doubt. To Naomi, Ms. Alice is a wounded bird. A creature deserving of empathy.

"Such a dear," Alice says. "You want to stay here with me, sweetheart? I'll teach ya how to be. How to *really* be. This crowd doesn't get it like me. It's good huntin' around here. We could eat good together."

"No," Henry says vitriolically.

"No?" Ms. Alice says. "I wasn't talkin' to you, was I?"

"We won't be separated," he says. "Naomi is with us. We'll give you two bags. That's all we can spare."

Ms. Alice's eyes burn red again. This time they stay that way. "That wasn't one of the choices. No deal."

Tatiana tucks her flask into her pocket and struts right up to Ms. Alice. "That's our best offer. I suggest you take it."

"Or what?" Ms. Alice gives a brief, bitter laugh. "No one's got any morals these days. No sense of gratitude or respect. But I'm stickin' to my guns. I get what I want, or you don't get your vehicle."

It happens so fast. Tatiana lunges for the keys, and Alice backhands her. I barely process the shock of the slap before Tatiana grabs Ms. Alice by the throat.

Alice scratches at Tatiana's face, so Henry takes her wrists, holds them behind her. I have to remind myself that they're not violently assaulting a helpless old woman. It's not what it looks like. But Naomi doesn't understand this. She didn't see what I saw, doesn't know about Ms. Alice's appetites.

"Hey!" she says.

Ms. Alice's red eyes shoot over to Naomi. There's an opportunity for manipulation, and she doesn't hesitate. "Please. They're hurting me."

"Let go of her!" Naomi shouts, pulling at Henry's arm. "I'll stay! I'll stay. I'll . . ."

Distracted by Naomi's declaration, Henry must loosen his grip, because Ms. Alice's hands break free. They're quick, flittering up to Tatiana's face. To her eyes.

Ms. Alice's thumbnails are atrociously overgrown, impossibly pointed. Tatiana screams, and then Ms. Alice is free and Tatiana is on the ground, silk pajamas soaking through with snow as she holds her face in her hands. She moans to herself, speaking in French.

"My girl," Ms. Alice says to Naomi, smiling sweetly again, arms open wide in anticipation of an embrace.

Naomi stumbles backward.

"Come on, now, darlin'. Oh, I think you'll do quite nicely. Anyone happens upon you in these woods, they'll be happy to follow you anywhere, I reckon." With her smiling like that, I can see there's skin between her teeth.

I wonder if Naomi sees it, too.

"She's not staying," I say. "We'll give you the blood. You can take the blood."

Tatiana spits at the ground. Her eyes are intact but a goopy pink, her face streamed with black mascara. She looks to Henry and says something to him in a foreign language.

"Here!" Ilie says. He and Elisa have the cooler. They open it, toss a bag of blood at Alice's feet, then another. But she doesn't seem interested anymore. She's focused on Naomi.

"I'll stay," Naomi says. "It's fine. I'll stay."

"What are you doing?" I ask her. "Stop. I'm not leaving you here. Not with her."

"What does it matter?" she says, uncharacteristically resigned.

"You heard her. She's stayin'," Ms. Alice says. Her body shakes, and suddenly she has Naomi by the hair, pulling her toward the woods. "No changing your mind on me, darlin'."

The first time Naomi was arrested, it was for assault. She came to my dorm to comfort me after Smith circulated the naked pictures I'd sent him. She told me she was going to step out to smoke, but she went and found Smith and punched him in the face and smashed his phone. This all happened outside, on the street, so instead of the campus security it was NYPD who showed up, and they didn't exactly care that Naomi was a nineteen-year-old girl. I finally emerged from my dorm when a classmate alerted me to the situation. The whole incident only brought me more notoriety at school, and sometimes I wonder if that's what really set me off self-medicating. Because it's always been easier to blame Naomi. Because whenever she tries to save me, she makes things worse.

But she does try to save me. It can be a burden to be loved the way she loves me. I'll never be sure if I deserve it. I can only love her back the best I can.

Ms. Alice yanks her hard by the hair, and Naomi winces, and then I'm there, and I've got Ms. Alice's arm in my mouth, and I bite down with all the force I have, and she screams this awful scream and falls back away from me.

Her blood is in my mouth, and it tastes like nothing, but that only makes me angry. Resentful. Rabid. Makes me want to chew her up and spit her out.

"Y'all belong on leashes," Ms. Alice says, cradling her arm, pressing on the wound to stanch the bleeding.

I remember what Henry said. *We bleed. There is blood in our veins. We have thick skin, but we aren't impenetrable. We need to be careful; we do not have much to spare. It's painful to lose.*

"Fine," Ms. Alice barks, tossing the keys and scooping up the two bags of blood that lie in the snow. "Get outta here. Get! But don't come back again. I'm tired. . . ."

Her voice breaks, and I feel sorry for her. I shouldn't. She's a murderous cannibal. But she's alone. And she's been alone for who knows how long? She could be alone forever. Maybe loneliness makes monsters of us all.

Maybe it's no excuse.

The bland stickiness of her blood lingers on my tongue and the roof of my mouth. I'm disgusted by it, and at myself for attacking her like that. I took from her body, a body she feeds with bodies. I bit into her. I cannibalized a cannibal.

With a final cry, Ms. Alice scuttles toward the hills. I see her red eyes watching us from the distant trees.

There's a moment of silence before Henry reaches down, picks the keys up off the ground, and says, "Let's go."

Elisa puts her arm around Naomi and loads her into the camper.

Ilie helps Tatiana to her feet. She brushes the snow from her legs and comes toward me.

"You are a savage," she says, before kissing me on the cheek. I'm not sure when she had her change of heart. Not sure when these strangers started to feel like family.

She gets into the camper, then Ilie. Henry waits for me. I walk past him without eye contact, embarrassed by my violent outburst, my savagery. He sits beside me inside the camper, puts a hand on my thigh. A simple act of reassurance that could alleviate my shame if I let it.

"Everyone in?" Elisa asks from the front seat.

"We're here," Ilie says. "Let's go!"

I'm fatigued from the scuffle, and I can no longer support the weight of my own head on my neck, so I rest it on Henry's shoulder.

"Sometimes there are weirdos," Ilie says. "Ms. Alice is weirdo. Not so good with people. In more way than one."

"Mm," Naomi says, shuddering. "How come she doesn't turn someone? Make herself a friend?"

"She's not old enough," Henry says.

"But she's old," Naomi says.

"In appearance. She was turned late. Cruelly. She was abandoned by the one who changed her. Left to fend for herself. She let her thirst consume her. She still has not learned the restraint it takes to turn someone. It takes centuries to master, and it can only be done so many times. When you turn someone, you give them part of yourself. Your essence. Your soul. If you give away too much, there will be nothing left."

I almost ask him how many people he's turned but decide I don't want to know.

"Right," Naomi says.

"Why did you volunteer to stay?" I ask. "Why would you do that?"

She shrugs. "If it was gonna be a whole big thing, I figured it'd be, like, easier if I just hung out with her for a while."

"She fucking eats people," I hear myself say. There's a tense pause, and I'm nauseous remembering the thick, rubbery texture of Ms. Alice's skin as I bit down through it.

"Wait. What?" Naomi asks. "What did you just say?"

"Never mind. You're better off not knowing."

"You're not going to tell me?" she says, her tone combative. "Okay. You know why I volunteered to stay? Because you don't seem to want me around, Sloane. You've admitted you think all of this is my fault. And you've ditched me two nights in a row now. Just gone off—"

"I guess now you know what it feels like."

"Really? Really?"

"How can you say I don't want you around? You have no idea what I just saved you from."

"I guess now *you* know what it feels like. What I've been doing for you for the last twenty fucking years."

"Forget it," I say. "Just forget it."

"Okay, sure. Sure, Sloane. Let's just bury it and see how that works out."

"Let's."

"Do not fight, loves," Ilie says.

"We're not fighting," we snap in unison.

247

Ilie raises his eyebrows, puts his hands up in surrender.

"Sorry, Ilie," I say.

Naomi sighs and lies down, using Ilie's lap as a pillow. She closes her eyes, and he plays with her hair.

After a while, once Naomi starts softly snoring, Henry asks me, "Are you all right?"

"No," I say. "No, I'm not."

I went through a phase when I read obsessively about the Donner Party. Cannibalism seemed so abstract, about as real to me as Santa Claus. To witness it was another bend in my reality that I'm not totally sure I can withstand. And this tension with Naomi, the wedge our thirst is driving between us, feels just as dangerous as the thirst itself.

"What are you thinking?" he asks.

"I'm thinking I wish that never happened," I say. "That I didn't know about Alice or feeders. That I didn't attack her like that. Bite her like that."

"Why? You were defending your friend."

"Yeah, but . . ." I want to believe there's a way forward here. Buy into this teenage dream of freedom and love and sex and friendship and excitement and no responsibility, no consequence, no guilt, no shame. I want to believe in a genuine second chance that won't end in disaster. But what if existing this way is too much for me to handle? What if the blood stops going down so smoothly, or if it starts going down so smoothly that I forget what it is that I'm subsisting on? What if it costs me Naomi? What then?

"I promised you. I will show you how we can live," he says, raising my hand to his lips, and he kisses my knuckles. "Will you let me? Will you trust me? Will you try?"

I want to, but it's too painful. And he can't promise me that I will ever learn how to live with myself.

31

We make it to North Carolina but not to Wilmington. The morning sun forces us off the road, bright and yellow, a cheery antagonist.

"We can stay here today," Elisa says, pulling into the parking lot of a Comfort Inn. "Or we can go to a campsite. Find a shady spot. All sleep in the back."

"No," Tatiana says. "There are too many of us. I want a proper mattress. Soft linens."

I doubt she's going to get either at a Comfort Inn, but since I don't want to sleep in the back of the camper, I keep my mouth shut.

Elisa parks in front of the hotel, and we wait under the awning while she and Henry get us rooms. Ilie kindly unloads our luggage and the cooler, with its lone remaining bag of blood. I watch Naomi twitch in its presence, unable to take her eyes off it.

Tatiana sips from her flask. Her eyes are hidden behind a pair of glamorous cat-eye sunglasses. She offers the flask to me, and I shake my head.

"No?" she asks. "You don't want?"

I do want. That's the problem. "How are your eyes?"

249

"They sting," she says. She tilts her head to the side, contemplative. Then she reaches out and tips my chin up. "You are unhappy when you deprive yourself. You are unhappy when you indulge. You are unhappy in your bones. Henry will not cure that. He will suffer trying. As your friend has."

She cradles my face, then leans in like she's about to kiss me. She whispers in my ear, "If only you could stare at your reflection. Be face-to-face with the one who holds your joy hostage. Perhaps then you could forgive her. Perhaps then you could hope to fall in love with your future."

She does kiss me. Kisses my shocked, open mouth. Her lips are impossibly soft, and she smells like roses.

"Eternity is a long time to wallow, *ma chérie*," she says, lowering her sunglasses to show me her eyes, which are oozing, crusted with pinkish gunk. "Too long."

She pushes her sunglasses up her nose and turns away from me. I touch my lips, now slick with gloss. Her words snake through my brain, and I feel naked, exposed. I zip up my coat, as if that'll do anything to cover me.

"Keys!" Elisa says, whimsically leaping through the hotel's automatic doors, holding up three key cards. "It is not the castle, but it will do."

The hotel lobby is small, dimly lit, with linoleum floors and a drop ceiling. It smells strongly of bleach, but at least that means it's clean. Elisa presses the button for the elevator. Naomi glares at the woman behind the counter, who smiles politely and waves, wonderfully unaware that the person she's greeting so amiably wants nothing more than to rip her neck apart with her teeth.

"Nay," I say, taking her arm.

"I'm fine," she says, pulling away from me.

The elevator dings, the doors open, and the six of us cram into the elevator.

I realize we're a sight—an eccentric bunch. Tatiana in her silk pajamas, Ilie in one of his hipster-pirate getups, Elisa in a long, flowing dress. Henry, Naomi, and I look relatively normal, though a little dirty. None of us are properly dressed for the weather—it's below freezing out. If we don't want to draw attention to ourselves, we're doing a pretty bad job.

Our rooms are at the end of the hall on the second floor. They're all next to one another. Elisa and Tatiana take the first. Ilie stands outside the second, looking at Naomi, who looks at me.

"Whatever you want to do," I say. The tension between us is supremely icky, and I hope she goes with Ilie so I can escape with Henry. So he can distract me from everything with his mouth.

"All right, Ilie," Naomi says, slipping her arms around his waist and giving him a tight hug. "Let's have ourselves a sleepover."

"So fun," Ilie says, smiling.

Henry and I take the last room. It's nicer than I anticipated. The carpet is torn up in some spots and the wallpaper is peeling, but it's clean. There are two queen beds, which presents an awkward predicament. Do we use the two beds? Or do we share one?

There's a knock on the door, and my stomach flips before I hear Ilie's voice.

"You have the cooler," he says. "Naomi needs to drink."

Henry opens the door and there they all are. Ilie, Naomi, Elisa, and Tatiana. They plop down on the beds, make themselves comfortable as Henry gets out the bag of blood. He takes the plastic cups from the bathroom, pierces the bag with his spile, and pours two even. They get passed around, with Naomi and I getting the cups last.

I consider abstaining, attempting to resist my thirst. But deprivation doesn't seem to work. Any attempt I've ever made to punish myself has only led me straight to my next mistake.

Also, it's not lost on me that this is it, the last of our supply. I don't know when we'll get more. How we'll get more. Maybe this goes unnoticed by the others. It definitely goes unspoken.

I bring one of the cups to my lips, and I close my eyes and I drink. Let it in. A taste like no other. An immaculate medicine. It settles me.

"The day is young," Ilie says. "Let us stay awake."

Tatiana yawns. "I am exhausted."

"Me, too," Elisa says. She gets up on tiptoe, pirouettes, curtsies, then says, "Sleep sweet."

Tatiana follows her out, pausing in the doorway to say, "Ilie, leave the lovers in peace."

I feel my cheeks go red.

"You are all no fun. Naomi, let us go have fun. We can watch TV. We can run around hotel, pretend we are spies," he says.

"Do you have drugs, by any chance?"

"Of course I have drugs," he says, laughing.

She jumps on him, and he piggybacks her out into the hall. Henry closes the door behind them.

"She'll be okay with Ilie," he says. "He's smarter than he seems."

"If you say so."

"I do." He takes my face in his hands to kiss me. He stops to yawn. "Sorry."

"You don't have to apologize," I say, catching his yawn. "I'm spent."

"Should we sleep?"

Looking at him, I get a very good idea that I'm almost too shy to speak out loud. Almost. "Could we shower first?"

He grins. His fox grin. His cat-that-got-the-canary grin.

We undress each other. We soap each other, use our hands to create a lather. We look at each other. We kiss each other. We clean each other. It's an intimacy like I've never experienced. Not even in all my years with . . . Joel.

For a second, I couldn't even remember his name.

A small part of me wonders if I should feel bad about it, acknowledges that I have yet to process or fully comprehend the loss of that relationship. But most of me is busy washing Henry's hair.

After we get out of the shower and towel each other off, we get into bed, one bed, and he holds me. His skin is still a little wet.

We lie in nectarous silence for a long time.

Then he says, "Do you want to hear my sad song?"

I nod, then rest my head on his chest, listening to his heart, the steady thump of it.

"I was a prince, once. Centuries ago. Far away from here," he says, his accent shifting, voice going deeper. "I have seen many battles. Fought many wars. I have killed. I have won. I have lost. I was married to a girl whom I did not choose, did not love, who did not choose me or love me, who died too young. My father was cruel, and my younger brothers resented me. I had no friends whom I could trust. I thought I would die alone on a battlefield. I became this so I would not, so I might prove myself to a kingdom that no longer exists. Be honored by history, which I know now does not remember me. I have spent centuries drifting in the dark, hating who I'd been, unsure of who I'd become."

He pauses.

"You remind me of what it once felt like to step into sunlight," he says. "To feel warmth. To experience true brightness. All that's tangible and intangible."

It's the most beautiful thing anyone has ever said to me, and I wish I knew how to respond. I wish I could believe his words, meet him where he is. I wish I knew how to trust this stranger—all his mischief, all his danger, all his beauty, and the pull between us that could be love.

My throat yearns, not for blood, but for sound, for the right words. I need to say something. I need . . .

"Thank you," I tell him. *Thank you. Thank you?*

He grins a new grin. Not goofy or devious. Despondent. The grin of a man on a sinking ship, admiring the sky.

"Get some sleep," he says, reaching over to the nightstand and grabbing his cigarettes. "I'm going out to smoke."

"Okay. All right."

He gets out of bed, gets dressed, kisses me on the forehead. Then he's gone, and I'm alone, and I wonder what I should have said to him. Anything but "thank you."

I close my eyes, and I see Ms. Alice, the skin between her teeth. I hear the echo of her horrible laugh. I remember her blood. The blood in the tumbler. Lee's blood on Naomi's lips. The blood of the man at the rest stop. Matthew's blood, our first victim, left in the woods behind our cottage.

I remember my reflection, the last time I saw it, will ever see it, in the dirty mirror at the lake house. I picture Naomi, imagine her across the hall with Ilie, snorting illicit substances off each other. And Elisa, her curls haloing her face, pulling her sleep mask down over her eyes. Tatiana, sprawled across the bed in her silk pajamas, beautiful and bitchy and maybe even wise.

Perhaps I could hope to fall in love with my future. This future. With these people.

With him. Henry.

If I can get past the guilt and the fear. Accept my thirst.

I open my eyes and stare at the empty cooler at the foot of the bed, weary myself until I drift off to sleep.

When I wake up, Henry isn't beside me. At first, I assume he took the other bed, offended by my tepid response to his romantic declaration comparing me to his fond human memories of sunlight.

But once I get the courage to look over, I see he isn't there. He isn't in the room at all. I don't think he ever came back.

The clock says it's four seventeen p.m. It could be wrong, but if it isn't, he's been gone all day.

I slide out of bed and put on pants, a T-shirt, my boots without socks.

When I open the door of our room, Naomi's standing there.

I slam my hand to my chest. "You startled me."

She still wears her Penny Lane jacket, despite its being blood-stained. The stains have faded to an inconspicuous brown, though. No one would assume it's blood. Hopefully.

"What are you doing out here?" I ask her.

"I don't know. Ask Dracula," she says, pointing to her room.

"What?"

"Your boyfriend knocked on our door, like, half an hour ago. They're all in there plotting. I went out for a cigarette," she says, tossing a pack up in the air. "Don't have to worry about them killing me anymore. You know how I love to look for that juicy sweet silver lining."

"What do you mean, plotting?" I say. "Let's not stand in the hall."

I pull her into my room and close the door behind us.

"Sharing a bed, I see," she says, flopping down on the other, still-made queen.

"What did he say? When he came in."

"They're robbing a bank," she says casually, lighting a cigarette. "I fucking missed smoking. Lollipops? What was I thinking?"

"Are you joking?"

"Blue raspberry doesn't hit the same, you know?"

"No, I mean about the bank. And put that out—you're going to set off the alarm."

She groans but does as I ask, getting up and putting the cigarette out in the bathroom sink. "They're robbing a bank tonight."

"Are you being serious? I can't tell."

"Sorry. *We're* robbing a bank tonight," she says, leaning against the wall. "A blood bank. And yes, I'm serious."

"What specifically did he say?"

"He knocked on the door, woke us up. Woke up Tatiana and Elisa. They all huddled in our room. He said he found a blood bank and they're going to rob it tonight. There was some hesitance because it's, like, short notice. I gather they usually plan these things well in advance. Ilie was, like, what's the rush? Henry didn't say but I think we all know."

"Know what?"

She gestures to me. "The rush."

"Me?"

"Well, and that." She points to the cooler. "Ms. Alice cleared us out."

"I don't want to hold up a blood bank."

"Seems like it's going to be more *Ocean's Eleven* than *Bonnie and Clyde*."

I fall on the unmade bed and put my head in my hands. She sits herself beside me.

"This clearly isn't their first time," she says. "We'll get what we need without . . ." She mimes chomping into me. "Sip it out of a cup like it's Diet Dr Pepper. What is Dr Pepper a doctor of, exactly?"

"I don't know. Physics," I say, flatly.

She laughs. "Buck up. We're not expected to participate in the heist. I have a feeling they want us to stay out of the way. It's kind of romantic. Him robbing a bank for you. Like a hot Dracula John Dillinger."

"He's not Dracula," I say.

"Do you know that for sure, or . . . ?"

I squeeze my head between my hands, close my eyes, clench my jaw.

"You don't want to talk about real shit, hash it out, so I'm keeping it light. Surface level."

"Should we try talking them out of it?" I ask, standing.

"Why? This is what you wanted, isn't it? I mean, under these circumstances. Obviously."

"Obviously."

"They're going in after hours. It's going to be more of a breaking-and-entering situation. A stealth operation," she says, eyes sparking.

"Are you into this?"

"Kind of, yeah," she says, swinging around so she's lying sideways on the bed, posing like a starlet. "Outlaws. Vampire bandits. What's not to like?"

"Other than all the bloodshed?" I ask.

"That's the best part," she says. "Kidding."

"Are you?"

She's suddenly, eerily, dead serious. "I don't know how to make it right, Sloane. I'm scared, too. I have my regrets. I've done plenty of things that I'm not proud of over these last few days. But what am I gonna do? I can't change it. What's done is done," she says, sitting up. "I can only move forward."

I remember Henry's observation. *She lives as though she's running out of time.* I used to think Naomi never considered consequence, that she felt no shame, or fear. I can see now that I misunderstood. She's burdened by the same things that burden me. Only her solution is to live harder, move faster, attempt to outrun, while I hide away, make myself small and static. I thought she was the reckless one. The dangerous one. But maybe I just wanted to believe that I wasn't.

"You're the person I love most in this world. I don't want to lose you. I need you. You can't be mad at me forever," she says. "Literally forever."

"I'm not mad at you, Nay," I say, and as the words leave my lips, I realize they're true. It's easy to project anger at the person closest to you when the person you're really angry at is yourself.

"You can't be mad at yourself forever either. You know that, right?"

I flip her off. "Mind reader."

She takes my hand and gives it a squeeze, and it's like we're in the back of Meghan's mom's minivan, like the moment we became friends. The moment we found home.

"I'm sorry, Sloane. For all of it."

"Me, too, hoss."

"Huh. Yeah, you can pull off 'hoss.' I mean, I kind of thought it might be my thing now, but . . ."

"I feel like I actually can't pull it off, but you don't want to tell me that, so you're using it so I won't use it. Taking a bullet for me."

"Nah," she says. "What do you say? Should we go crash their party? Find out the grand plan?"

"I guess."

She leads me out of the room, across the hall. She takes out her key card but pauses before opening the door.

"Wait," she whispers. "First, you have to tell me what's going on with you and probably-not Dracula."

"Now?"

"Yeah. Real quick. Spill it," she says. The way she's looking at me, her stupidly beautiful face bright as a firework, her giddiness contagious, I'm defenseless. So I tell her. And she gasps and giggles and we're teenagers again and everything is perfect and normal until I remember it isn't.

32

When Naomi opens the door, the room falls silent. Ilie sits on the floor, Tatiana and Elisa are on the beds, and Henry hovers over them. They stare at us.

"Hello, loves," Ilie says after a beat.

"Hey," Naomi says. "Are we interrupting?"

"They shouldn't come," Tatiana says. "They will mess it up somehow."

"Thanks!" Naomi says, maybe offended. I'm not. Tatiana's probably right.

"You think we should separate?" Elisa asks.

"We're not separating," Henry says. "They'll come. They'll be lookouts."

"Yes, lookouts," Ilie says. "Good idea."

"It's getting late," Henry says. "Gather your things."

He strides past us out the door without acknowledging me. I follow him across the hall into our room.

"Henry," I say as the door slams behind us.

He grabs my suitcase and the empty cooler. "Do you have everything?"

"I think so. But, hey. Wait. Slow down," I say. He won't look at me. There's a shift in his posture, in how he carries himself. He's tense. "I didn't mean to . . . I don't know—pressure you into a blood heist tonight."

"This is what we do." He attempts to pass me, but the space between me and the wall is too narrow.

"Wait. Henry." I reach out and turn his face to mine.

Our eyes meet, and he sighs. "Let me keep my promise. Let me do something good for you. Please."

My mouth falls open, but no sound emerges, no words. He has once again rendered me speechless. "I . . ."

"We need to leave now so we arrive just as it closes. The timing is important."

I don't have an argument, since this whole thing is motivated by me. By my angst over how we acquire blood. By my blabbing to Ms. Alice about our supply. So I step aside and let him pass. I trail him out into the hall, where Tatiana and Elisa whisper to each other. Ilie opens the door for Naomi, who dances out of their room wearing Tatiana's cat-eye sunglasses, which I assume she stole.

"How do I look?" she asks me.

"Like a reclusive movie star who's murdered every husband she's ever had."

"That's *exactly* what I was going for."

We all head to the elevator and ride it down. Tatiana snatches her sunglasses back from Naomi, who pouts. We step out into the lobby, and thankfully no one's there. Because there's a phantom ache in my throat. I'm thirsty. I wonder if Naomi is, too.

We go through the doors, emerge from under the awning, and bristle at the light. The sun faints into the horizon and orange hues seep through the trees, branches reaching up toward a purple darkness. I beg the night to come faster. We need it. Need its cover.

Naomi lights a cigarette, takes two drags, then tosses it into some dirty parking-lot snow.

"This isn't exactly an inconspicuous getaway car," I mumble to Naomi as we climb into the camper.

Ilie's in the back with Tatiana. He's completely naked and she's lying across the seats with her arms crossed—bored or displeased or both.

"You could have knocked. I am modest, you know," Ilie says, winking.

"Um . . ." I say, trying to avert my eyes, but the space is too small.

He pulls on a pair of slacks. "This is my new look. Regular guy. Very professional."

"It's a good look," Naomi says, sitting opposite Tatiana. I squeeze in beside her.

"Everyone ready?" Elisa asks rhetorically, turning on the radio before anyone can answer. It's an oldies station playing "La Bamba" by Ritchie Valens.

"Oh, hell yes," Naomi says, shimmying.

"This is a bad sign," I whisper.

"How?" she asks.

"First we hear a Buddy Holly song in the hotel shuttle. Now Ritchie Valens."

"It's not like we're on our way to the airport," she says, which shuts me up.

Tatiana yawns, stretches to sit. She wears jeans and a sweater, and it's the first time I've seen her in anything other than lingerie or pajamas. She pulls her cherry red hair into a bun while she looks from me to Naomi and back to me.

"Do not involve yourselves," she says, "if things go wrong."

"What do you mean, if things go wrong?" I ask.

She rolls her eyes.

"We will handle," Ilie says, zipping up a navy fleece. "That is all she means."

"Got it," Naomi says.

Ilie ties his hair back, pulls on a beanie, clears his throat, and in a startlingly good American accent asks, "How do I look?"

"So handsome," Naomi says, swooning. "Like an Ivy League dropout who ended up modeling for J.Crew."

I doubt he understands the reference, but he laughs anyway. He grabs her by the waist, tilts his head so he can go for her neck, kiss her there. She gives a playful squeal. I wonder if she misses Lee or if he seems like a distant memory, the way Joel does. It's been five days, I think, since I last saw him, but it might as well be fifty years.

He'll move on fast in my absence. Maybe he'll cheat on the next one, or maybe he'll be happier with her. Maybe he'll be faithful. Maybe he'll put all my things in a box in the basement, and eventually his new wife will donate them or throw them away. All the things I was attached to, that made it seem too difficult to leave. My things. The house. The peach tree.

My whole world, everything I cared so much about, abandoned, and it bothers me not at all. I wish I could do the same with my emotional baggage. Just let it go.

Elisa makes a sharp turn, and Ilie rolls onto me.

"Sorry, my love," he says, slipping back into his own accent. "Don't tell Henry. He will get jealous."

He's chipper as ever, and that should put me at ease about the imminent robbery. But there's this persistent nag, anxiety pinching me from the inside. I'm thirsty, but this is something else. A different sensation. There's an urgency about this excursion that seems ill-advised.

"Tatiana," I say. "Should we not do this?"

"There's no talking Henry out of something once he makes up his mind," she says, which is and isn't an answer.

"Do not worry," Ilie says. "We do this many times. Do we usually stake out the place for a few nights? Yes. But it is no problem. Everybody thinks about money, not blood. Most places, the security is not so much."

"Most places," I say.

"Here," Henry calls from up front.

Elisa parks the van and I peer out from behind the curtain. We're in the mostly empty parking lot of a strip mall. There's a deli, a post office, an eye doctor, a nail salon, an AutoZone. And at the corner, an American Red Cross donation center.

My throat is bone-dry, my tongue like sandpaper, and I itch all over. That itch. That fucking *itch*.

Henry and Elisa come into the back.

"The collection will be sometime in the next half hour. That's our window," Henry says. "I'll get the lights and cameras."

Tatiana speaks in French. She's animated, using her hands.

"When Tati goes in the front to distract, I will go to the back," Ilie says. Henry tosses him a lanyard with a key card at the end, encased in plastic. "Go in, get the good stuff, get out."

"And on your signal, Henry, I will pull the camper around the side, blocking access," Elisa says.

"Good," Henry says. "Sloane, you will be with Elisa, and Naomi will stay out front to make sure no one goes in behind Tati. Okay?"

"Um, okay?" I say, looking to Naomi, who nods.

"Now," Henry says. He pounds his fist to his chest and opens the door of the camper. When he's gone, Elisa returns up front, and I pull back the curtain to watch. He strides coolly across the parking lot with his head down, hair hanging in his face. It's snowing, flurries appearing fast, like a magic trick, as zealous as confetti. The sun is gone, and Henry's a shadow among shadows.

A minute passes. There's a murky silence inside the camper. Outside, the wind sounds pained, like a scream smothered under a pillow. The illuminated signs, the streetlamps, suddenly fizz and then go dark. I think of the gas station, and a shiver hikes up my spine.

"Go," Elisa says, and Tatiana opens the door. Naomi moves to follow her.

"No," Tatiana says, without looking back. "Stay here."

"But, Tati," Ilie says, "Drago said—"

Now she turns around. "His judgment is clouded. He likes this one because she's a beautiful waif full of angst and self-loathing, because she is like him. She inspires his need to be heroic. Once a prince, always a prince. And this one . . ." She points to Naomi. "This one has beguiled you and Elisa because she will go down on you both and you can all have a laugh after. *Ha-ha*. You do not see. They are a danger to us, and to themselves, until they commit to their existence. Until they learn that they must embrace their thirst if they ever hope to control it. The problem children will stay in the car because *I* say so."

She steps out and slams the camper door shut.

Naomi and I exchange a look. She sucks air through her teeth and says, "Could be wrong, but I don't think she likes us."

"Elisa?" Ilie says.

"It's okay. They'll stay with me," Elisa says. "Your turn."

He shifts back into his American accent. "Awesome."

He adjusts his beanie and then gets out of the camper, letting in a gust of cold air and snowflakes.

"Is everything cool?" Naomi asks. "I can still go out there. I won't fuck it up. I'm not thirsty."

"You're not?" I ask her, the words scoring my throat.

"I feel all right," she says. "It's not as bad as it was."

"No, no," Elisa says, starting the engine. "We've got this. We—"

She's interrupted by the groan of the camper. It makes the same horrible grumbling it did right before we ended up in Ms. Alice's cannibal murder town.

The stench of exhaust is immediate and overpowering. I retch and cover my nose.

Elisa pulls out of the parking spot. The tires screech and slide, and a calamitous rattling noise harmonizes with the grumbling.

"Something tells me Ms. Alice is not as good a mechanic as she claims," Elisa says. "On further thought, I do not think she really wanted to help us this time."

"Well, fuck," Naomi says.

"We should call this off, right?" I ask.

"It is already in progress," Elisa says, turning to go behind the strip mall. "It is too late to stop it."

"Um, I know I'm a rookie, but I don't think it's smart to commit a crime if you can't then flee the scene of said crime," I say.

"I'm with Sloane on this," Naomi says, and it's so good to finally be back on the same page, to be back in sync with her.

"No one will know there was a crime. If anyone notices at all, they will assume whatever is missing is due to a clerical error. They always do," Elisa says. She doesn't seem particularly stressed, considering the circumstances, but that does nothing to reassure me. "I will try to fix the camper."

"And what if you can't?" I ask.

"Then we will find another way," she shouts over the engine. "Do not despair."

Naomi furrows her brow, equally put off by Elisa's optimism. She draws back the curtain as we pull up next to a dumpster on the narrow stretch of pavement behind the strip mall, which bumps against a patch of winter-bare woods. There are two cars parked in spaces that run parallel to these woods. A silver Toyota Corolla and a beat-to-shit 1990-something red convertible, the top up, one of the side-view mirrors adhered with duct tape.

As I look at these cars, inhaling the exhaust from the camper, it dawns on me.

We'll be stealing more than blood tonight.

33

Elisa gets out and gets to work on the camper, which continues to sputter even with the engine off. It's obviously a lost cause.

Through the window, we watch Ilie emerge from the bank with two coolers. He takes one look at Elisa, drops the coolers, and goes back inside. He reemerges moments later with a set of keys. He unlocks the Toyota and drags the coolers toward the car. He pops the trunk, and Henry appears next to him, helping him load.

"We're not all gonna fit in that car," Naomi says.

"Nope," I say. "Not to mention, if he took those keys without anyone noticing, I'm willing to bet someone's going to notice soon enough and report their car stolen."

"Unless . . ."

"Unless . . . ?"

"Do you think our new friends would leave that kind of loose end? Or do you think they'd . . ."

"Henry promised me no one would get hurt," I say.

"Do you believe him?" she says, turning to me, letting the curtain fall.

I hesitate, fearing speaking it out loud will jinx it somehow. But I'm tired of cowardice, so I go ahead and say it. "Yeah. I do. I believe him. I trust him."

"Well, that's something."

The camper door rips open. It's Henry.

"We need to go," he says.

We stare at him, not sure what to do, what to say.

"We need to go *now*." He reaches for me and pulls me out of the camper. I hang on to Naomi, and she stumbles after me. The snow is dense and heavy, the wind severe.

"You two in the back," he says as we hurry toward the Corolla. "Ilie and Elisa will get you out of here."

Elisa slips into the driver's seat and starts the car; Ilie gets into the passenger side. Tatiana comes up behind Henry, and it allows me to momentarily dismiss the sense I have that someone else is approaching. Momentarily. But the man's heartbeat is so loud. His scent so strong. There's a stink about him.

A problem. A complication. An inevitability. There will be no clean escape. Whoever stays behind will meet him, decide his fate.

He's coming. He's getting closer.

And with him, a sudden crystal clarity. Not horror, or anxiety. Not even thirst. Only a calm resolve that's eluded me for so long.

I look at Naomi. I can read her; I can tell. She senses him, too. And she knows what I know. Tatiana was right. We need to commit to our existence. The two of us, together. And I need to learn how to save myself.

"Naomi and I will stay," I say. "Okay?"

Naomi doesn't flinch. "Okay, hoss."

"*Bonne chance,*" Tatiana says as she gets into the back seat.

"Sloane," Henry says, his eyes finding mine through his tangle of overgrown dirty-blond hair. I trace my fingers across his face, still trying to solve the mystery of what makes it more strange than beautiful.

I slide my hands to his chest, lay them flat, feel him beneath me. I want to thank him for ending my drought. I want to tell him that once I figure this out for myself, accept it, embrace it, can control it, I'll gladly risk heartbreak for the chance to love him. But there's no time for all that, so he gets one word.

"Dare," I say, and I push him back.

He grins. That grin.

And then he's in the car, and the door is shut, and the vampires— our new friends, our new loves—are speeding away. And then they're gone.

Naomi and I start toward the dead, smoking camper, moving against the snow, the wind.

"So, this is an exercise in self-control, yeah? I mean, I'm not typically pro-abstinence," she says. "But in this case . . ."

"We're on a case-by-case basis," I say, thinking about the man at the rest stop. "We'll see what happens."

"Happy to follow your lead."

"Car trouble?"

His voice reaches us before he does. But then there he is. Maybe in his fifties. Camo coat. Jeans. Baseball hat. Boots. He swaggers up to us with a wide gait, thumbs hooked on his belt loops.

"Yes," Naomi says, not missing a beat. "This stupid old thing."

"Ah, yeah, yeah. You got a dinosaur," he says. He's a particular kind of genial that women learn early to be skeptical of. The jolly drunk uncle who will turn on a dime. "What are you doing parked back here?"

"We're lost," I say. "Go figure."

"We turned in here by mistake," Naomi says. "Thought there was a way out. It's so hard to see with all this snow. Then the engine started making this noise."

The man sighs and shakes his head. He stares at the camper, hikes up his jeans. "Where you ladies headed?"

"Raleigh," Naomi lies.

He whistles. "That's still a ways."

"Is it?" I ask.

He lifts the brim of his hat, looking us over. "You know why women are bad drivers?"

Naomi and I are silent. The sound of distant sirens slinks through the night.

"No guesses?" he asks. "Because there's no road from the kitchen to the bedroom."

There's a pause, and I have no idea what's about to happen. But then Naomi laughs. A big, fake laugh.

"That's a good one," she says, flirty. She turns to me. "Don't you think?"

The sirens fade. They're not for us. At least not yet.

"You're funny," I tell the man. I reach up to the delicate skin of my neck. I can feel my thirst vibrating underneath. I push against it. *Patience. Restraint. Control.* We can't drain every asshole we come across. Ignorance isn't enough to justify our kind of bloody retribution. Though maybe it should be.

I understand in this moment that there is no right thing to do, no good way to exist as what we are, or even as what we were— mortal women. My worldview, my rules, my morality, were all constructed as a cage for my shame—shame forged by forces outside myself. I've related restriction to virtue, nourishment to gluttony; associated satisfaction with guilt ever since I learned about the Atkins diet, ever since I heard the word "slut," ever since I was young. But I'm not young anymore. I'll never be young again.

"Ah well. Can't really tell jokes like that anymore 'cause everyone gets all sensitive. You two are good sports, so I'll help you out," he says. "I work over at the AutoZone. There's nothing we can do with this thing here, but a buddy of mine owns a shop that's not too far. I'll get you a tow. No charge."

"Really?" Naomi says, petting his arm. "You're a lifesaver."

He looks us up and down again, takes a set of keys out of his pocket. "Might be a while, though. Got some issues with power. Weather ain't gonna let up. I could, uh, give you a ride somewhere. If you need it."

"That your car?" Naomi asks, pointing to the beat-up convertible.

"Yup," he says. "Only a two-seater, though. One of you might have to ride on my lap."

Naomi laughs again. "Oh, you're bad! What's your name?"

"Dave," he says, smiling, revealing brown teeth. "What do you say? You want the ride?"

Naomi and I lock eyes, and she answers for us. "We'd love it."

"Yes. Thank you. We do *need* a ride," I say, still looking at Naomi.

"You know," Naomi says as we follow him to his car, "it's so lucky that out of everyone we could have come across, we found you. We so appreciate you coming to our rescue, Dave."

"Do you, now? I could think of a few ways you could, uh, show your appreciation," he says, laughing as he unlocks his car. "This ain't my usual ride, by the way. Just a loaner."

"Is it?" Naomi says, whipping a pistol out of her jacket and pressing it to the back of his head. So much for following my lead. "Actually, don't answer that. Don't make a fucking sound."

"Naomi! Where did you get that?" She doesn't answer my question, but I answer it for myself. I recognize the gun. It's from the gas station. It's the little one that woman pulled on us after Naomi bit her face. Naomi must have taken it. I don't know if there are any bullets left.

"Give me the keys," Naomi says to him.

"What the fuck is this?" he asks. I can sense his heart beating faster, blood pumping faster. "What the fuck is this?"

"This is us stealing your car. Figure you won't mind, since it's just a loaner. Now, give me the keys or I'll shoot your fucking brains out."

The man reels back, knocking the gun from Naomi's hand. It falls somewhere on the ground, somewhere in the snow.

He's still got the keys, and Naomi fights for them, digging her nails into his arm.

He cries out. "You bitches! You bitches from hell!"

He's being too loud. Someone will hear.

"A little help," Naomi says, trying her best to wrestle the keys away. He isn't making it easy.

We could find a way out of this without bloodshed. We could. But then this motherfucker spits in Naomi's face. And I make a conscious choice, make it without guilt or shame, without second-guessing.

I move closer.

Closer.

Close enough.

I grab his arm, and I bite down hard. My mouth floods with blood. So delicious. I wish I could savor it more, but I'm thirsty. I swallow. And swallow.

Naomi, too. She's got his other arm. Drinking. For a moment, I dip into my imagination, where we're sharing a milkshake, each with our own straw. Something innocent. Something sweet.

The man's knees give; his head slumps over. He slips from my grasp and hits the ground. Alive. Still alive. A glass half-full.

Naomi and I stand still for a minute, staring at him, licking our lips. My mind goes quiet. I drift into that state of bliss, but the screaming drags me right out.

Someone's screaming.

I look up, and there's a woman. I don't know who she is or

where she came from, but I know she's seen too much. She turns around and takes off running.

Naomi slips off her boot and chucks it. It hits the woman square in the back of the head, and she falls forward. She does nothing to catch her fall, so I assume she's unconscious.

"Really?" I say.

"I should've played softball."

"We need the keys," I say. I check the man's hands. He must have dropped them somewhere. "They're in the snow, I think. Fuck!"

"Should we just leave him here?" She takes him by the legs and starts to drag him toward the patch of woods at the edge of the pavement, leaving red streaks in the snow.

"The bloody snow is a sort of dead giveaway, don't you think?" I say, feeling around in slush. "Got them!"

"Should we take him with us? Put him in the trunk? If he wakes up, he'll report the car stolen. He'll report us."

"What about her?" I say, pointing to the woman laid out near the dumpster.

"Shit, shit, *shit*. I'll drive," she says, dropping the man's legs. "You're too slow."

"Fine. But if you get us pulled over . . ." I say. I'm climbing into the passenger seat when I hear it. A scuffle, a grunt, and then . . .

It's a distinct sound. I know exactly what it is.

A gunshot.

I slam the back of my head emerging from the car, dizzying myself as I turn to see what just happened.

He shot her.

He shot Naomi.

She staggers backward, her eyebrows rising in surprise as her chest smokes.

The man, laid out on his back, gun raised, smiles, contented in his violence.

He turns toward me, and I watch the realization sweep across his face. That he needs to use that stupid weapon again. He aims at me. He pulls the trigger.

But there are no more bullets.

I fly forward and rip the gun out of his hands and bash his head in with it. I hit him again and again, so his blood sprays into my mouth. Then I toss the gun aside so I can watch his eyes bulge as I choke him, as I squeeze, as I feel the blood rushing. He looks at me with such horror, such disgust, and I don't care at all.

He curses at me, so I shove my hand into his mouth and dig my nails into his tongue and tear it out and show it to him, and then it slips from my grasp and then it's beside us on the snow, like a fillet of tilapia in a grocery-store seafood display. I bite into his neck, and I drain him, and while I'm doing it I don't even notice that I've crushed him. I've caved his chest in. My eyes roll back, and the blood comes in, warm and gratifying. It tastes so good. Even better than before. It might be the best I've tasted yet.

It frees me from the false righteousness of deprivation, introduces me to the glorious, necessary selfishness of vampirism.

I drink him dry.

When I'm done, I stare at my trembling, bloodstained hands, and then I lick my fingers clean.

"Sloane . . ."

Naomi. I snap out of my bloodlust, and I turn to her as she collapses to her knees, holding her chest.

Her eyes are open. I think she's breathing. Do we even need to breathe? Aren't we supposed to be immortal?

"Naomi?"

She winces in pain.

"Are you okay?"

"Are you seriously asking me that?" She lets her head back, looking up at the night as her face twists in pain. "We need . . . to get out of here."

She stumbles as she attempts to stand. She hobbles toward me, crying out. I want to help her but I'm too afraid to touch her. She looks down at what's left of the man, then up at me.

"Sheesh," she says, reaching out for my arm. I give it to her.

"I thought I was the judgmental one."

"I thought . . . I was . . . the violent . . . one."

The pile of man pulp is ever present in the corner of my eye. I made such a mess. The guilt creeps in, but I kill it quickly. He shot Naomi.

I help her into the passenger seat of the beat-up convertible. Tears stream down her face. Red tears.

"Okay," I say, hurrying to the driver's seat and starting the car. Foot on gas. I go. "Okay. We'll find Henry. We'll find the others. They'll know what to do."

I drive around the side of the blood bank, cut through the parking lot, pull onto the main road. There are potholes, and the road is slick, and my palms are slick, and with every swerve, every jolt, Naomi wails in agony.

"I think it went through . . . my fucking heart," she says. "I think . . . I think I'm bleeding. . . ."

"No. No, you're not. You're . . ." Henry's voice echoes in my head. *We don't have much to spare. It's painful to lose.* "It's going to be okay. You're going to be okay. You're going to be okay."

If I say it enough, maybe it will become true.

34

I don't know where I'm going. All I know is I'm not going the speed limit.

"Maybe . . . Wilmington? The summer house still? Yeah?" I ask Naomi, who fades in and out of consciousness.

I get on the highway but then change my mind and get off, drive back roads. But it's too quiet, and the snow is bad, and I regret my decision.

"Maybe we should ditch the car?" I ask. "Naomi?"

She groans.

"Should I pull over?"

"I'd say . . . avenge me . . . but you . . . already did."

"You're going to be fine. We can't die," I say. "We're not supposed to die."

"Of . . . natural causes," she says.

Can a vampire survive a bullet to the chest? Can anything?

Distracted, I speed through a stop sign. "Shit."

I make a quick turn onto a narrow, nowhere road.

"Ah!" Naomi screams. I've never seen her in so much pain.

"I'm sorry. I'm sorry. I'm . . ."

My eyes flick up to the rearview mirror. Red and blue lights flash behind us. A single whoop of a siren rings out, and I'm suddenly boiling alive in my skin. The terror is so intense, I might combust.

"Fuck! *Fuck.* Where did he come from?"

"Sloane . . ."

"We're in a stolen car. You're clearly injured. What do we do?"

"You could . . . pull over . . . and . . . take care of it . . ." she says. "Temporarily . . . incapacitate. Or have . . . the . . . whole . . . tall drink . . ."

"We shouldn't have separated from the others. I'm sorry. I thought I could . . . I don't know. I wanted to believe I could do this. Be this."

"Or . . ." she says. "You can drive."

We look at each other. I don't see her as she is now. I see her as the fourteen-year-old girl who sat across from me in the food court of a New Jersey mall, fidgeting with her straw. Smart, and stunning, and funny, and cooler than anyone has any right to be. Who chose me to be her best friend. Who sees me when I can't see myself.

I slam my foot on the gas.

The acceleration is better than I expect, and we fly.

"Told you," Naomi says, "you're . . . the engine- . . . revving type . . ."

"I don't know about that," I say, watching the cop car in the rearview. It's catching up.

"Hiding away . . . in the burbs."

"Shh, shh," I tell her. "Save your energy."

"For . . . what?" she asks, giving a weak laugh.

The cop is on us. He tailgates me. He's at the back bumper. The road is covered in snow, and I can't go any faster. This is it.

"Hang on," I say, drifting over into the other lane and then hitting the brake. The cop clips us, and Naomi gasps.

"What the . . . hell was that?"

The cop gets on his PA. "Engine off! Out now! Hands where I can see them! Hands! Hands!"

"Don't move," I say. "Three, two—"

"What . . . happens on . . ."

"One!" I shift into reverse, sliding my foot off the brake and onto the gas. I smash into the cop car's driver's side. Take off its mirror, dent the door.

I shift back into drive and spin the wheel hard, and we slide, the snow squelching under the tires. I regain control and pass the cop going the opposite direction. Sixty miles per hour. Seventy. Eighty. Ninety. So fast that the convertible top rips back, that the duct tape fails and the side-view mirror dangles free.

We approach a four-way stop, and I blow straight through it. The cop hasn't caught up to us yet, but it's only a matter of time. I hear the sirens. More are on their way.

There's snow in my hair, piling up in my lap. I look over at Naomi. She's quiet, slouching against the passenger-side window. Her eyelids wilt.

"Nay?"

We reach a fork, and I take the left. There's some traffic on this road, which isn't good. Other cars. Obstacles. Witnesses. I clench the steering wheel. It's a two-way street, and we're now stuck behind an SUV going so slow, I could scream.

Its driver is smart to be careful in this weather. But I've stopped being careful, forfeited the game and all rules along with it, and there's no going back now. So I speed into oncoming traffic to pass the SUV.

The driver of an approaching sedan hits their brakes, avoids hitting us but spins out, colliding with the SUV. There's an ugly crunch, followed by a screeching, an awful sort of music. It's a fender bender. An inconvenience. For them. Not for us. The accident will cause a roadblock. Another distraction for the cops.

I listen, though, and the sirens are drowned out by fierce wind. The visibility gets worse, oncoming headlights merely faint smears. The snow falls harder. The road gets messier. I'd be grateful for this storm if I thought I could continue to drive through it. The tires lose traction, and we start to skate all over the road.

"We might need to find somewhere to pull off," I tell Naomi.

"It's . . . okay," she says. "This is . . . as far . . . as we'll go. . . ."

I make the next left, which leads us past a Home Depot, a movie theater, to . . .

"No way," I say as a mall comes into view. "No way."

"The . . . dream mall."

It's clearly abandoned, entrances boarded up. There's what was once a Lord & Taylor—ghost sign lettering reading white against the rest of the dirty exterior. Sections of the parking lot are enclosed in chain-link fence.

"We . . . have to . . . go . . . in," she says, breathless.

She's so pale. She needs help. We need help.

I need help.

"Sloane . . . please . . ."

I never could say no to her.

I park the car behind the Home Depot and help her out. She can barely stand on her own, and she's cold. So cold it hurts for me to touch her.

It's a hard walk to the mall.

"Are you thirsty?" I ask her. "I can get you . . . someone."

It's not lost on me that I sound like Ms. Alice.

Maybe the world makes you callous. The longer you live, the less you care. I wonder if that's a good thing, or if it's tragic. I wonder if it's possible to ever know for sure.

"That's . . . okay . . ." she says.

I carry her to an entrance. I pull back the boards and find it's chained up with a big padlock. I pull on it. Yank hard. I don't know what I expected to happen. It's a lock. It won't magically spring open at the touch of my hand.

"Use your . . . teeth," she says.

At first, I think she's joking. Then I realize I don't care; I'll do whatever it takes to get us inside. Into the dream mall.

I lean over, and I spread my jaws, and I start to gnaw. I bite down hard, and I snap right through the chain. I spit it from my mouth, wipe off my tongue. It tastes sour, like everything. Except blood. Except Henry.

"Look . . . at you . . . crashing . . . into cops . . . chewing through . . . locks . . ." Naomi says as I push open the door for her. "You're so . . . fucking cool."

I hold my breath, waiting for an alarm to sound, but it doesn't.

A stroke of luck. If I can call anything about this situation lucky.

Naomi tumbles forward, into the dead mall.

It's dim. There are some skylights, but other than that, darkness. Shadows cross the ugly white and pink and turquoise tile. Diamond patterns. Rats scurry around. I can hear them, smell them. Their scent is powerful and specific, cutting through the rot. Leaking pipes leaving puddles, spots of mold on the walls, fountains with an inch of stagnant water covering dirty coins—abandoned wishes.

We come to an escalator, half-collapsed in a two-story atrium.

There's a carousel off to the side. A small one, with only a few horses. I can tell it was beautiful once, though the colors have faded, and the whole thing is covered in dust. I feel sad for the horses, trapped in here, frozen. Unable to dance around their forever loop. There are so many ways to be stuck, aren't there?

"This is it," Naomi says, falling to her hands and knees. "It really is the . . . dream mall."

"It is," I lie. It looks nothing like the mall in my dreams.

"We made it," she says, smiling as she lowers herself down onto her side. I cringe because the floor is so filthy. Because I don't know what to do. "I bet . . . you have . . . a sad mall story . . . one of your . . . disasters."

"The Sampoong Department Store collapse," I say, sitting beside her. "South Korea, 1995, I think? Lazy builders. Greedy executives. There were structural issues that went ignored. Didn't want to close and lose revenue, even when there were huge cracks in the ceiling. And then, yeah. Five hundred people died. More than that injured."

"In- . . . in- . . . inspiring," Naomi says, pointing to the crumbling escalator.

"That was a department store, technically not a mall. I don't know. I don't know." I peel her coat back. She was right. She is bleeding. Dark, thick, strange blood. For the first time since I was bitten, since I was changed, the sight of blood doesn't make me thirsty. It makes me nauseous.

"They found . . . those two bodies . . . at Pompeii," she says. "The lovers."

"Maybe they were just friends."

She smiles. "Best friends?"

"Yeah. Or they were together but not exclusive, and then at the last minute it was like, well, fuck it."

"Don't . . . make . . . me laugh," she says. "Imagine. Not that . . . into each other . . . but it's . . . the end . . . of the world . . ."

"Yeah," I say. "Nay, maybe I should—"

"Maybe they . . . were having . . . an Armageddon bang."

"Naomi, are you, um . . . Should I . . . ?"

She shakes her head. "Give me . . . a minute."

"Okay," I say, wiping my hands on my shirt before I touch her, sweep her hair out of her face. "You're going to be fine."

"We should have . . . spent more time . . . together."

"Maybe they'll find us. Henry, Ilie . . . Maybe they've been following. They'll know what to do. . . ."

She looks up. "Is that . . . a carousel? Definitely . . . the dream mall."

She writhes in anguish. She's leaking. There's blood on the floor.

"Naomi. You need blood. You need—"

"It's okay, hoss," she says, smiling. "My time's up."

"Don't say that."

"Just . . . promise me . . . you'll live. Drink . . . smoke . . . fuck . . . fuck up . . . *live.*"

"Don't say that! Stop. Just stop talking like that. I can't do this without you. If you go, I—"

"You should . . . be with . . . your prince. The way you . . . look at . . . each other . . . he's so into . . . you. He . . . must be . . . smart," she says. There's no color left in her. She's withering away right in front of me.

"You don't get it. I can't survive a minute without you. Not a second."

"I'm not . . . I'm not . . . afraid . . . anymore. It's . . . okay."

"I am! Nay . . ." I get an idea. I push my sleeve up. "Bite me."

"R-r- . . . rude."

"Seriously. Bite me. Drink from me. Take my blood," I say. "I bit Ms. Alice. It's possible. I think—I think we can take from each other. Give to each other. It won't taste good, but—"

"I . . . don't . . . have it in me. . . . I'm . . . tired. . . ."

"We have to try to do something! Please." I lower my wrist to her lips. "Please. Please . . ."

She shakes her head.

282

"Please!" My pleading echoes through the mall. "Please."

Naomi's eyes glaze over.

"Fuck it," I say, lurching forward and sinking my teeth into the visible blue veins where my arm goes skinny, where the metal once was, which was meant to fix me but didn't, couldn't. It doesn't taste like anything, and it hurts like nothing I've ever felt before. What I imagine it would be like to have a tooth extracted without anesthetic, a bone hammered broken, a limb axed off. A removal. An unwelcome alteration.

"Here," I say, allowing the blood to leak into her open mouth, like Elisa did that first night. Only now it's my blood instead of Naomi's own. Vampire blood. Thick and dark and strange and maybe not good enough. Maybe this is a useless transfusion. "Drink."

Her head lolls.

"Swallow it. Please? Stay with me."

I keep bleeding. I keep giving. But there's no response. It's so quiet, until it isn't. Until there are footsteps. Until we're no longer alone in the mall.

My vision blurs, and I know if I lose any more blood, I won't have any more to spare. But if I stop, if I tie off my wrist, it'll be over.

I'm suspended in time.

If I don't accept that she's lying on the floor, eyes closed, teeth bloody, motionless, maybe it won't be real. If I don't accept that we have company, likely the police closing in, maybe they'll just disappear.

I don't call her name again, because if she doesn't answer, that's an answer. One I don't want.

I let my eyes wander. I find a greening penny on the floor, heads up.

This really is the dream mall.

283

I crawl over to the fountain, rubbing the oxidized penny between my fingers. Making a wish as I continue to bleed, as the approaching footsteps hurry closer. I toss the penny in, and it makes a satisfying splash. The ripples go out, and out, and when they fade, I can still see them. Even after the surface of the water goes still, they're there. In my eyes. In my mind. The hope of the moment, of the wish, rippling out endlessly.

When I finally turn around, it's to the sound of a familiar voice calling my name. To Naomi, sitting up, color in her cheeks, smiling at me, in the arms of strangers we met a few days ago, who are not strangers anymore.

The view is too good to be true. I choose to trust it anyway.

When I turn around, it's to something better than a dream.

It's to beauty and friendship and love.

To my life.

I want it, want to savor it to the last drop. The delicious mess of it.

All of it. Everything. Forever.

EPILOGUE

Two women sit outside a café in Prague. They're both twenty-four years old, American, and this is their first trip to Europe. One of them made lists, read travel books, brought an adapter for the outlets. The other brought outfits.

They drink strong black coffee, even though it's late. They're tired, still not quite adjusted to the time zone. And they're intimidated. The world is so big, so much bigger than they ever imagined. They don't speak the language. They're not sure if they have enough money. They don't understand how much they need to tip or if they even need to tip at all.

One wishes she'd brought more stylish clothes, like the other. That one wishes she'd brought more comfortable shoes. That one wonders why she doesn't miss her boyfriend, if maybe they should break up. The other wishes she had a partner, someone to wonder if she missed.

The women have been friends for a long time, so they don't need to say any of this to each other. They already know. They're content to just sit in silence.

Though it's not silence. There are people all around them, mostly speaking Czech.

Not the people at the next table, though. They speak English.

But that's not what first draws the two young American women's attention. It's an odd cast of characters. There's a redhead wearing head-to-toe lace, what's essentially lingerie. There's a tall, regal, curly-haired blonde in velvet. There's a man with a buzzed head, tattoos, gold teeth. A pixie sits in his lap—a petite woman with short dark hair. Then there's the loud one—a beautiful man in a black T-shirt and leather pants, his hair coming loose from a messy bun.

And the mysterious one. He leans back in his chair, smoking a cigarette. His shaggy hair is dirty blond, and maybe actually dirty. He's distracted, staring off into the distance. Like he's looking for someone. Like he's waiting for someone.

"Hello, loves!" says the loud one.

At first, the young American women wonder if he's speaking to them. They blush, sit up a little straighter.

But they soon realize his hello wasn't for them. It was for the two women behind them, walking down the street hand in hand. One with strawberry blond hair, wearing a white blazer over a short dress, a pair of Chuck Taylors. The other with black hair in a braid that falls down past her hips, wearing a bright yellow peasant blouse, cutoff jean shorts, and over-the-knee boots.

They move in sync, whispering to each other. Laughing.

The two young American women watch them, awestruck. There's something about them. They seem so sure of themselves. So confident. So content. Like they've walked these streets a thousand times before. Like they know exactly where they're going. Like they want for nothing. The black-haired one rests her head on the strawberry blonde's shoulder.

"That'll be us someday," one of the Americans says to the other. "That'll be us."

"Maybe it already is," says the strawberry blonde as she passes their table. The black-haired one turns around, blowing a kiss.

Acknowledgments

To Lucy Carson, always and forever my MVP! Thank you for your brilliant ideas, your dedication, your diligence, your enthusiasm, for everything. You get my vote for every superlative. You're a wonder.

To Jess Wade, thank you for your spot-on insights, for making me a better writer and storyteller, for your talent and support and hard work. I can't believe how lucky I am that I get to work with you.

To Danielle Keir, Chelsea Pascoe, Jessica Plummer, Gabbie Pachon, Katie Anderson, and the entire dream team at Berkley. My gratitude is deep and eternal. No amount of exclamation points in my emails could ever convey how thankful I am, but that won't stop me from trying!!!

To the booksellers and librarians, oh how I love and appreciate you. To the podcasters and reviewers, I see you and the work you put in and it's invaluable—thank you. To anyone who has ever picked up one of my books, come to an event, told a friend—it means so much to me. Thank you, thank you, thank you.

To my family, I'm so grateful for your support. If you've read this book, let's just go ahead and pretend you didn't. Mom, thank you for being the best horror fan.

To Deanna, for the trips to the mall. To Christy and to Melissa, for running around New York City with me in those early days. To Abby, Maria, Heather, and Courtney, for all the wild times that made me feel so alive. I love you forever.

To my writer friends, you genius lot! Kristi DeMeester, for talking me off a ledge, and for being so smart and talented and cool, I'm so thankful for you. Clay McLeod Chapman, the legend, thank you for everything but especially for being an early reader and specifically for that bedbug line. Molly Pohlig, Eric LaRocca, Nat Cassidy, and Brian McAuley, for being there and for dazzling me with your words. May Cobb, bestie, for the early encouragement, friendship, stories, and stiff drinks. To Steph Kent, Jai Punjabi, Amble Johnson, and Doug Chilcott, for all the lovely Sundays. To Agatha Andrews, for the conversations and inspiration. To Courtney, again, and again and again, for being my turtle and my sounding board.

To Nic, for making my life so wonderful, thank you, I love you.

And to you, dear beautiful reader! Thank you so much for picking this up. May you always be brave enough to go after what you want.